Praise for the

"We are very proud to announce that *Letters From Wishing Rock* by Pam Stucky is a 2013 B.R.A.G. Medallion Honoree. This signifies that this book is well worth a reader's time and money!"

— *Indie B.R.A.G.,*
www.bragmedallion.com

Letters from Wishing Rock has been awarded the Awesome Indies Seal of Approval

— *www.awesomeindies.net*

"Just what the doctor ordered, fresh, quirky, funny in places and seasoned with wisdom. Light without being frivolous, it follows the story of a woman trying to find someone to fill her desire for true love and family. The inhabitants of Wishing Rock embody this sense of family in the most delightful way, and I fell in love with the characters in a flash, especially Gran. The rhythm the author created with the different length emails and occasional texts was skillfully done and gave an almost musical undercurrent to the text. The characters are delightful and the recipes a nice touch. The travels in Scotland made me want to visit." (referring to *Letters from Wishing Rock*)

— *Tahlia Newland, author of* Lethal Inheritance

"This was a book I stayed up late to read, because reading it felt like sitting comfortably by the fire, talking with my nicest and funniest friends, all of whom had uplifting and sometimes hilarious thoughts to share. As the story progressed, not only did I become more curious about how all the characters' adventures would turn out, but I found myself thinking along the same philosophical lines as they were, regarding how to make one's life happier. Her writing, in the voices of the various characters, is witty and wise, and I found myself grinning or giggling at several of the observations."

— *Molly Ringle, author of* What Scotland Taught Me

"I wish this series would have been around when I was younger and still trying to figure out what I wanted in a relationship and in life in general. So many wise words, and more than once I went back and reread a page or two because it struck such a chord with me."

— *PLL, Amazon reviewer*

"Both of Ms. Stucky's novels are fantastic! A fresh approach to writing that takes readers into the lives of the characters (which are all interesting and fun). I never wanted the books to end! The concepts of happiness, joy, and love are all addressed in ways that are thought-provoking and so much fun to read. I love the fact that the characters are so real, and the story is so believable. I recommend this book to anyone, but especially someone that you think might benefit from a new way of looking at happiness in life. Thank you Ms. Stucky! "

— *SJ, Amazon reviewer*

"This second book in the Wishing Rock series was well worth the wait! I read this just as quickly, if not more so, than the first! Pam Stucky brought all the favorite, familiar characters back from our introduction to the world of Wishing Rock. At the same time, we got to see these characters grow and adapt to some pretty big changes and surprises along the way. Learning even more of the backstories of some of the beloved residents of the town was a joy and I can absolutely admit to some jaw-dropping revelations while traveling through the pages of the story! It was wonderfully written, a lovely escape from 'real life,' and provided opportunities aplenty for self-reflection. Underlying it all was a message we all need reminders of... take the time to cherish what you have. I can't wait to see what happens next for the residents of Wishing Rock!"

— *Amy Bednarik, Amazon reviewer*

Books by Pam Stucky

FICTION

The Wishing Rock Series
(novels with recipes)

Letters from Wishing Rock
The Wishing Rock Theory of Life
The Tides of Wishing Rock

NON-FICTION

Coming Soon:
Pam on the Map (travel/humor series)

Iceland
Retrospective: Switzerland
Retrospective: Ireland

www.pamstucky.com
twitter.com/pamstucky
facebook.com/pamstuckyauthor
pinterest.com/pamstucky

The Tides of Wishing Rock

a novel with recipes

third in the Wishing Rock series

PAM STUCKY

Published in the United States by Wishing Rock Press.

Cover photos and design by Pam Stucky
Author photo by Haley Christine Photography

ISBN: 0985125225
ISBN-13: 978-0-9851252-2-6
eBook ISBN-13: 978-0-9851252-3-3
eBook ISBN: 0985125233

www.wishingrockpress.com

for Mom and Dad
who believed in me from the start

November

Text from Ed to Ruby
Sent: November 27, 2010

Hey, gorgeous. Do you have a lot of cups?

~

Text from Ruby to Ed
Sent: November 27, 2010

Excuse me? Do I have a lot of cups? Um, what kind of cups?

~

Text from Ed to Ruby
Sent: November 27, 2010

Weird echo in here. Stackable cups. I challenge you to a cup stacking contest. Do you have any cups?

~

Text from Ruby to Ed
Sent: November 27, 2010

I believe I have a normal person amount of cups. Do you want me to check?

~

Text from Ed to Ruby
Sent: November 27, 2010

No worries. I'll ask Millie; I have to stop by the store anyway. Also, in case you didn't know, it's your birthday in three days. Do you want to go to my island for your birthday?

~

Text from Ruby to Ed
Sent: November 27, 2010

You have odd questions today. Do I want to go to your island for my birthday? Is that a euphemism? Is that related to the cups?

~

Text from Ed to Ruby
Sent: November 27, 2010

No, I mean my actual island. Unrelated to cups. Did I not mention I own an island?

~

Text from Ruby to Ed
Sent: November 27, 2010

    I think I'd remember if you'd mentioned you own an island. That seems a bit of a detail to leave out. Where exactly is this island? Do you mean Dogwinkle? I know you pretty much own this town; do you own the whole island?

~

Text from Ed to Ruby
Sent: November 27, 2010

    Not Dogwinkle. A separate island. Very near by. As yet unnamed. Just big enough for you and me.

~

Text from Ruby to Ed
Sent: November 27, 2010

    You own an island. Of course you do. Well in that case, yes, I would love to go to your island. Overnight or for the day?

~

Text from Ed to Ruby
Sent: November 27, 2010

    Just for the day. Too cold for overnight. No cabins. Groovy, I'll set it up. Wednesday, you, me, my island. Put it on your calendar! I'll tell your boss to give you the day off. And tonight: Tonight, we crown a new cup stacking champion. It's on, my friend.

~

Text from Ruby to Ed
Sent: November 27, 2010

Ah, cup stacking. Bring it.

~

From: Ruby
To: Alexandra
Sent: November 27, 2010
Subject: Vancouver?

Hey, lady! How are you? How is Canada? How are David's parents? How is your trip? You're coming back on Wednesday, right? I miss you! And, oh, hey, did you know Ed owns an island? I swear, this place keeps surprising me. Did I mention I miss you? Enough questions? See you soon! x

~

From: Alexandra
To: Ruby
Sent: November 28, 2010
Subject: RE: Vancouver?

Hello, my love!
We've only been gone two days! Surely you can't miss me all that much yet. Give it some time. Maybe three days. Yes, David and I are coming back on Wednesday. Vancouver is fine. Educational. One learns so much from meeting the people whence someone sprang forth, does one not! I haven't "met the parents" in … well, I've only ever done it the once. When I was dating in high school I dated boys I'd known my whole life, so obviously I knew their parents, too. Jimmy was the first and only man I dated whose parents I didn't already know, and I went and married him. I haven't really dated since he

4

died, which feels like so many lifetimes ago. Do we revert back to the age we were the last time we did something? Meeting David's parents and family, I felt eighteen again.

Having said that, of course they – the parents, anyway – are lovely people and I had no need to be nervous. Mildly introverted and quite intelligent. The kind of people who give space to their words; who listen intently to what you're saying and only when you're done do they form their thoughts in response and then speak. Alice and Leonard DuBois, a professor and a banker.

David's sister Lola is an interesting being. Though her name is Lola, she is neither showgirl nor transvestite as were those most famous Lolas, but did spend some time as a stripper, "purely out of curiosity," she says. She made lots of money but simply lost interest after a while. Lola is the family rebel with the requisite tattoos and eyebrow piercings, calls herself "the underachieving starving artist." Curiosity of the workings of the human mind seems to drive her to push people's buttons as she can, not necessarily to harm but not necessarily out of kindness, either. More simply, she does it to amuse herself. In my opinion she'd do well to put her intelligence to some other use, but it seems she's a bit bored by the world and finds what ways she can to counteract that boredom.

Looking at Lola, then at David and their parents, one does find oneself pondering genetics. What rascally regressive genes got loose when the Lola egg and Lola sperm met, on some sordid summer night? Did David's mother, I even found myself wondering, have an affair; the great family secret? Mr. and Mrs. DuBois were a marked contrast to Lola: calm to her clamorous, polite to her pushy. Where she stares with a smirk that makes me feel she knows something embarrassing about me and will share it with the world at any moment, Alice and Leonard could not be more accommodating. Charming, witty, humble. Fascinating folk, but you'd never know it if you didn't engage them; they'll spend the whole evening asking you about your own life, for all the world making you believe you're the most interesting person they've ever met. But, like David, they are active in the world. Last summer, they hiked the Pacific Crest Trail. Tuesday nights they volunteer: he at the youth center; she at the library. Alice served on the City Council for a term, a decade or so ago. Seats at the local symphony hall bear their names, David tells me. Paragons of virtue and class.

So those are the happenings up here. My love to you and Ed.

Oh! Ed! Yes, I vaguely recall his having bought an island several years back. He didn't make much of it and I'd frankly forgotten all about it. Does he go out there much? If he does, he doesn't talk about it. A small thing, if I remember right. Is he planning to do something with the island? Sell? Build?

Love again, and hello from David,
Alexandra

From: Ruby
To: Alexandra
Sent: November 29, 2010
Subject: RE: RE: Vancouver?

Do you know what I noticed in that there email there? Did you notice you said "we," rather than "I"? As in, "We've only been gone two days." Hmmm! Interesting, Alexandra! Things are going well, are they? I'm so happy for you! I know you say it's been hard for you to open up again, but girl, looking from the outside you're doing all right. That David is one lucky man.

Speaking of David being a lucky man, Erin is still sort of moping. No, not moping. Thinking very loudly, I guess. You can practically feel the thought clouds around her. That is, I can practically feel them. You probably always could, right? The joys of being a psychic.

Speaking of the joys of being a psychic, have you done more research into … what was it you were going to study? Brain stuff? Neuro-something or other?

I'm afraid I can't tell you any more about the island, except that I am (we are) (Ed and I, not you and I) going out there! At which point I'll be able to report back. I asked Ed about it but he won't tell me anything. He's taking me out there first thing tomorrow. Spending my birthday with the kindest guy on the planet, on his own little island. The stuff of fairy tales!

Except: I gotta admit, I do wish the island had some plumbing. Having to dig holes and pee behind bushes on my birthday isn't exactly living the dream. (The stuff they don't talk about in fairy tales. Because, I ask you: Did the Seven Dwarves have indoor plumbing? And don't even get me started on Sleeping Beauty.) I'm so curious to see what the island does have. Lots of bugs, undoubtedly. There are a hell of a lot of bugs in the world.

Interesting points you make there, about Lola and genetics. Maybe she was adopted? Or abducted by aliens early in life, and replaced with a replica? That would explain the lack of emotion, perhaps. Ed was telling me that once when he, Michael, and Tom were camping out near Balky Point (which begs the question: why would a person from Wishing Rock need to go camping up near Balky Point? Is Wishing Rock itself not remote enough?), they all swear they saw a UFO. I know it would be so out of character but I suspect our dear gentlemen may have been imbibing at the time and/or spinning some tales. But what if not? What if they were right, and their UFO made a left turn to head on up to Vancouver?

Anyway. Meeting the parents, that's a big deal, right? I've still not met Ed's mom. Iceland's a ways to go, I suppose. Would you ever take David to meet your parents? When was the last time you saw them? Has spending time with his parents got you thinking about yours?

Well, I'll be out in the woods tomorrow on this fantasy island. I doubt I'll be in cell phone range, so don't worry about calling. Happy birthday to me! I'm off to challenge Ed at cup stacking – we got started on it the other day and now we can't stop! Talk to you later!

xx

~

7

From: Alexandra
To: Ruby
Sent: November 30, 2010
Subject: Happy Birthday!!!

Happy, happy birthday, dearest Ruby Parker! You're likely out on Ed's island as I write this. I hope and am sure you're having a wonderful time. Funny, you've got me trying to remember what I know about that island. I really don't think Ed ever talked about it much. As far as I know, no one else has ever been out there. Why in the world is that? It's not like life in Wishing Rock is so scintillating and busy that none of us ever had a moment to head out. But, I guess we all had other things to do. Life fills up to fit the time allotted. Write and tell me all about it.

Your powers of perception are sharp, young one. Being here with David's parents did indeed get me thinking about my own. We haven't spoken in years. At first it was intentional but now I suppose it's just habit. I'm not even sure they're still living in Mt. Vernon. Maybe I'll think about looking into that. What a coward I can be about some things. I don't know why I feel this hesitation about seeing them again, but I do. It's not as though they can hurt me now. Dad can't hit me now. I wouldn't stand for it. They're powerless over me, and yet … and yet they're not. Old wounds, Ruby. They are always with us. Another thing for me to let go of in the new year, I suppose. I'll add it to the list. It's growing.

Well, then. We are – that is, I am – back tomorrow and I will want a full report on the magical mystery island and all its charms. I simply can't believe this is your first birthday since we met, and I'm not even there to share it with you. You will come to my home soon, and I will make you birthday pie. We will invite the men, or we won't; the choice is yours. We will chat, and have deep conversation, and solve the problems of the universe, and toast the stars with a prayer of gratitude for bringing you to Wishing Rock and into my life.

Again, the happiest of birthdays to you, Ruby.
All my love,
Alexandra
P.S. You have inspired a cup stacking craze in the DuBois household. I mentioned Ed's new diversion, and next thing I knew, Leonard was researching the best cups for cup stacking, and running to the store to get them. We are stacking cups at every spare moment. I assure you, should you challenge either me or David to a contest, you will not win.

November 30, 2010
Letter presented from Ed to Ruby on the island

My Ruby,

Life is a funny thing. You go through your whole life not knowing someone, and then suddenly they're there, as critical to your life as the air itself, and you wonder how you ever managed to breathe without them. The only thing you can figure out is that the existence of this person in the world at the same time as you, even if you didn't know them, was enough to keep you alive.

I'm not old, Ruby, but I'm also not young. Here you are turning thirty-six today, and there's a part of me that feels ripped off that for thirty-five-and-a-half of those years you existed and I didn't get to know you. It feels like precious lost time that I didn't even know I was squandering, but yet I can never get back. I have few regrets in life; I'm not the kind of guy who regrets. Yet somehow, inexplicably, I regret that time. I regret missing out on all those years with you.

I'm not a particularly serious man, either, you may have noticed. Ruggedly handsome, yes, but not serious. Even so, I've learned a thing or two in all my years. Having just passed the fortieth birthday milestone myself, I am excited to know I'm finally wise enough – or at least old enough – to make commentary about being forty. And, having earned this right by taking that trip around the sun the requisite number of times, I will.

There are things a man comes to know by the time he's forty. He knows whether he'll ever be any good at horseshoes and lawn darts. He knows how he likes his steak and his art. He knows how to take care of himself, or knows that he can't. He knows whether he's the kind of guy to ask forgiveness or permission. He knows that his own character has only to do with himself and there's no one else to blame. He's known too many people who've up and died without giving notice, so he knows not to take life or loved ones for granted. He knows that even knowing that, he still fails, too often, but the grace is in the trying. He knows what makes him happy and what – or whom – he has to walk away from. He knows you can't take back what's been said, so he's more careful with his words. He knows that you can make a pretty good argument that laughter is the most important ingredient in a relationship. He knows the difference between being honest and being kind, and he knows when to be each. He knows you regret the things you didn't do more than the things you did. He knows how little he used to know about fear, and that he used to fear all the wrong things. He knows there's no shame in letting go or in admitting he was wrong. He knows what's worth fighting for.

And, by the time he's forty, if he's not already married, I suppose, a man has a pretty good idea of what kind of woman he wants. More than that, though, deeper than that, he has a pretty good idea of what kind of woman he deserves.

I'm showing my hand a bit here, Ruby, but I'm going to let you in on a secret: My deepest fear is that one day you'll wake up and realize I'm not good enough for you. My only fear, really. Anything else, I could cope with. Anything but losing you. I don't deserve you but yet by some glorious twist of fate or some mistake of the gods, here you are, with me. I may as well tell you now. You're smart; you'd have figured it out eventually.

The ancient Egyptians. Of the mummy times, the pharaoh times, those ancient ones. Did you know that when they made mummies, they pulled out all the organs to preserve them, except for the brain? The brain, they pulled out through the unlucky dead person's nose and discarded. They thought it was useless. The other organs they preserved in little organ jars that they packed in alongside you. Except for the heart. These ancient Egyptians thought you'd need your heart in your next life, so you'd better have it with you. They thought all thinking was done with the heart. Brain: useless, pulled out the nose. Heart: saved, sent along with you into eternity.

It's hard to argue with them. When I think about you, it isn't my brain that feels it. It's my heart, my chest, that fills up with searing warmth, with almost unbearable joy. It's my heart that grows too big and starts climbing up my throat. When I think about you, my breath catches.

I love you, Ruby. I can't possibly give you everything you deserve in life and on your birthday, but whatever I have, it's yours.

Happy birthday,

Love,

Ed

December

December 1, 2010
Wishing Rock News
Millie Adler, editor
Letter from the Editor

Dear Rockers,

Happy Hanukkah, everyone!

Oh my stars, here it is December, where did the year go! Seems like just yesterday we were all gathered around the telly up at Claire's and Tom's, wondering if the world was going to end the moment the clock struck midnight, as 1999 turned into a pumpkin. And now here it is, almost 2011. Did we make the most of the year? Did we love enough, laugh enough, potluck enough?

If not, then, another month begins in which we can try to get it right.

And December it is! You know what that means! I get dizzy just thinking of all the activities this month. No comments from those who might suggest I am just normally dizzy! Be careful or your mail might not get delivered right, and it's a big month for bright packages, you know!

All right, here we go:

1. Hanukkah dinner. Don't forget the Hanukkah dinner on Friday. The Blausteins are sponsoring the dinner and are inviting every-

one to join them in the fifth floor commons room at 6 p.m. Bring a dish if you like; I know Carolyn is supplying the applesauce and I'm bringing roasted green beans. Check with Rachel to see what else is needed if you haven't already signed up for something. Starting around 7:30, Adam and Rachel will talk about Hanukkah traditions.

2. Secret Santas. Secret Santas begin with the name drawing tonight at 7 p.m. in the second floor commons room. Anyone who would like to participate is welcome. Participants are encouraged to put on their creative hats rather than spend a lot of money.

3. Our ambitious new Open House. As you may have heard from the constant buzz, we're having an Open House on Dec. 11 to let the world, or at least any wanderers who may venture out here by intent or by accident, see what Wishing Rock is all about. There are myriad components to the Open House, so let's just dive in!

a. Concert: Walter's band has been practicing away with great determination, and is almost ready for prime time. Not quite ready for prime time, though, so the concert will be a 3:00 matinee on the 11th. Location: auditorium downstairs. Free, but donations are welcome and will benefit the town's maintenance fund.

b. Open House Tour: We're inviting people to open their homes as a part of the Open House Tour so visitors can get a real sense of living here. Let me know if you're willing to participate, and then plan some snacks for those who come by. We'll add you to an Open House map for visitors and give you a special sign for your door.

c. Decorations: People of all faiths, denominations, non-faiths, etc., are invited to help wrap up our Box and make it festive! Whether your decorations are Christmas-related, Hanukkah-related (yes, I know it will be over by then, but who takes down decorations that quickly?), winter-related, present-related, or just pretty, you can join in the fun. To encourage active participation I am – that is, the Wishing Rock General Store is – sponsoring a contest. Best decorated home wins a $10 certificate at the store. Most festive commons room get a 10% off coupon at the store for everyone on that floor. Let the competition commence!

d. Open House Potluck: If you don't know how to potluck by now, you must be new here. The Open House potluck will commence at 6 p.m., this one downstairs in the auditorium lobby. Bring your best dish! Since we'll have visitors, if you'd like to print up some recipe cards to share with passers by whose taste buds you seduce, that might be a nice touch. I know many people also appreciate it if you post a notecard by your dish listing its ingredients, in case someone might be allergic.

4. The Inn: Claire reports that the Inn is full booked up over the dates of the Open House, so if visitors are going to stay overnight, I guess they'll have to go to Moon Bay. Ed and Michael are looking into staging a couple empty units in our Box, buying nice furniture for them and whatnot. They'll look all pretty (the rooms, not the Brooks boys) for the Open House, and then can be used as vacation rentals after that (again, the rooms, not the Brooks boys).

5. New Year's Eve "Formal": And, last but not least, don't forget our Formal New Year's Eve Ball! As you may have guessed, this is a dance that takes place on New Year's Eve. All are welcome, with or without a date. Define "formal" however you wish, we just want you to be there. If you want to come dressed to the nines, come dressed to the nines; if you want to come in your pajamas, come in your pajamas. After the traditional yearly discussion of moving the Ball to Moon Bay, since they have that lovely conference center, it was once again decided there is no place like home. Sign up in the lobby to be on the decorations committee. So we may all concentrate on our gorgeous gowns and handsome suitors rather than cooking, the Ball will be catered by a cafe from the Bay. No charge for the tickets, but please "purchase" one anyway by December 24 so the committee knows how many people to expect.

Is that all? I'm sure I've forgotten something and I'm sure you smart people will remind me. I have a good stash of Christmas cards in the store now, and I've stocked up on the makings for fudge. What's more, Walter made a batch of his Aunt Marie's traditional "pfeffernüsse" cookies, and by golly one batch makes about a million cookies. I've brought some to the store for visitors to munch on, so come on by and say hello! Recipe below. Yes, Walter does realize it contains neither "pfeffer" nor "nüsse." They do, however, contain a good deal of delicious.

Happy holidays, everyone!

Millie

Aunt Marie's Pfeffernüsse
Ingredients
 2 cups sugar
 1 cup dark corn syrup
 1 cup butter
 1/2 cup evaporated milk
 1/2 cup shortening
 1 tsp baking soda
 1/2 tsp anise oil
 1/2 tsp allspice
 1 tsp cardamom
 1 tsp nutmeg
 1 tsp cloves
 1 tsp cinnamon
 6+ cups flour (enough to make a fairly stiff dough)
Directions
1. Mix all ingredients thoroughly and chill overnight in refrigerator. Next day, take the dough and roll into ropes about 1/2" in diameter.
2. Freeze rolls in freezer until hard but easily sliced. Slice about 1/4" thick.
3. Bake on ungreased cookie sheet at 350° for 6 minutes. Do not let the cookies touch on cookie sheet before baking. Do not overbake. Watch cookies closely; because they're so small, the moment between "done" and "overdone" comes quickly!
4. Cool on tea towel. Store in airtight container.
Questions? Ask Walter.

From: Ruby
To: Gran
Sent: December 2, 2010
Subject: Hello!

Hi, Gran! I'm so sorry I missed your call on my birthday. As it turns out, Ed owns a tiny little island not too far from our own Dogwinkle Island, and he took me out there for the day. A lovely little almost-midweek escape. Cold and a bit damp, but that's the way end-of-November birthdays always are, so it was nothing new.

The island, however, was of course new to me, and a great birthday adventure! I've never given much thought to what a private island would or should be like, but now that I've seen this one (as yet unnamed – something we need to rectify!), I think, honestly, it's about the most perfect little island a person could ever hope to own. It's not too tiny; rather, it's actually quite a nice size. Ed says it's a bit over nine acres. Right now, it's completely undeveloped except for a make-shift boat dock, but Ed says it's zoned for a home if he should ever want to build one out there. I'd initially thought, well, you'd need to build roads, right? But I suppose you wouldn't really. Paths for hiking and for your bikes or golf carts or whatever, maybe, but not really roads. Nine acres is pretty small. You can get up late and still walk around the whole island before brunch.

As for shape, the island itself is somewhat long and narrow, with a meandering coastline with bites taken out of it here and there. Along the west side, facing out into the sunset, there's a beautiful sheltered bay (or cove? What's the difference between a bay and a cove?) with a sandy beach and a good-sized area, fairly level and more or less clear, beyond the beach, so that's where he'd probably build. The level area is raised up a bit from the beach area, so you're not right on the beach and you have to climb down a bit and through some dunes to get to the water – oh, that's the other bit of construction on the island, a rough boardwalk and steps leading from the beach through the dunes to the level area – but on a small island such as this, there's no such thing, really, as a far distance. We spent the day hiking around;

it made me realize how much we take for granted all the trails that workers have spent hours and days and years creating in parks, to make it easier for us all to make our way around! I made Ed walk in front of me with a stick, to sweep away any spider webs. It wasn't too bad, actually, but it was the least he could do for me on my birthday, right? We didn't explore the whole island, but Ed showed me some of his favorite places. We hiked to the top of the low cliffs on the south side, meandered around the bay area, hacked our way through a forested area on the east, explored another clearing in the northeast that might have room for a tiny little landing strip, should a person want to make the island accessible by air. Then we went back to the boat, where Ed brought out a bottle of wine and a picnic basket of goodies, and toasted the day and me, and us.

Anyway, I could tell he loves this little island and even if he doesn't come out here much, and though he hasn't done much with it yet, he has given it lots of thought. I'm honored that he took me out to see it. He's so often giving and doing for others that it was almost surprising to see something he dreams about just for himself. This is his. Not Wishing Rock's, not the Brooks family's; it's his. And it's beautiful. If I had an island like that, I think I'd build a castle on it. Remember when we were in Scotland? Even as I write that, I realize the error of my ways: of course you are still there! But remember when I was there with you, and we were driving around? All those castles, they still play around in my brain sometimes. I know people say they're drafty and damp and cold, but you have to admit, there's something undeniably and indisputably romantic about a castle.

Enough about Ed's island, though. How are you? How is Liam? Are you enjoying being "home" again? Do you think of Liam's house as "home" now? What else is going on?

Love you and miss you so much!
Ruby

From: Gran
To: Ruby
Sent: December 3, 2010
Subject: RE: Hello!

Happy belated birthday, my dear granddaughter! It sounds like you had a spectacular day. And how could you not, out on Ed's private island! Not that Wishing Rock (which I must visit sometime) doesn't sound grand, but Ed's Island sounds idyllic. I was talking with Liam about Ed owning his own island, and both of us had our interests piqued at the idea. We went onto the internet to find out what we could find out. As it turns out, buying one's own island isn't as much of a pipe dream as one might think. Definitely some islands range into the millions of dollars, but some are quite affordable by almost any standard – cheaper, even, than an average house in Seattle. Unbelievable! Liam even found one out here near Oban that's available for sale right now. The idea of owning an island is, I agree, somehow so romantic (but why?) that I must admit, I was tempted. But I'm at an age where I'd best be getting rid of possessions rather than acquiring them. An island will not, therefore, be amongst the things I leave behind when I go.

You said Ed has plans to build. Did he say when? A little cabin escape would be so nice. Isolated as Wishing Rock is, you're all right on top of each other. A chance to breathe away from prying eyes would surely be nice.

Now, to get you up to date on the latest in my little Oban, my charming town of scattered homes and steep hills!

I talked with Pip last night and she, Gavin, and the baby are all doing well. The rest of Scotland has been caught tight in winter's icy grip, but luckily Mull is only today starting to get the snow. Pip is nearly halfway through the pregnancy, and while I would never be one to accuse one of my perfect granddaughters of any imperfections, let's just say I think Gavin's life is getting easier again, after Pip's somewhat trying first trimester. Fewer eggshells to tiptoe on now; she isn't gagging quite as much at the smell of him; her emotions are not tripped quite as easily; the world is a calmer place. For now! As for great grandma, I haven't knit an afghan in decades but I've borrowed a neighbor's knitting needles and am working on a baby blanket for my great grandbaby-to-be. Keeps my lap warm on these cold winter nights, and warms my heart, too, to think maybe this child might cherish an afghan knit by dear old great grandma, long after I'm gone.

Not only is it cold and snowy but the nights are getting quite long, and one starts to realize how far north Scotland is. We are getting just over seven hours of daylight each day now – more than an hour less than you. And I feel it! The sun – or rather, the light, since there really is no sun – is barely up before it starts going down again, and the gray lingers in the sky and our minds; the chill lingers in our bones. I am more than ready for the tides to turn again at the end of the month, for the light to return to our days and our souls! An old lady does start to wonder how many more long dark winters she'll be blessed to endure, or how many more springs she'll have the joy to welcome. Much as I try not to be fatalistic, every day I am aware of the time I have left. Even with the kindest of fates it's unlikely I'll see Pip's baby graduate, and certainly not marry. Even with the kindest of fates I won't have many years with Liam, and at my age those years go so fast. Even with the kindest of fates I simply don't have nearly enough time left.

Having said that, though, Ruby, I want you to know your old Gran has led a good life with no regrets. While I might want more years – and a younger back and knees – I wouldn't want to live forever. If we lived forever, we couldn't appreciate today. It is the temporary, limited nature of our time on earth that bring the moments into sharp focus. Our mortality is a blessing. Remember that. All the moments, even the bad ones, are blessings.

Well, I'd better get to my knitting. If I finish this blanket early I might like to make a matching cap and booties. And then another set, just in case another baby comes along! I'd forgotten the peace that can be found in the gentle, rhythmic clicking of two needles.

Wishing you another wonderful year of joy, love, and grace,
All my love,
Gran

~

From: Ruby
To: Erin
Sent: December 4, 2010
Subject: Out the door

Hey lady!

We're just about out the door. Ed and Michael wanted to catch the early ferry in to Seattle for this furniture-shopping expedition. Carolyn and I are so excited, getting free reign to furnish two whole condo units, top to bottom! I suggested that we could just move all my stuff into one of the homes they're staging, and they could buy me all new stuff, but somehow they disagreed. Whatever, we get to shop! And, don't tell Ed, but I suspect that if we happen to buy some things that I absolutely love, it would not be impossible to convince him that these items truly belong in my home. Even if that's not the case, I still am more than a little excited about going into the stores and pointing at things and saying "this, and that, and that, and oh this too, put it on that gentleman's charge card." Since these units are to be rented out, we're doing a three-bedroom unit and a two bedroom unit, to start with. That would suit a good number of families, I'd think. Whether anyone will actually want to vacation at Wishing Rock is an interesting question, but that is not my concern at this point. My concern is, bamboo sheets or cotton? Love seat or full couch? And so on. Whee!

Ed confirmed with Ben that Ben will be by to help out at the office Monday if we're not back yet – there's so much to be bought that it wouldn't surprise me if it takes a while. It is so handy that that kid takes his classes online and is so flexible. I think he's taken on about every job there is at Wishing Rock, for a day or two anyway, sort of our own live-in temp worker. Good thing he's a quick learner! Besides which, there aren't many jobs in Wishing Rock that can be messed up in only a day or two. I like to think of it as aiding his education.

At any rate, we're just about off. I'll talk to you soon!

xxx

Ruby

Text from Erin to Ruby
Sent: December 4, 2010

Got your message. Ben and I will hold down the fort! Be home by Tuesday. I'm heading to Hawaii Wednesday.

Text from Ruby to Erin
Sent: December 4, 2010

Wait! What?? For how long?

Text from Erin to Ruby
Sent: December 4, 2010

A couple weeks anyway. I bought tickets for the 8th through 22nd for now, but if I like it, who knows, maybe I'll stay longer.

Text from Ruby to Erin
Sent: December 4, 2010

Well of course you're going to like it. It's Hawaii! But I thought you were going to Iceland? What happened to Iceland?

~

Text from Erin to Ruby
Sent: December 4, 2010

December happened to Iceland. I may go some other time. I'd like to, still. Right now, though, there are only about four hours between sunrise and sunset in Reykjavik. Not really prime real estate for someone who needs to lighten her mood! Hawaii sounds a lot more like what I need.

~

Text from Ruby to Erin
Sent: December 4, 2010

Good point. You're going to miss the Open House, though! Okay, we'll be home by Tuesday for sure. Get packed early so you can plan on dinner at my house Tuesday. We're off to the kitchen store – I'll talk with you soon. x

~

Text from Erin to Ruby
Sent: December 4, 2010

Somehow I will survive missing the Open House. I'll leave a potluck dish with Millie and it'll be like I'm there. And I'll be home in time for caroling. Don't worry, it's just a vacation! See you soon. xx

~

From: Alexandra
To: Ed
Sent: December 5, 2010
Subject: Danger

Mr. Edward, how are you? How goes the furniture hunting? Our dear Box is certainly getting a good makeover, isn't it! Claire has Tom and Ben running around the whole place with paint cans, touching up walls and baseboards and window frames. Good thing you and Michael aren't here "helping" or I'd worry the whole thing would turn into a paint war. Don't deny it. Claire told me today about the time they were gone and you and Michael drywalled over the doorway between their bedroom and their bathroom. Clearly, the best use of your time, energy, and creativity. Men! I will never understand you with that silly Y chromosome.

And, in fact, that's why I'm writing. To warn you. Ever since David got a taste of the adventures the poker gals and I were having the last few months, he now wants to devour the whole smörgåsbord. He has decided Dogwinkle needs a zipline somewhere, and he's decided you and Michael are the ones to make it possible. My gentle banker is becoming a wild man. As we speak he's working on a business plan and will be approaching you with it soon for your consideration as an investor. I don't know whether to plea his case with you or encourage you to discourage him! A zipline! Good heavens. Because what we need on this island is people falling to their untimely deaths. Can you even think of a place on the island where the ziplining would be good? I can't really picture it, unless it's out between Balky Point and Moon Bay, somewhere around Knot Mountain maybe. I haven't explored much that way, but I'm sure it'll happen soon. David has made mumblings about "winter camping" and I'm not all too pleased to hear him including me in those plans. Why would I leave a perfectly warm and dry home to drive five miles to lie on rocks in the cold and rain? Something about that just doesn't seem so hospitable. Perhaps I should encourage a boys' camping trip with you and the others? Then again, your combined testosteroney influence may not be what I want for him either. It seems the spelunking was just the start.

Having said that, he's still the same old David at heart. After the Open House is over, he has told me, we are going to spend some time getting together my Home Emergency Kit. You might recall he has three kits himself: home, work, car. The fact that these three kits are generally located within walking distance of each other now that he lives and works in Wishing Rock is a moot point. David assures me that in case of disaster our biggest challenge won't be the earthquake or hurricane or whatnot itself, nor will it be treating our injuries. No, our biggest challenge will be food poisoning, stemming from the fact that if we even have kits to begin with, none of us can be bothered to change out the emergency food more than once a decade. I believe he was kidding on this point, but then again, he might not have been. I can barely keep my pantry current. I just dumped out broth with a "best if used by" date of 2007, and I am still not convinced it wouldn't have been perfectly fine to use.

Food poisoning due to lazy people. Who would have thought this is how our civilization will end. Thank goodness I have David here to save me! It must be fate.

I'm sure you've heard by now that our Erin is heading to Hawaii Wednesday. I'd tell her we can't run away from ourselves but that's the sort of thing a person has to figure out for herself. Wherever we go, our brains and our hearts and our fears go right there with us. Besides which, I've done the same myself more than a time or two. If one is going to delude oneself into thinking a change of scenery will fix everything that is wrong in one's life, one might as well be warm whilst doing it.

So, there you go. Ziplining, business plan, Hawaii.

You did talk with Claire and Tom, didn't you, before deciding to spruce up a couple rooms for rent? I'd hate for there to be strife at home over your competing with the Inn.

Love to all,

A.

From: Ed
To: Alexandra
Sent: December 6, 2010
Subject: RE: Danger

Ziplining? Ziplining! How did we not think of that before! Lex, you're brilliant! Must talk with Michael immediately. Oh, the liability. First we dabble in liquor, now in high-risk adventure. What next, teaching people to juggle with fire and swords? Ziplining! Lex! Your man is brilliant.

Yup, Rubes told me about Erin. Well, hell, as you in your wisdom pointed out, ain't nothing wrong with a little Hawaii in December. We've been driving and walking in the rain for two days now, and I can't say as I'm all that charmed. Frankly, I think maybe we should all follow Erin and make sure she's okay.

Seriously, don't worry about our girl Erin. Just having her midlife crisis a little early, that's all. She'll be fine, will come through it better than ever.

Our shopping is almost done. It's pretty simple. Or would have been, had Michael and I come alone. Good golly Molly but those ladies had to look at everything before deciding! Carolyn more so than Ruby. She has a good eye; I just wish it were a little quicker. If you see something you like, must you really check to make sure there's nothing you like more? This isn't whiskey distilling. This is furniture.

Yes, we talked with Claire and Tom. We're not trying to steal business; just trying to add flexibility. We'll always try to steer people to the Inn first, but for some families a whole apartment will make more sense. Hopefully we can drive some business to Wishing Rock. Also, we can pay someone to do the cleaning and whatnot when renters leave, which will be a little more money in the local pocket, which is good. Gotta do what we can to help our people.

So, shopping nearly done, tonight we celebrate with a late night happy hour overlooking the water. I'll wave out toward you all, and we'll be home tomorrow, probably early afternoon.
Ed

From: Alexandra
To: Ed
Sent: December 6, 2010
Subject: RE: RE: Danger

Wonderful, we will see you tomorrow, then. I'm glad to hear you've had such success with the shopping, and very glad to hear there will be no Brooks/Stewart feud in our midst.

Erin tells me Ruby was going to have dinner at her house tomorrow, but since she won't have much time to plan, tell her we've arranged a going-away party at my house instead. The usual crowd. Cocktails and cup stacking. You do not know what you have started. David is a cup stacking machine. Be warned. Be afraid.

We'll start early, heavy hors d'oeuvres and drinks rather than the fuss of a real dinner. Bring an appetizer if you have time to put something together.

A.

~

From: Ed
To: Alexandra
Sent: December 6, 2010
Subject: RE: RE: RE: Danger

Ruby's right: You do say "we" a lot these days. You rascal, you, Alexandra! Who knew, David and Alexandra. You know I'm certified to perform weddings, right? Or I could be, just say the word.

Message about hors d'oeuvres and drinks has been passed along; Ruby heaved a sigh of relief and said thanks. We'll see you tomorrow!

~

From: Ruby
To: Pip
Sent: December 7, 2010
Subject: hey

Oy vey, it's late. Thought I'd say a quick hello before heading to bed. Erin is leaving tomorrow for Maui for two weeks, with the threat of staying longer if she likes it. Who wouldn't like it? She can't move away; I won't have it. She just needs a break from ... hm. From what? She just needs time to think, I guess. I think the whole David and Alexandra thing still sort of bugs her. She broke up with him, but still, we like to keep our options open, don't we? Who am I to say anything; I picked up my whole life and moved to Wishing Rock after Pete dumped me. In retrospect, though, I'd say it worked out pretty well for me.

How are you guys doing? How's the wee baby growing in there? Gran is so excited. I can't tell you how glad I am she's over there for you. You're such a long way from home, Pip! I miss you. Can't we convince Captain Gavin to move here? We have water here, too, and an island, and boats. He's needed here as much as he's needed there, and you are needed here very very much.

I swear it's not just because I want to see the baby. I want you around, too.

That's so selfish of me! I want you to do what makes you happy and be where you're happy and with the people who make you happy. But I can't help missing you. Ed has been talking about visiting distilleries in the U.K.; maybe I could come visit with him sometime? Hopefully soon.

Because after all, from what I hear, the weather in the U.K. in winter is lovely! Haha. Or not so much.

I'm about to fall asleep at the computer. Going to bed now. Give the baby a kiss for me.

Love you,
Ruby

From: Pip
To: Ruby
Sent: December 8, 2010
Subject: RE: hey

Wow, it was indeed late when you sent that email – we were already up for the day! We go on walks almost every day now, morning or evening depending on Gavin's schedule, which is more unpredictable this time of year due to weather. The walking is supposed to help with growing-baby-related mommy issues. Who woulda thunk having something growing inside you would be so hard on a person's body? Anyway, today it was a morning walk, with us bundled up in eight hundred layers each. It is so cold! For a long while we managed to escape the snow that has shut down the rest of the country, but it finally caught us, too. Even so, despite my misgivings of Mull being so isolated and remote, and despite the fact that Scotland in general is insanely cold and snowy right now, this really is a nice little island. I know you miss me there and I miss all of you, too, but my little corner of Scotland, my baby, my husband, my tiny bakery business, my home, my hearth, my life, these are all so, so good right now. Every bad thing I ever went through was worth it to get to this.

I've read that at about sixteen weeks, the baby is now about the size of an avocado. Ruby, I never imagined I would be someone who would be tracking my baby with online pregnancy calculators, but I am. I'm fascinated! Sometimes it's a little creepy, though. Fingernails and toenails gross me out in general, so the idea of a creature growing inside me with its own fingernails and toenails (not present now, but they will be by thirty-two weeks) is something I just try not to think about. They say I'll be able to feel the baby kick in a few weeks, and I'm right at the point where they could probably tell if it's a boy or a girl. It's a good thing we have twenty-four weeks left because there's not a single name we agree on yet. I know I'm not supposed to want a girl over a boy or a boy over a girl; I'm supposed to just want him or her to be happy and healthy. Gavin just wants happy and healthy, because he already has one of each, Riley and Alina, and on top of this

his brothers and sisters have produced legions of nieces and nephews as well. But me, well, I guess there's just something about Scotland that makes me want a boy. I can't explain it. A hearty, healthy boy to romp amongst the heather and wear kilts and be the spit-and-image of his da, play the bagpipes at Grandpa Liam's knee and learn to dance with Grandma Adele. But in the end, happy and healthy is enough. You know, they don't tell you that when you're pregnant your heart's capacity for love grows at eight times the rate of your belly. I love this little kid so much. Gross toenails and all.

I'm assuming you guessed this, but we're not keeping the pregnancy secret anymore. Tell anyone you like, if you haven't already.

Gavin says hello, and he says to tell you we'd love to have you come visit, with or without Ed, anytime. We would. Come soon.

Hello to all,
Pip

~

From: Ruby
To: Pip
Sent: December 8, 2010
Subject: RE: RE: hey

That's it. I have to visit. Keep the light on for me. I'm going to start planning, and one way or another, we'll be there as soon as we can! Maybe we'll wait for the Deep Freeze of the U.K. to thaw before we head over. Bundle up and stay warm!

Love you,
Ruby

~

From: Erin
To: Ruby
Sent: December 9, 2010
Subject: Maui

I'm here! Basking in the muggy, glorious Maui heat. Got in about 2:30 yesterday afternoon, then what with car rental, stopping at the store for some groceries, and driving time, I didn't get to my condo until just before 5:00. Oh, and also a stop at a tiny farmer's market right next door to the condos! How handy is that?

First on the agenda last night: wine on the balcony while watching the sun lower itself into the ocean. The condos I'm staying at are right on the beach, literally just feet away from the sand and a perfect little bay. Humpback whales are migrating now, and their route takes them right past my balcony. I was sitting on the deck, Riesling in hand (that is, Riesling in glass in hand), when I heard a loud "Oooooh! Good one!" from two decks away. Thinking with great hope that it wasn't one of THOSE kind of neighbors, the creaky bed kind, I looked up and saw a man pointing out to the ocean. I followed his gaze just in time to see the splash of a humpback that had just "breached." Pulled out my binoculars and watched for a while longer to see if it would resurface, but it didn't. Nonetheless, I have a mission: see another whale breach while I'm here.

The man, smiling, looking relaxed and happy, somewhere in his late 30s or early 40s, saw me and waved, then went back into his room. Single?

After the spectacular sunset, which happened just moments after I'd just settled onto the balcony, I fixed myself dinner of fresh local tomatoes and mozzarella and olive oil on crusty bread. By 7 p.m. I was exhausted. Made myself stay awake until 8, but I fell right asleep to the sound of the waves and the gentle caress of the wind through the blinds. It's funny how dark it gets so quickly after sunset. Makes it feel like it's the middle of the night when it's only 7:30. On the other hand, I was wide awake well before 5 this morning. Sleeping in until after 6 a.m. felt luxurious and sinful! Got up, went on a sunrise run, picked up a plumeria blossom that had dropped from a plumeria tree on the trail back to my room, and came in and made a mango pineapple smoothie. Now here I am again on the balcony, plumeria in my hair, watching for whales.

I don't know what the agenda is for the day. Maybe I won't have an agenda until after lunch. I do think a nap is a requirement. This warm weather feels so sultry after the cold of Wishing Rock. Maui was a good choice.

Chat soon, Ruby! If you're online sometime look and see if I am and let's IM.

E.

~

From: Ruby
To: Erin
Sent: December 9, 2010
Subject: RE: Maui

Erin Paige Anderson, I am so jealous of you right now! We had intense wind and thunderstorms all day yesterday. Not a bad thing, really; I love thunderstorms and it feels like we never get them. Ed and I went up to the Inn and joined Claire and Tom on that covered part of their porch to watch the lightning strikes and count the seconds before the thunder. Even so, beautiful as that may have been, it was wet. It is so wet. And our sunset is just after 4 p.m.! Wet, cold, and really short days. I would give an awful lot to be sipping a frou frou drink on a balcony in Hawaii right now. Soak up that sun but please don't come back too tan. I might have to hurt you if you do.

Wishing Rock is in a frenzy getting ready for the Open House. It's actually quite fun, with everyone so excited! People have decorated their doors to look like gifts, and the commons rooms are starting to look like Santa threw up all over them. Shiny everywhere! Bells everywhere! Silver and gold everywhere! Snowflakes everywhere! It's quite a sight! I'll take some pictures and send them on to you.

I'll try to catch you on IM soon. Relax and enjoy life, my friend!

x

Ruby

~

From: Ruby
To: Mom
Sent: December 10, 2010
Subject: fudge

Hey, Mom,

Can you send me the fudge recipe? I can't find mine anywhere. I don't know how I lost it, but it's severely missing. Our Open House is tomorrow. I think I have all the ingredients; just need the recipe! Thanks!

Love, Ruby

~

From: Mom
To: Ruby
Sent: December 10, 2010
Subject: RE: fudge

Hi, sweetheart,

Recipe below. I made some four days ago and your father has already eaten a quarter of it. This year the chocolate bars are down another fraction of an ounce again and you'll have to buy three if you want to do the recipe just right. Soon the baking bars will be smaller than the eating bars. My last batch turned out a little dry. I don't understand how it could be dry with the humidity and all the rain. Maybe I boiled it too long. I think my candy thermometer might be broken. Did you find your candy thermometer? I think it's safer to revert to the old-fashioned method of simply bringing to a boil and then boiling for five minutes. I've never had as much success since I started using the candy thermometers. Next time I'm going to go with the boiling method.

I used that kitchen scale you gave me last year to help measure out the marshmallow creme, as that's just so hard to measure. 1 1/3 cups turns out to be about 4.13 ounces, I think. Try that and see if that works for you.

Hello from Dad.

Love, Mom

Fudge
Ingredients
    2 cups (12 oz) chocolate chips
    9 oz milk chocolate bar, broken into bits
    1 1/3 cups marshmallow creme (about 4.13 ounces)
    2 Tbsp butter
    2 2/3 cups chopped nuts (optional)
    1 1/3 cups evaporated milk
    3 cups sugar
    Dash salt
Directions
- In mixing bowl mix the chocolate chips, chocolate bar, marshmallow, butter, and nuts.
- In large and deep pan, mix evaporated milk, sugar, and salt. Bring to a boil over medium heat; boil 5 minutes or to 225°, stirring constantly.
- Remove from heat and pour over chocolate. Stir until chocolate melts and mixture is smooth.
- Pour into ungreased 9x13 pan. Cool completely and cut into 1" squares. If it seems a little too runny, wait a bit and it still might set up just fine.

From: Ruby
To: Mom
Sent: December 10, 2010
Subject: RE: RE: fudge

I had all the ingredients but I messed up! The last few years my fudge has been too dry, and when you said yours was dry this year too I got fudge-scared, underboiled, and it was a mess. The consistency of frosting! I'm going to have to make it again. This time I'll just boil it five minutes no matter what the thermometer says and if it's runny, I'll just hope it sets up overnight. Millie has some of the ingredients downstairs but Ed has run into the grocery store at Moon Bay for me to get more marshmallow creme before I can make another batch. Darn it! All that effort, wasted. Well, Ed says we can put it on graham crackers. Like we need more sugar this time of year!

Take "new candy thermometer" off my Christmas list. I can't believe that every year this fudge comes out different. You'd think we'd be pros at it by now. I guess that's part of the tradition, the yearly mother-daughter kibitzing over the size of the chocolate bars and the state of the fudge. If I'm ever President I'm going to do a State of the Fudge address every December.

Ed just got back so I'm firing up the stove again. Wish me luck. Love you, love to Dad!

Ruby

From: Erin
To: Ruby
Sent: December 11, 2010
Subject: peace

Hey, Rubes. So it's the big day there – the Open House! I imagine the Box is bursting with people inquisitive about our odd way of life. Actually, I'll be really curious to hear whether anyone shows up. It's a great idea and all, and I know they've been marketing it like mad to anyone who will listen, but will anyone really come? Getting to Wishing Rock takes some effort. Give me a full report. Make sure someone records Walter's concert, too. I'll want to watch that, for sure. If you get this before the concert begins, tell everyone I said good luck or break a leg or whatever it is one says to musicians that doesn't jinx them to oblivion.

Maui is divine. One thing you should know: if there's an apocalypse and I am called on to rebuild the earth in some fashion, If I'm in Hawaii you should just give up hope. Being here has an intensely relaxing effect on me. Almost like a lobotomy. Like a forget-it-all serum. As I write this it's just after my morning run, I'm sitting on my condo's balcony, staring out at the ocean, and I keep thinking "Focus, Erin, focus! We ..." (speaking to myself in the royal "we") "We came here to sort things out, to make some decisions about life, to figure out a path, to discern what we need to do on our quest for our Declaration-of-Independence-given right to pursue happiness." But somehow my focus shifts, and I spend the greater part of each day lulling in serenity, watching the migration of the humpback whales. This isn't a tedious pursuit, mind you. Somewhat fruitless, but not tedious. It consists of watching the vast ocean for little puffs of water, then trying to determine whether that puff was just a wave crashing against the water, or a whale spouting off. It's mesmerizing. It may even be close to meditation. Watching the ocean for signs of whales has a way of emptying the mind of all worries and cares.

In fact, if it weren't for my morning runs, I don't know that I'd have any focus at all. My runs bring me back to my goals and keep my brain from going off the deep end. Without them I'm sure I'd go insane. I'm still getting up at 6 a.m. every day – so much easier here than at home in the drizzly rain. By 8:30 it's getting too hot to run. Most walkers and runners are out around 7:00 so I have that magical hour from 6 to 7 to myself. The sun hasn't quite risen at six; it's awake, but lollygagging in bed reading the paper, not quite up yet. In those morning hours I renew.

I have decided my aim here is to embrace my imperfections and to learn and live with abandon. I'm going to hula, to tackle the ukulele, to do everything I can without worrying about doing it right. I don't care anymore about consequences. I can deal with consequences. What I can't deal with anymore is hiding from life. Don't tell Alexandra I said that. I know she thinks I'm hiding from things, running from things. The way I see it, in coming to Hawaii I was running away from noise. Turning down the volume so I could hear the quiet whispers. They're coming through.

I'm heading off in a bit to drive the road to Hana. Actually, I think it's supposed to be in title case: The Road to Hana. Whether I will get there is yet to be determined. I'm told that with The Road to Hana, the journey very literally is the destination. There's not much "there" there at Hana, so one must enjoy the trip along the way. I've packed up suntan lotion, a floppy hat, my camera, some water and snacks; I've noted the various famous banana bread stops along the way; I've marked what are supposed to be the "best" waterfalls on my map; I'm ready to go.

I could get used to this.

Love you,

Erin

~

Text from Alexandra to Ruby
Sent: December 11, 2010

Come get my potluck dish. I can't go.

~

Text from Ruby to Alexandra
Sent: December 11, 2010

Alexandra is texting? A text from Lex?? As Ed would say. Must be a special occasion! What's up, buttercup? Why can't you come? Sure, I'll swing by now.

~

Text from Alexandra to Ruby
Sent: December 11, 2010

My mother is here. My mother, whom I haven't seen since the Lincoln administration. My mother is here. She just got here. I don't know. We'll talk later.

~

Text from Ruby to Alexandra
Sent: December 11, 2010

Holy moly! We will talk later for sure! I'm on my way. Let me know if you need anything else!

~

From: Erin
To: Ruby
Sent: December 11, 2010
Subject: shaving

Aloha again! Just wanted to throw you a bone. Maui is divine, but I'd forgotten one thing: shaving in winter. Normally my razor is settled in for a long winter's nap at this point. Now, I'm going to be shaving every day for two weeks. In December. So, you know, yes it's warm and the sunsets are gorgeous and the whales are playful and the drinks are fruity and the male hula dancers are indescribably yummy and the sand in my toes tickles and the plumeria smell like heaven, but also, I'm shaving every day. Does that help make you feel better about my being in paradise while you're getting drowned?

I was thinking about shaving. I came to the conclusion that the first woman ever to shave her legs was probably a hooker. And here we're all following suit. Yet, I don't have it in me to rebel. That darned first leg-shaving woman! Ruined it for the rest of us.

~

From: Ruby
To: Erin
Sent: December 11, 2010
Subject: RE: shaving

Just in from the potluck. Exhausted, will write more later. Yes, yes of course, if you have to shave in winter then Hawaii is hardly worth the trouble! I see your point. Now I'm curious about the history of shaving. Lucky for me I'm too tired to bother looking it up. Will chat more soon! Alexandra has news. Love you, goodnight!

~

From: Alexandra
To: Erin
Sent: December 12, 2010
Subject: family

Hello, my love, aloha, how are you?

I am whirring. My brain awhirr. You know the feeling, I suppose.

Yesterday was, of course, our Open House. All manner of people came to discover our little haven; who would have thought? A great deal of interest in our simple world, our simple lives.

But that fact, astonishing as it is, is not what is on my mind. What my brain is whirring about: My mother showed up.

She didn't call first to warn me or to ask. Just showed up. The Open House committee blanketed the region with flyers and posts online and all imaginable types of advertisements for weeks, trying to boost our little population here. Did you see the flyers? My picture was on some of them. Mom somehow saw one of them and recognized me and researched. I changed my name but, stupid me, I kept my middle name as my first. So, she found me.

Half an hour before the potluck I got a knock on my door. There she stood. I had Ruby come get my casserole, and then Mom and I talked the rest of the night.

It's tempting to get angry. It's tempting to lash out, give voice to all the vicious accusations that come to mind. It's tempting to ask why she never did anything to get us away from my father when he was hurting us all. I chose, however, to listen instead, to see if now, now that I'm in my forties rather than a naïve child, I could understand her perspective. I chose to listen and to ask questions.

Erin, it is wise to remember that each of us is the protagonist of our own story. Each of us is a master at justifying the things we have done, at believing we've done the best we could. I suppose it's true. None of us can do any better than we know how. My mother – who of course was quite young herself then, however old she may have seemed to my young eyes – simply did not know any better about how to get us out of that situation, away from that abuse.

She didn't apologize. She still doesn't really believe she did anything wrong. She believed and believes she had nowhere else to go, didn't believe she could support us without him. Unbeknownst to me, though he wasn't working last I saw him and seemed to spend all his time in a drunk stupor on the couch, he did in fact dapple in selling soft drugs, just enough that my mother felt she couldn't make do without his "income." She knew things weren't perfect but couldn't see a way out. I could get angry now that she didn't have the courage to try, that she didn't believe in herself or value us enough to try, but what would be the point?

It does seem that "wrong" can't always be a relative term, but it might be more relative at some times than others.

My father, she told me, is dead. Liver failure. Not a shock. What did I feel when she passed on this news? Curious, I suppose, that he'd never tried to come talk to me from the beyond. Even dead, he still doesn't care about me. It's mutual. Is it? Is that true? No, it's not. I suspect every one of us, whether it's logical or not, reasonable or not, forever wishes for the love and acceptance of our parents.

Somehow he must have been the protagonist in his own story, too. Somehow he must have justified everything he did. Somehow he must have felt vindicated, felt he was in the right.

Mom saved the biggest surprise for the end of the evening. After I told her about how I lost my visions recently, and how it's been so good to feel my deceased husband and children around me again, she paused for a good while. I thought she was going to say something about her grandchildren, about how she'd wished she'd known them, something like that. Instead, when words finally came out of her mouth: "You have a sister, you know. An older sister. Your dad had a daughter with another woman before he met me. He left them behind and never bothered with them again. I found out a year before he died when she came looking for him. She's in Bellingham now."

A half-sister. In Bellingham. We were just there. Did we pass her on our poker outing? If I'd been connected to the spirit world at the time could I have sensed her somehow? Does she know about me?

"She doesn't know about you. We didn't talk much about you after you left home. When I tried at first, your father would …. So, anyway, we didn't talk about you. We didn't tell her."

Ouch.

I didn't ask any more about this woman, my half-sister. I was in too much shock, I think.

Now to decide what to do about her. Really, there's no deciding to be done. I will have to find her, meet her. I can't not know.

I'm reminding myself to look at it from her perspective, impossible as that feels. Each of us, doing the best we know how at the time. I don't think I was the person my parents thought I was, and as it turns out they were simply humans too, as broken as the rest of us. Was it Ruby's Gran who said that none of us can ever really know another person? The older I get, the more I see it's true.

My mother stayed in Moon Bay and was gone in the morning before I had a chance to find her. She left me the name of my half-sister, and that's it. The next move is mine.

Well, that should keep me occupied for a while! As for the rest of the Open House, I missed it completely. Hopefully people weren't too turned off by the rain. Wet yesterday and even wetter today. The pineapple express has arrived, the weathermen tell us! All the way from your neck of the woods. We appreciate it, thank you so much!

Miss you,
Love
A.

From: Erin
To: Alexandra
Sent: December 13, 2010
Subject: RE: family

That's crazy about your mom showing up out of nowhere. Do you think she thought you'd refuse to see her if you knew she was coming? What would you have said if she'd asked? As for your dad, I'm sorry … I'm sorry for your loss? I'm not sure what to say here. There's a loss there, whether he was kind to you or not. There are lots of losses there. I'm sorry for your loss.

How are you going to go about meeting your sister? Calling her? Stopping at her house? Makes it a little inconvenient that your parents never gave her a hint that you exist. Well, keep me in the loop. You know I'm here for you.

As for Hawaii. Alexandra, it's almost bedtime and I just got home from … a date. I think it was a date. I'm not entirely sure, but it sure felt like a date.

I know what you're thinking. "This is Erin. Doesn't Erin have rules? No new relationships between Labor Day and her birthday in March?"

Yes, this is Erin. This is Maui, though, and the rules seem to be flying out the window.

The other day I headed out on the Road to Hana, expecting waterfalls and dramatic vistas and a slow, curvy drive. I was determined not to overplan – some have accused me of such in the past – so I stopped when I wanted to stop, drove on when I wanted to drive on, took detours when intriguing detours presented themselves.

One of these detours was a road that branched off to the left of the main road to a tiny little village. I'd read that at the end of this road was a lovely little beach that sounded absolutely quaint and peaceful, so I veered off at a curvy-road crawl and headed on down. Immediately I was reminded of our drive through Scotland – this one-lane road barely qualified as a road, but this time there were no handy Scottish road turn-outs. A jeep came flying up in the other direction and I hardly had time to pull over to the side before they were already past me, barely missing the side mirrors on my rental car. Carefully, I edged my way along, the road a lot longer than I'd expected, which got me wondering if somewhere amongst the ti plants and palm trees I'd missed a turn. There was nowhere to turn around, though, short of pulling into someone's driveway, so I continued on.

To say I was rewarded for taking the road less traveled is an understatement. When the road finally ended, it opened up to an empty parking area overlooking a rocky bay, waves whipped into a frothy white as they crashed into the jagged black volcanic rock. I'm sure I gasped at the sight. I got out of my car with my camera and took a few dozen pictures, then put the camera away and just sat on the edge of the rock wall, staring out at the waves, thinking.

After quite some time, I realized I wasn't alone. Off in the shadows, someone had at some point hung a hammock – and it was occupied. When I finally noticed him, the man in the shadows smiled a half smile, like he was thinking "About time you saw me, lady."

So this is him: tan. Very tan. Maybe 5'10" or 5'11". Slender but broad-shouldered. Blond, made blonder by the sun. Longish baked blond hair, very wavy but not quite curly. Some wrinkles around his eyes. From squinting? From laughing? I don't know yet. I'm guessing both.

Without getting up from his comfortable perch, he offered: "My name is Roone."

"Rune?" said I. "Like the little divination rocks?" See, Alexandra, I have learned something from you!

The little smile widened. "It comes from that. Dad was from Norway, Mom from Iceland, and they both moved to Canada, Newfoundland, where they met before getting married and running off to Minnesota. My name is Nordic. Usually it's spelled R-U-N, but my parents were worried people would call me 'run.' So they spelled my name R-O-O-N-E. And yes, it comes from the little rocks. It means secrets, magic. Secrets and magic, that's me. Middle name, Gunnar. Warrior. I'm a man of mysteries, warrior of life."

Somehow, that felt like more words all strung together at once than I expected from this man in the shadows. I thought he'd be the quiet observer type, but turns out he's the talkative philosophic observer type. Bouncing around questions like a Zen master. And a little cheesy. Warrior of life?

He moved to this village a few years ago, he told me. "Plan A was to work an office job in Minnesota for the rest of my life. That didn't work out so I'm going with Plan BE instead." Smiled at me expectantly. I bit.

"Plan B?"

"Plan BE. B-E. Existential. Being. Living. In the NOW." He said it like that, all caps. "People spend all their days trying to work for something and they don't even know what they're working for. I spend my days BEING. It got me here," he said, indicating the paradise of hammock and bay, and the ukulele and the small cooler I finally noticed by his side. "I have everything I need and nothing more. Plan BE."

So I changed my own Road to Hana plans, and instead sat and talked with Roone all day, into the afternoon until the sun started to set. He played the ukulele for me, just a little bit, the soft sounds mingling with the wind and the waves. We exchanged phone numbers, and he went off to dinner. I sort of thought he might invite me over, but he didn't.

I didn't text or call him yesterday, and he didn't text or call me either. Nothing yet today. I may head back down to the village tomorrow if I have to. I'm only here a few more days. I have to take advantage of the time I have here!

Stay tuned for the ongoing adventures of Erin and Roone. I will keep you posted.

BE well, Alexandra,

Erin

~

From: Ruby
To: Erin
Sent: December 14, 2010
Subject: Hey

Hey, lady!

I had dinner with Alexandra last night, who told me all about your ROOOOONE! Your magic mystery rock warrior man. What's up? Tell all! I want every juicy detail! Tell me or I'll make it all up and spread it around like it's the truth, and everyone will believe me, and you don't want that.

Can you believe about Alexandra's mom coming to visit? What a shocker. She's still mulling it all over. I talked with Ed about it, about his own parents. He hasn't seen his mom in forever, you know. And then there's that mysterious Aunt Meredith — we never hear about her! The tales of the Brooks men and there escapades abound in these parts, but where are the women? I'm becoming a little obsessed with the question. I suggested a Brooks family reunion and Ed seemed intrigued, so maybe we can get these women out here to check them out for ourselves. Ed's mom, of course, is in Iceland, but it seems the whole family has all but lost track of Meredith, Ed's dad's sister. I'm creating stories about her in my mind. She ran off to the circus, she's a nun, she's an astronaut on a secret mission to Venus, she's in the FBI, she created an underground city, she's the mayor of a big city under an assumed name, she invented a true invisibility cloak. Who can say? Until we know, anything is possible.

In other news, the Open House went well. The place was chock-full of people! That's how Ed described it. This led us to a discussion about chock:

Me: "What the heck is chock, anyway, and how is it possible it's always full, never empty? You never hear 'chock-empty.' Whatever it is, I want someone to make me a wallet out of chock skin. Send the boys out chock-hunting, and bring back a chock, and make me a chock-skin wallet so it's always full. That is your Christmas present to me."

Ed: "You know you have to be specific with the universe, or so Alexandra tells us. If you just ask for a wallet that is always full, you might end up with a wallet always full of peanut butter. The universe has that kind of sense of humor, you know."

Me: "Money. I want a chock-skin wallet that is always chock-full of money. Tens and twenties. Hear that, universe? Tens and twenties in my always chock-full chock-skin wallet. Tens and twenties, ten dollar bills and twenty dollar bills, in good old United States cash. Not old. Current. Good, current, fully usable, United States ten and twenty dollar bills." That universe. It can be very, very tricky.

So I've become obsessed both with the Brooks women, and with chock. You need to come back. I clearly am no good at entertaining myself. Soon I'll be making art out of elbow macaroni.

One of the people at the chock-full Open House was a guy named Glen Nelson. He came to scope the place out for his family, looking for somewhere to vacation this summer, he told us. He was so charmed by Wishing Rock that he's going to bring the whole family out for winter vacation, arriving this weekend, I think. From what I gathered, they'd prefer to rent a house over summer, but while they're here the next couple weeks they can look around the island to see what's available. A dad, mom, and two kids. That's all we know.

You're lucky to be there in the sun. It's been raining all over the area like no one's business since what seems like before the beginning of time. Since the Big Bang. Since before the Big Bang. It is raining. It rains in the morning and then it rains in the late morning and then in the afternoon it rains and if we had tea time it would be raining at tea time and then it rains through dinner and then it rains some more. Some places have been flooding the last few days. We've escaped it so far but we're watching the roads.

All this rain reminded me, though, how much I miss the sound of the rain on the roof. Being in one building with everyone else is nice, but sometimes I miss having my own roof. The music of the rain, the soothing steady beat, the heartbeat of the rain. Aborigines made it into a musical instrument, you know, a rain stick. It's beautiful. I told Ed how I missed it, and he drove me out to a lookout point – sort of near where Jake first told me about dogwinkles, remember that? – and we cuddled up in blankets and snuggled with each other and drank hot chocolate and listened to the rain tap on the roof of the car. It was nice.

And speaking of Jake, he'll be home for the winter break soon. Seems my boy is a man now – too old to stay with his parents anymore. He's convinced Ed and Michael to suit up an empty one-bedroom unit, which he'll rent while he's there. I suspect he's using Ed's residual guilt about taking me away from him – though that's totally not what happened – but I suspect so nonetheless. Ed won't even confirm that he's actually going to charge Jake rent for the two weeks. On the other hand, what's the price of healing a friendship, right? And Ed's a grown man. He can deal with it himself. Guess which floor they're doing up a one-bedroom on, though? Ours. They're making 309 a one-bedroom rental. I asked Ed if they couldn't put Jake on some other floor, but they're already putting rental units on every other floor. Two-bedroom rentals in 401 and 207, and a three-bedroom rental in 504 – that's the one the Nelsons will be renting, for the parents and two kids. So we get Jake just down the hall from both of us! I wonder if Ed is doing it on purpose, as a test of my loyalty. Creep. My heart belongs to Ed and none other! Jake will just have to deal.

In other news, I called Gran this morning to wish her happy birthday. She's doing well, still powering full-force ahead. Eighty-one. Still young, but not as young as she once was. It makes me sad to know there are fewer years ahead with her than we have behind us. I love that woman. I hope I'm like her one day.

So, that's the news from here. Chock-full, Open House, mysterious Brooks women, rain, rain, rain, Gran's birthday. Miss you! Come back!

Love, Ruby

~

From: Millie
To: Adele
Sent: December 15, 2010
Subject: National Wishing Rock Day

Dear Adele,

How are you, my friend? I hear it was your birthday yesterday! Happiest of birthdays to you! I hope it was wonderful. Wishing you many more.

We are drenched and drowned out here in wet rainy Wishing Rock. Ruby tells me you all are getting frozen under and frozen over, so I suppose we're half a step up from that but not much! It's about now that I wish for those days in the summer which at the time seemed far too hot. We're never happy with what we have, are we?

Preparations abound for our ongoing December activities. We just had our first Open House, trying to attract new residents, and on the whole I'd say it was a success. Walter's band was just fantastic, if you aren't so particular about whether people are always playing in tune. Details, details! Now we're focusing on Christmas and the

New Year's Ball. Keeping ourselves busy this year. We drew Secret Santa names and I drew Old Henry. Old Henry! Do you remember my telling you about him? Grumpy Old Henry. I'm shocked, honestly, that he even is participating. I guess if Scrooge and the Grinch can find Christmas spirit, then maybe even Old Henry can. Finding small gifts to surprise him with has stretched the limits of my creativity, since I barely even know him, but I guess that's the whole point of Loving thy Neighbor. If loving thy neighbor were always so easy we wouldn't have to be reminded, now would we!

As if I weren't busy enough, I got a bee in my bonnet recently with the idea that there should be a National Wishing Rock Day (regardless of whether anyone outside Wishing Rock knows about it). There's a Day for everything under the sun – a National Lemon Cupcake Day, a National Flashlight Day, Ferris Wheel Day, National Sugar Cookie Day, everything! My birthday is Random Acts of Kindness Day, I'm quite pleased to say, as well as National Indian Pudding Day and Champion Crab Races Day. But, there's no National Wishing Rock Day, and I'm on a mission to change that. I am now in the process of learning more than I even knew there was to learn about towns, villages, cities, and the like. Educated on the history of Wishing Rock I may be, but I did not know until yesterday that we are officially a town. It is only by the grace of being established decades ago that we even have the right to be incorporated. In 1994 the state decided any areas under 1,500 people couldn't incorporate. As even Dogwinkle's biggest town, Moon Bay, doesn't have twenty percent of that, we couldn't incorporate as a town today even if we combined all our little hamlets. (Note: when I say "hamlet" I mean so only in the colloquial sense, as Washington does not have "hamlets," nor "villages" for that matter.)

In my research I've learned that it would, in theory, be possible to get a National Wishing Rock Day established officially, but it literally takes an act of congress – something I have no interest in spending my time on. The next step is simply to pick a day and declare it, so I'm doing just that. I'll be polling the people of the town to see what date they'd like to pick as our Day, though I have my own preference and might well just tell everyone it was picked even if it wasn't.

And that's about all that's new here in Wishing Rock. Busy as ever in our cozy tiny town.

I hope you are well; my love to all.

Millie

⁓

From: Erin
To: Ruby, Alexandra, Claire, Millie, Carolyn
Sent: December 16, 2010
Subject: Update

Hello, my dear and beautiful poker group gal friends,

How are you ladies? I'm having a great time but I miss you all. I've been told – one might say in a thinly veiled threat – that I must send details on my latest escapades. To prevent any miscommunications or rumors (inadvertent, I'm sure), I'm writing you all at once.

As I suppose you've all heard by now, I've met a most intriguing gentleman here on the island, a lovely man who goes by the name of Roone. (He goes by it because that's his name. Just trying to be poetic there.) The last time I wrote I didn't know his last name, but now I do: Solberg. Roone Gunnar Solberg. Norwegian/Icelandic descent. You may now all unleash your sleuthing skills on the internet and find out all you need to know to assure yourselves I am in no danger from this mysterious young man (or axe murderer?).

If you're going to ask me what he does for work, there's not an easy answer to that. He used to do odd jobs: telemarketing, sales, even some contract project management. He still does odd jobs: serving as a waiter at luaus, giving guitar and ukulele lessons, contracting with a friend who does home construction. Once a nomad, always a nomad. The difference, it seems, is that in his prior jobs he was at a desk with a tie, and now he's outside or playing music. The difference is subtle, but he says it's all the difference in the world. I can't imagine him with a tie at a desk. He's one of those people who can't be tied (haha) down. Works to live rather than the other way around. He's a minimalist in material goods; I wouldn't be surprised if he told me he only has two pair of shoes.

As for what we have been doing together: We've been having fun. He asks questions, lots and lots of questions. He's challenging my thoughts right now, challenging my thinking ruts, which is just what I needed. Yesterday he took me out on a tour of parts of the island, first up to a lavender farm, then out to a forest with what he called "trampoline trees" – trees with roots growing in mats on top of the ground in such a way that they formed, for want of a better phrase, a great and delightful boinginess. We boinged, and he pointed out the forest destruction caused by wild pigs, and then we went on to a bay that's a local favorite for snorkeling with turtles. As our day had started somewhat late in the morning, that was quite enough, but tomorrow he's invited me to his house (finally!) for a "pupu" party – pupus being appetizers. He lives in a little village off the Road to Hana, and though his house isn't right on the water, he's on the wrong side of the island anyway to watch the sun dip into the water as it sets. A sight, I might add, that I've been watching from my own balcony every night. I'm going to miss the sunsets and my whales when I come back! If I come back.

So tomorrow, a pupu party. Roone says one of his friends is a hula dancer so I may try to convince her to give me a lesson or two. (I've been assuming it's a her, but I just realized I could be wrong!) I wonder if Roone has a grass skirt and coconut bra at his house that I could borrow? Sort of doubtful, but I have this severe craving to wear a grass skirt and a coconut bra. Maybe I'll just wear a tank top and shorts.

Which reminds me, sorry to hear about the rain there! The flooding and the storms – sounds like a real mess. You all keep safe! I'll get extra sun on your behalf. Don't hate me because I'm dry and warm.

That's about it from this end. Just getting to know the guy and having fun doing it. Relishing the sun, savoring the chance to explore my mind and my life with the help of a new friend, enticed by the world of possibilities. Anything could happen, right?

Love to all,
Erin

⁓

From: Millie
To: Erin, Ruby, Alexandra, Claire, Carolyn
Sent: December 16, 2010
Subject: RE: Update

Erin! We miss you! You are so right, though: if ever there were a time to escape our miserable weather, the time is now. The power keeps flickering and I'm just sure we're going to lose it at any minute. I have the heat turned up in case the power goes out. I hate being cold! The store is completely sold out of flashlights and candles. Everyone's been stocking up. Lucky for us the town installed battery-operated back-up lights in the hallways and stairways a few years back so we won't kill ourselves wandering around in the dark, but still, I just hope everything stays on. Every time we have storms like this there's talk of getting a generator, but it just hasn't happened yet.

On to more important things, though! This Roone: please clarify, are you romantically inclined? Have you gone on an official "date"? Status, please! We old fuddy duddies have to live through you and that means you need to send more information!

Pupu party? I'm glad you clarified what a pupu is because I would have been worried. If anyone makes a good pupu, send on the recipe, we can always use more pupu recipes!

Millie

⁓

From: Erin
To: Millie, Ruby, Alexandra, Claire, Carolyn
Sent: December 16, 2010
Subject: RE: RE: Update

To clarify Roone: We are not yet romantically entwined. He took me on a tour of the island; I'm not sure, is that a date? Or just someone showing me around? Something about it felt rather non-date-like, but I definitely feel chemistry with Roone. I think he feels it too. I hope so. I can't believe I'm leaving in six days! I hate the idea of a long distance relationship. No fun at all. Hawaii is so far away from home.

~

From: Claire
To: Erin, Millie, Ruby, Alexandra, Carolyn
Sent: December 16, 2010
Subject: RE: RE: RE: Update

If Roone went by "Roo," he could have "Roo pupus."
Or if Roone moved here, he could have "Roopetizers."
It's all so Roomantic.
In case you're wondering, cocktail hour started early up here at the Inn. Ladies of Wishing Rock, come up and join me soon!

~

53

From: Erin
To: Claire, Millie, Ruby, Alexandra, Carolyn
Sent: December 16, 2010
Subject: RE: RE: RE: RE: Update

Oh my lord. Is that the cocktails talking or the rainy weather cabin fever? Roopetizers. Claire. Really. You have been around Tom too long.

~

From: Millie
To: Claire, Erin, Ruby, Alexandra, Carolyn
Sent: December 16, 2010
Subject: RE: RE: RE: RE: Update

You should definitely seize the day, Erin. Live with no Roogrets.

~

From: Claire
To: Millie, Erin, Ruby, Alexandra, Carolyn
Sent: December 16, 2010
Subject: RE: RE: RE: RE: RE: Update

You two should see if there's a Roodeo in town where he could lasso some Roominants. Has he been to the Roocky Mountains? Does he play tennis with a tennis Roocket?

~

From: Millie
To: Claire, Erin, Ruby, Alexandra, Carolyn
Sent: December 16, 2010
Subject: RE: RE: RE: RE: RE: RE: Update

Getting him to fall in love with you shouldn't be Roocket Science. You're a lovely young girl. Soon he'll be bringing you Rooses and Rooseberry sherbet or perhaps a Rootabaga. He will bring you these gifts when you go off together on a rendevRoos.

~

From: Claire
To: Millie, Erin, Ruby, Alexandra, Carolyn
Sent: December 16, 2010
Subject: RE: RE: RE: RE: RE: RE: RE: Update

RendevRoos! Millie, you have outdone yourself! Well done!

~

From: Erin
To: Claire, Millie, Ruby, Alexandra, Carolyn
Sent: December 17, 2010
Subject: RE: RE: RE: RE: RE: RE: RE: RE: Update

Oh. My. Stars. You ladies are Roodiculous!
Speaking of which, where is Rooby? Alexandroo? Caroolyn?
Also, Claire, I was telling a woman at the condo unit next door about that Birthday Granola you make, and she asked for the recipe. I forwarded it to her but she pointed out the recipe you sent us doesn't have the amount for the flax seed. You list it in the directions but not the ingredients. This was an email from October 27; maybe you still have it in your sent mail. How much flax seed?

~

From: Alexandra
To: Erin, Claire, Millie, Ruby, Carolyn
Sent: December 17, 2010
Subject: RE: RE: RE: RE: RE: RE: RE: RE: RE: Update

I'm here! Just back from the clinic for medicine for a UTI. Perhaps this is indelicate but then so are you all: may I say, speaking of pupu, I do not know who invented the procedure for giving a urine sample but undoubtedly it was a man, and one who could aim, at that. I had to give a sample at the clinic and as you know this feat is all but impossible. I surely can't be the only woman who has never spent time studying her private parts in a mirror, and frankly, I have no idea just precisely where to hold that tiny vial to get the sample they want. I drank a gallon of water before going to the clinic but by the time I got there had to go so bad that I couldn't wait. Then when the time came for the urine sample, there was nothing left. They want "mid-stream" but my friends, they're lucky if any of it gets in the vial at all. And yes, shall I point out it was a vial this time? Not a cup, but a vial, a little bottle with an opening only 1/2-inch in diameter. And I'm supposed to figure out how to get urine in there? Not just urine but clean mid-stream urine? I can't understand how with modern technology we haven't developed something more advanced and easier than peeing in a cup. This doesn't even begin to discuss the pre-peeing procedures they ask of you, and the fact that completing the procedures as directed by the various How to Give a Urine Sample posters on the wall would take two more hands than I currently have. Peeing in a cup. It's one step up from bleeding people with leeches for disease. Primitive.

I was trying to think how to incorporate "Roo" into my story but the only thing I could come up with was uroone for urine. Millie and Claire, I will leave the comedy hour to you two clever beings. Though I do believe that now we know Roone's full name, we can begin our investigative Rooconnaissance.

~

From: Claire
To: Millie, Erin, Ruby, Alexandra, Carolyn
Sent: December 17, 2010
Subject: RE: RE: RE: RE: RE: RE: RE: RE: RE: RE: Update

You enjoyed our witty Roopartee then? Yes, we'll have to Rooconnoiter! Find out if he has a Roocord or anything. That one was "record." Like a police record. Not sure that one was clear. Witty Roopartee can be difficult, with unforeseen Roopercussions.

So sorry to hear about your UTI, Alexandra! Those are just awful. And I know exactly what you mean. At any clinic where they take urine samples, they should have pubs set up. People could go and drink and be merry, and then give copious urine samples, all the urine samples in the world, and then shuttle on home. Urine samples. One of the most undignified lab tests around!

No Rooplys yet from Rooby or Caroolyn yet, though. Were they going somewhere with Ed and Michael to get more furniture?

Erin, forgive my Roocipe erRoor! It's 1 to 2 Tbsp, and it should be ground up or otherwise it'll just go straight through you undigested. Here's the Roocipe again – coRoocted!

Birthday Granola – again!
Ingredients
    4 cups regular rolled oats
    1 to 2 Tbsp flax seeds, ground
    1/2 cup raw almonds, chopped
    1/2 cup raw pecans, chopped
    1/2 cup dried coconut
    1/4 tsp nutmeg
    1 tsp cinnamon
    1/4 tsp sea salt
    scant 1/2 cup maple syrup
    scant 1/4 cup oil
    1 tsp vanilla
    1/2 cup raisins or currants, optional

Directions

- Preheat oven to 350°. In a large bowl, combine oats, flax seeds, almonds, pecans and coconut. Mix together nutmeg, cinnamon, salt, maple syrup, oil and vanilla in a small bowl and pour over oat mixture. Mix ingredients thoroughly.
- Thinly spread the mixture on two baking sheets covered with parchment paper. Bake for 10 minutes, stir well and return to oven for another 7 to 8 minutes until granola is lightly toasted. If using raisins, add them after the mixture is cooled. Store in a sealed jar.
- Makes 7 cups.
- Note: I rotate the baking sheets (move the one on the top rack to the bottom rack and vice versa) after the first 10 minutes. It prevents the top batch from getting too toasted.

From: Ruby
To: Claire, Millie, Erin, Alexandra, Carolyn
Sent: December 17, 2010
Subject: RE: RE: RE: RE: RE: RE: RE: RE: RE: RE: RE: Update

Hello, ladies! No we weren't out getting more furniture, but yes we were up getting all those rooms (or Rooms? Ah, doesn't work, does it!) put together. Carolyn and Michael are finishing up painting and furniture arranging in the unit Jake will be renting, while Ed and I were working on the unit the Nelsons will be renting, since they're arriving tomorrow! Funny how adding five people to Wishing Rock feels like a huge infusion.

Erin, you're not allowed to move to Hawaii! Please Rooconsider. Haha! See what I did there? So what if I'm late to the party; I still brought my lampshade hat!

Erin, are you going to be home at your condo tomorrow? I'm going to try to catch you online to IM. Answer if you're there!

I have to get back to our new rental units. Just taking a quick break, but that Ed is a merciless boss! I just heard the power has gone out at Balky Point and the northern half of the island, so we're in a race against a potential outage. Fingers crossed! See you all later! xxx

~

From: Erin
To: Ruby, Claire, Millie, Alexandra, Carolyn
Sent: December 17, 2010
Subject: RE: RE: RE: RE: RE: RE: RE: RE: RE: RE: RE: RE: Update

Thanks for the recipe, Claire! Miss you all. Stay safe and dry, everyone! Love you!

~

Instant Message (IM) from Ruby to Erin
Sent: December 18, 2010

Hey! It looks like you're online. Are you there? How are you? Sorry I couldn't write much with the ladies yesterday. Are you out on your balcony again, watching the waves go by? Throw back a chi chi for me, please!

So in the midst of the rental room renovation chaos last night, Ed officially invited me to the New Year's Eve Ball. Got down on one knee to do it. Seriously? For serious, who does that? I was about to throw up, thinking he was going to ask me to marry him. I haven't the slightest idea what my answer would have been. But, the question turned out to be "Will you ... go to the ball with me?" I accepted with grace. I'm in panic mode, trying to figure out what to wear. Millie says it's "anything goes" but is it really? Do people all wear formal gowns? If I actually were to show up in flannel pajamas, would I be laughed out of the room? You're going to go too, right?

~

IM from Erin to Ruby
Sent: December 18, 2010

Yup, I'm here, wifi is actually slightly better on the balcony side of the unit. It drops every now and then so if I disappear I'll try to come back. Or I'll just go get another drink.

Ugh, I'd forgotten all about the ball. Has everyone been claimed already? What about Ben? Surely he can be my back-up plan.

Yes, you really can wear whatever you want, and chances are whatever you wear, we've seen worse! One year someone's guest showed up in bike shorts. BIKE SHORTS. I did not dance with said gentleman. Creepy.

So the point is, you can wear what you want, but yes, you'll be mocked if you show up looking crazy. This is Wishing Rock, after all. We live for that sort of thing.

~

IM from Ruby to Erin
Sent: December 18, 2010

Oh, sorry. Ben moved quick. I told you about the Nelsons, right, that family moving in for the winter break? They got here yesterday, and last night they joined us up in the fifth floor commons room, where we were playing an impromptu game of charades. The daughter is sixteen or seventeen, I'd guess, and Ben managed to invite her to the ball within minutes of meeting her. Ha! Taking after his suave older brother, Ben is. So he's taken. Backup plan two?

~

IM from Erin to Ruby
Sent: December 18, 2010

His suave older brother! You said Jake is coming home, right? Does he have a date to the ball? He can't have a date already, right? Would you mind? I mean, it's been months, and you're the one who dropped him.

~

IM from Ruby to Erin
Sent: December 18, 2010

I don't mind at all. Actually, he's arriving tonight, I think. Want me to have him call you?

~

IM from Erin to Ruby
Sent: December 18, 2010

Yeah, I guess I'd better catch him as soon as possible. What other choice do I have?

~

IM from Ruby to Erin
Sent: December 18, 2010

Surely there's someone. How in a town of a hundred people do we not know everyone intimately?

~

IM from Erin to Ruby
Sent: December 18, 2010

It's like language. There are hundreds of thousands of words in the English language, but the average person uses only about two thousand of them. A hundred people in Wishing Rock, and we only really know a handful. Our poor brains, they can only take so much.

~

IM from Ruby to Erin
Sent: December 18, 2010

Hmm. Okay, well, I'll ask around and see who I'm not thinking of. What about someone from the ferry? You're always on the ferry doing distributor runs. Ever see anyone there? I mean other than Bradley, unless you want to get back together with him. Or someone from that figure drawing class we took? Does the Balky Point lighthouse have a bachelor lighthouse keeper or anything?

~

IM from Erin to Ruby
Sent: December 18, 2010

The idea of anyone ferry-related is awkward ever since Bradley. There must be someone watching over the lighthouse, but I have no idea who it is. I wish Roone lived in Wishing Rock. How the heck is everyone already attached?

~

IM from Ruby to Erin
Sent: December 18, 2010

It's about choice. Too much choice makes people picky. If we
don't have much choice, we make do with what's around. Even Eve
might not have picked Adam if she'd had ten other men to choose
from. She might still be sitting there, undecided, while Chris Harri-
son told the men that five of them would be going on group dates,
two would have one-on-ones, and the rest would be out of luck.

~

IM from Erin to Ruby
Sent: December 18, 2010

Too much television, my dear.

~

IM from Ruby to Erin
Sent: December 18, 2010

Whatever. It's raining buckets. We're indoors a lot. I'm sorry
Roone can't be here for you. If you want, you can go as Ed's other
date. We can be sister wives.

~

IM from Erin to Ruby
Sent: December 18, 2010

Too. Much. Television. Step away, Ruby. Don't worry, I'll figure
something out.

~

IM from Ruby to Erin
Sent: December 18, 2010

Okay. If I hear of some dateless guy, I'll let you know. I'm sure you can go solo, right? Surely no one would frown on that. Surely it's been done before.

Anyway, speaking of Roone, how are things going? What's going to happen when you come back here? You are coming back here, right? On the 22nd?

IM from Erin to Ruby
Sent: December 18, 2010

I am coming back, yes. Possibly coming back to think about packing it all up to move here. I've got some thinking to do. Things are so great here, Ruby. I feel like I'm undergoing a metamorphosis of some kind. And I'm getting soooo much sleep. I feel renewed. Roone told me not getting enough sleep shortens life. He's all about getting enough sleep. It feels decadent, almost illegal. Nearly every night now I get nine hours of sleep, and it's amazing. But it's not just about the sleep. It's so much more than that. Just being on the island, and around Roone, heals me. This guy is good for my soul. My soul needs this.

But he hasn't officially asked me out yet. I wonder if that's because he knows I'm leaving? I hope when we do go out that he doesn't try to serenade me. He plays guitar in addition to the ukulele, you know, all the time. Men playing music or singing to women on dates – that's creepy. What am I supposed to do? Sit there and smile awkwardly? Even if they're good, they can only get away with it now and then. I'm happy to surprise them while they practice, softly, and listen in. But if they're all awkwardly mooning all over me and singing awkward tunes off-key, that's just awkward.

IM from Ruby to Erin
Sent: December 18, 2010

Does that happen to you a lot? Men serenading you?

~

IM from Erin to Ruby
Sent: December 18, 2010

Yes, it does. Every day I go home and someone is outside my door, singing to me. There's probably someone outside my condo unit right now, waiting to sing to me. The life I lead, it's so hard. You don't even know.

~

IM from Ruby to Erin
Sent: December 18, 2010

Your life is indeed a hardship. Men serenading you, and no date to the formal.

~

IM from Erin to Ruby
Sent: December 18, 2010

Don't try to rub it in. You're stuck in a state-wide downpour flood and I'm in Hawaii. I win.

~

IM from Ruby to Erin
Sent: December 18, 2010

Ha! You win. Okay, I gotta go – Ed just texted me that Jake is here. We're going to go show him his new room. I'll ask Jake about the formal for you. I'll keep thinking about a date for you. Maybe Ed knows someone. Don't despair! We'll find you someone! Tell Roone I said hi. Love you!

~

IM from Erin to Ruby
Sent: December 18, 2010

Love you too. Hi to Jake! And Ed, of course. Chat soon! X

~

From: Erin
To: Roone
Sent: December 19, 2010
Subject: Home!

Hey! I'm home safe. Those roads are really curvy in the dark, aren't they! Just wanted to say thanks again for such a fun night out. Your friends are so nice. So young but so nice. Don't you feel old around them? Not that I'm saying you're old.

I can't believe I have to leave Hawaii in just a few days. Being here has been transformative, and a lot of that is due to you, you know. Thank you for that. Life at home seems so difficult sometimes. Here life somehow seems easier. It makes more sense. At home, my brain is a constant whirl. Here, sometimes it's a whirl. Right now, it's a whirl. I've always felt like there's something I'm forgetting, that there's something I'm supposed to be doing. I feel it right now, not as intense as at home but as the time draws closer to go back to Wishing Rock it creeps back in.

But you have such a calming presence on me. You're like the Erin Whisperer. I'll miss you. Promise to stay in touch?

Erin

~

From: Roone
To: Erin
Sent: December 19, 2010
Subject: RE: Home!

I'm glad you're home safe. You're welcome. Erin Whisperer, that's a good one. I'll add that to my resume. Here's some whispering for you to remember: Life isn't difficult. You are making life difficult. Life just is. Let it just BE. You have all these thoughts in your head but look around you right now, what is there? You're in a chair, maybe, or sitting on the bed. The lamp next to you is turned on low. The waves outside are crashing against the sand, louder than you thought waves would be. There's a slight breeze pushing through the open windows. The ocean is carrying night sounds to you across the bay, sounds of people who are still out, occasionally glasses clinking, laughter, but mostly it's quiet. That's this moment. Nothing outside that matters. Don't fill this moment with things that aren't in it. Be generous with this moment. Let this moment have its due.

What you are right now is enough. Who you are is enough.

I'm glad you came to Maui. It's been fun getting to know you. I will keep in touch.

Roone.

~

From: Adele
To: Millie
Sent: December 20, 2010
Subject: RE: National Wishing Rock Day

Dear Millie,

Thank you so much for the birthday wishes! I had the chance to talk with all my family, which was wonderful. The time zone difference makes it difficult to connect sometimes, but everyone managed for old Gran. They are dears!

How is National Wishing Rock Day coming along? Have you decided on a date? What does one then do with a National Wishing Rock Day? Do employees get the day off? Will there be greeting cards? I'm not quite sure I understand the concept but I fully support your efforts. Best of luck in getting that all set up.

That Old Henry. I'd almost like to meet him, just to get a chuckle.

Not much going on here except trying to stay warm as our deep freeze continues. On the news they're saying it could end up being the coldest month since February 1947. I haven't mastered the celsius scale, but I can tell you it's below freezing. Liam insists that the best way to stay warm is to dance, so every night he's been teaching me jigs as best as I can keep up, and what do you know, he's right. I'm staying warm and we're having a fantastic time. The weather is making it more challenging for me to get over to see Pip, or her to come over here, even though it's just a boat ride away. Everything seems more difficult when the world is frozen. It's a wonder we Earthlings ever managed to grab a hold of life on this planet, what with so much of it being barely hospitable. I can't imagine living in this land without at least some of our modern comforts. Maybe I've gone soft in my old age. In my youth I mightn't have thought a thing of it, but these old bones like the heat more than they used to. Dancing, lots of blankets, a good cup of tea with a wee dram of good Scottish whisky. That's the way we're making it through.

This will be my first Christmas away from Seattle for quite some time. We're having the whole MacAlpine gang to Liam's house for dinner on Christmas Day – if, that is, they can get here. Oban is a tumble of hills, and driving can be treacherous on this ice, if not downright deadly. The kids who live nearby can walk, possibly, but I have my doubts as to whether Pip and Gavin and all Liam's other kids and their families will make it. If not we'll postpone and have it another time. I'll miss Ruby and her folks, though, all the people back home. Give my friends in Wishing Rock all hugs from Gran. The world has gotten smaller, they say, but at times like this the distance seems so vast.

My love to all,
Adele

December 20, 2010
Wishing Rock News
Millie Adler, editor
Letter from the Editor

Dear Rockers,

I have one question for you all: Who is in charge of making sure Old Millie doesn't die of exhaustion? What a month we've had already, and it's not even over.

First, a welcome back to our dear prodigal son and doctor-in-training, Jake Stewart, who is here for two weeks while on winter break from med school. If you're looking for him don't go looking up at the Inn with Claire and Tom and Ben; he's on his own now, Box 309. I think we all know where the good parties will be this season! Also, if you have a moment, swing by Box 504 and say hello to the Nelson family: father Glen, mother Amy Renee, and twins Emma and Ethan. Amy Renee tells me she does indeed go by both her first and middle names. Noting a tinge of a southern accent in her voice, I asked her if the double names was a southern thing. "No, I just got in trouble all the time as a kid so I got called by both names a lot," said she, her eyes flashing with mischief. "Plus, I like both my names. They're good names." I have a feeling we will need to keep an eye on her! Wishing Rock seems to be a magnet for all you troublemakers. Lovable troublemakers, but troublemakers nonetheless. Behave yourselves!

With those welcomes taken care of, here's a run down of the week ahead:

Tomorrow (Wednesday): Holiday cookie exchange, 6 p.m., third floor commons. Contact Carolyn for details.

Note for the curious: Erin returns late Wednesday night. Ruby's heading to Seattle in the morning to go pick her up and they'll both be back Thursday.

Thursday: Secret Santa ends. Gather in the second floor commons at 8 p.m. if you've been participating.

Friday (Christmas Eve): Caroling by floors. 6 to 6:30, any caroling should be done on the second floor. 6:30 to 7, caroling on the third floor. 7 to 7:30, caroling on the fourth floor. 7:30 to 8, caroling on the fifth floor. End at fifth floor commons for building-wide holiday sing-along, hot chocolate and cookies. Bring cookies, fudge, whatever you'd like to share. Walter will be leading the show on the piano. Anyone else is welcome to bring an instrument and join in. Be sure to bring a stocking to hang in the fifth floor commons; rumor has it a man with a beard will be filling them up overnight! The commons will be locked at 10:30 p.m. so make sure your stocking is hung with care by then.

Saturday (Christmas): Claire has volunteered to lead our annual Christmas morning yoga and meditation at 8 a.m. in the fourth floor commons room. Fifth floor commons room will be unlocked at 10 a.m., so come see if we had a visitor fill your stockings or if you earned yourself some coal! Alexandra will present the seasonal blessings at 7 p.m. down around the bonfire, or if it's raining, in the auditorium. Everyone is welcome at both.

Sunday: 12th Annual Boxing Day Wishing Rock to Moon Bay Almost 6K Fun Run and Walk. Be at the starting line, a.k.a. the west end of the parking lot, at 10 a.m. to get your number and so on. Walk/run begins at 10:30. Anyone who would like to staff a water station or a safety van, let Carolyn know; there is still room for a couple extra people. If you're not already registered, don't worry, you can do that on the day of the walk. Registration fee is $10 to cover costs. Proceeds above and beyond costs will be donated to the food bank.

Ongoing: Speaking of which, don't forget we're collecting food for the food bank, down at the store. You can also leave a donation which will be forwarded on to the food bank. With your $10 they can buy something like forty meals, so donations of both food and cash are most certainly welcome.

That's about all. I will be seeing you all over the building nonstop this week, I am sure!

Happy holidays, everyone!

Millie

~

From: Ruby
To: Gran
Sent: December 21, 2010
Subject: Old flames

Hey, Gran!

I miss you and Pip so much right now. I've missed you since Thanksgiving and before that even but right now I miss you more than ever. I wish you could be here with me. Why must everyone spread so far and wide across the globe? Why must the globe be so big? That's the answer: we all need to move to a tiny planet. Mercury. Mercury's small. We could road trip anywhere on Mercury in a day. Maybe. I'd have to look that up. So what if it's a little hot? That's what sunscreen is for! I'll bet you all would like a little warmth right about now, and we'd sure like a little something other than rain. Or graupel. Everyone's talking about graupel this year. How have I lived this long and never heard about grapuel before? Did they just make that up this year? It's sort of like hail, sort of. Look it up. We had us some graupel, which they invented just for this year and this month of crazy weather.

Anyway, Mercury. No, actually, I just looked it up. It's more than nine thousand miles around. While that means, in theory, that as the Mercurian bird flies nothing is more than forty-five hundred miles away (right?), that's still too far. Someone is going to have to find us all a much smaller planet.

Or you guys could move back.

Just a suggestion!

I'm holding down the fort here by myself right now. Ed, his brother Michael, and Michael's wife Carolyn (you've heard of them before, right?) all went up to Alaska to visit Ed and Michael's dad for a few days before Christmas. They left yesterday morning, and will be back on the 23rd. Ed called up that woman Laurel Payne, from Anchorage – do you remember her? She came here a few months ago, fuming and claiming to be Ed and Michael's long-lost half sister, and that part turned out not to be true, but they all became friends. Ed keeps in touch with her and called her up to charter a flight from Wishing Rock to Alaska yesterday, then flying back on Thursday. It cost a bit more than your traditional flight, but he and Michael were happy to pay it, and Laurel was happy to fly them around. After all, it was because of them and that 1976 "no-S" dime Ben found in Meriwether's long-lost treasure box that she was able to keep her plane! She flew down here earlier in the week, and we had a little dinner party, Ed and me, Michael and Carolyn, and Laurel. She seems to be doing really well. So much happier than when she first graced the halls of Wishing Rock. We had a nice time, got all caught up. They took off early yesterday morning. Ed is determined to get me up to Alaska at some point, but I just keep thinking about bears and mosquitoes!

Last night, knowing I was all alone and could use some company, Jake called up and invited me to his place for dinner. Did I tell you he's back in Wishing Rock for winter break, and he has his own apartment while he's here? He's renting from the Brooks men. No more room at the Inn! Well, that's sort of true, actually. Claire said the bookings were pretty full for the season, but I'm sure they would have made room for their son if he'd wanted to stay with them. He's reached the point, apparently, where he needs a little more space, so we furnished up a one-bedroom unit, and that's where he's staying until ... early January, I think. I can't remember exactly.

Somehow when he and I were dating, I never discovered what a good cook he is. Either he hid this skill or he's gotten better. He made a delicious chicken cordon bleu, with a side of caramelized butternut squash – delectable. Salad was a spinach-cranberry-avocado-pecan mix, drizzled with a dressing of blackberry balsamic vinaigrette and olive oil. For dessert he made crème brûlée, the sugar topping browned and crisped to perfection with a little hand-held torch he borrowed from Carolyn. He's going to make some lucky woman very happy one day.

After dinner we sat and talked into the wee hours. We haven't really talked like that since we broke up. Finally, it felt comfortable again. Finally, it seemed we both felt safe again. Like the trust was back. It's easy to forget the bad stuff, isn't it? When you have that connection with someone, and spend time with them again, late into the night with a bottle (or two) of wine ... well. I remembered why I loved him. He's a good man.

And so is Ed.

Tomorrow I'm heading in to Seattle to pick up Erin at the airport. I'm going in the morning so I can see Mom and Dad, have an official Christmas lunch together and catch up and have some quality time. It's been a while and I miss them, too! Erin's flying in really late – her plane gets in around 10 or 11 at night – so we're staying at Mom and Dad's overnight and will head across the water to Wishing Rock in the morning. I can't wait to hear her stories. She went to Hawaii with a troubled heart, and met up with a guy while she was there. To me he almost feels like a rebound guy – not that Erin is rebounding from anyone, but ... he feels impermanent, I guess. But to her, I think she's pretty smitten. Watch this space for more news on Erin! I'm hoping we don't lose her to Maui. I need my people around me.

All right, give all my love to Liam and the family. I'll raise a toast to you all at Christmas, and I always have you in my heart. Warmest of holiday wishes to you, Gran. I love you.

Ruby

~

Text from Ruby to Ed
Sent: December 22, 2010

Hey sweet cheeks! I'm just about to head off to Seattle to see Ma and Pa for the day. This time last year my whole brood was in Seattle, now everyone has spread far and wide. How did that happen? What about you – how are Alaska and Dad?

~

Text from Ed to Ruby
Sent: December 22, 2010

Hey gorgeous! Alaska is great, Alaska is always great. But I miss you. Next time you should come along. No fun not having you here when Carolyn and Michael are making goo-goo eyes at each other.

~

Text from Ruby to Ed
Sent: December 22, 2010

Carolyn and Ed are making goo-goo eyes at each other?? Did you spike their drinks?

~

Text from Ed to Ruby
Sent: December 22, 2010

In an old-married-couple sort of way they are. I can feel the
goo-goo, even if they're not overt about it. Anyway I miss you. Dad's
good. I love Alaska. Wishing Rock is home – home is you – but this
is home too. I'm bringing you here sometime, if I have to carry you
in a mail sack.

Text from Ruby to Ed
Sent: December 22, 2010

You don't have to carry me in a mail sack. I will come willingly, if
you can guarantee my safety from all things wild. I'd better go, ferry's
coming soon. Love you, miss you! See you tomorrow! xxxxx

Text from Ed to Ruby
Sent: December 22, 2010

Of course I will always protect you from all things wild. Except
myself! Rawrrrr! Ahem. Love you too. Miss you something awful.
See you tomorrow. xxxxx

From: Erin
To: Roone
Sent: December 22, 2010
Subject: On my way

Hey,

Well, this is it. I'm in the airport lounge, waiting for my flight. Thank you for driving me here, and thank you infinitely more for convincing me to pack up and check out of the condo early to head down to Haleakala last night. The sky-gazing last night was stunning. That sunrise this morning, up at the peak of Haleakala, above the clouds, was transcendental, even in the bitter cold. I had no idea it could get so cold anywhere in Hawaii! But it was worth getting up early for. I did hate having to get out of our cozy bed, away from those warm arms of yours that held me through the night. So sweet, so comfortable, so right. The best possible end to an amazing trip. Thank you, for everything.

I'll talk to you soon. xo

Erin

From: Gran
To: Ruby
Sent: December 23, 2010
Subject: Liam

Dear Ruby,

I'm so sorry I didn't write sooner. We've had the worst happenings here! Two nights ago Liam had quite a fall on the ice. He cut open the back of his head; it turns out it wasn't serious, but good heavens did it bleed, all over the snow, freezing right up into a red-black slick of blood and ice. Apparently head wounds are known to bleed profusely. They thought he might have had a broken tailbone, but luckily it's only bruised. Still, he is very sore. He has to sit on a blow-up donut if he wants to sit at all; otherwise it's just too uncomfortable. His son Will came over with fabric paints and colored the donut in the MacAlpine tartan colors. These Scottish men have their priorities straight! It kills Liam not to be able to move about, but that's what he gets for not listening to me. I told him to watch out, that the road was icy, but he thinks he's still as agile as his sons. Oban's hills are treacherous in this weather, the fog coming off the sea, crawling up and freezing on the slopes. Well, that's it, then, all holiday festivities have now been moved to our house. Liam is going nowhere for a few weeks. We'd been talking about heading to Ireland next week for Liam's son-in-law's birthday – Stephen, who's married to Katie, you remember them, Pip visited them recently – but that will have to wait. Better to do it when the weather isn't so miserable, anyway.

Liam's daughter Kenna (who is married to Stephen's older brother James, while we're speaking of the O'Neill boys, so many people to keep straight!) came over and helped me decorate the house and put up the lights on the tree the other day. She's a lovely young lady. Reminds me of you in some ways. I've missed you all a good deal, too, Ruby. The world is big but our hearts are bigger. You are here with me always, and that online computer chat, amazing as it is, well, we have that too. You know anytime you need to talk to me, I'm here. I love hearing from you anytime. Keep your computer video chat open on Christmas and if Liam and I can figure it out on this end, I'll give you a call.

Keep me updated on Erin. Somehow, even when we disperse we all end up on islands. Why do you suppose that is? Tell her to trust her heart and she'll be all right.

All my love,
Gran

~

From: Ruby
To: Gran
Sent: December 24, 2010
Subject: Merry Christmas Eve!

Dear Gran,

Merry Christmas Eve, Gran!

Poor Liam! That's awful! What bad timing, right at the holidays, though I guess a person is more likely to slip on ice in winter than summer. Still, that's terrible. I'm glad he wasn't seriously hurt. Tell him to keep still or do his exercises or whatever the doctor orders. I was looking up "bruised tailbone" and it doesn't sound like much fun at all. I'm glad some of his kids are still in town to help, but make sure they're all taking care on the ice, as well! The last thing we need is all those MacAlpines in the hospital and no one around to help you.

I suppose I should actually be wishing you Merry Christmas as it's already morning there, but we are still in early evening here. We have adult nog and fudge and strands of sleigh bells and an abundance of Christmas cheer, and in about an hour the caroling, done by floors, will begin. Millie printed up song sheets for us and everything. I can't wait. For a cold, rainy, miserable town, this place couldn't be cozier. Caroling for a couple hours, then sing-along and dessert, and then we all snuggle down for a long winter's night.

I'm staying at Ed's tonight. All our presents from each other and our friends are nestled up under his gorgeous tree, which is done up in white lights and white ornaments and red bows. We had to have a discussion about Christmas morning – do we sleep in, or get up early? I was in favor of a nice leisurely morning, but he tells me that Brooks tradition demands we get up at six. I reminded him I am not a Brooks, and we settled on seven, provided he brings me hot chocolate and makes me cinnamon rolls for breakfast. He agreed.

Ed spent part of the week up in Alaska, along with Carolyn and Michael, visiting his and Michael's dad. I keep trying to get Ed to organize a Brooks family reunion. For someone who so dearly cherishes family tradition, you'd think he'd be more keen on the idea.

He hardly ever talks about his mom, and his aunt is practically a non-entity in the family stories. This makes me want to get to know them all the more! I get the feeling there's more to the family story than we've been told.

On Christmas Day, Ed's having all our gang over for dinner, since his house is the biggest. It's a huge rambling suite, two units joined together, spanning the whole short edge of the building with the longest wall facing the water, and balconies on each corner facing northeast and southeast. Claire and Tom's Inn is on top of the building, but it only takes up part of the old part of the building, and Ed's unit is in the new part of the building, so he's essentially on the top floor. He's been working with an architect on plans to build a rooftop deck above his rooms next spring or summer, whenever the weather will cooperate enough for construction. I can't wait – then he'll have a three-sixty view. From that high up, on a clear day it feels like you can see almost the whole island. You can't, but it feels like it.

Then, the day after Christmas is the Boxing Day run/walk. Erin convinced me to run with her, and Ed agreed to run/walk, too, since Erin is sure to leave us in the dust. I'd say about a third of the people in town are participating in the race, another third are involved in registration, logistics, that sort of thing, and the final third will keep the Box warm for us for when we get home. It's going to be a wet run. The organizers thought they might have to re-route it a bit due to some flooding, which posed a challenge since there's really only one road between here and Moon Bay. But, the water went down enough that we can go on as planned. We'll be sure to be extra careful so we don't end up like Liam, sitting on donuts!

At least the road is mostly level. I just found out the other day there's actually a mountain on Dogwinkle Island! It's not quite a mountain; officially it's a hill, at 1,840 feet, but they call it Knot Mountain because it's ... not a mountain. Get it? Knot Mountain is sort of in the hinterland between Moon Bay and Balky Point. Ed tells me he has some property out there. I guess when you have lots of money, you end up having lots of things all over. First an island, now property out by an island. Surprises never cease.

Erin is back from Hawaii. On my way to get her at the airport the other day, I stopped by Mom and Dad's house. You knew, didn't you, that they had their kitchen and bathrooms remodeled this summer? It's so weird now. I know, logically, that the house is still the same house. Even though furniture and cabinets and even some walls are all moved around, it's like the old configurations are still haunting in the background, ghosts of themselves, like a transparent layer lying on top of or shimmering underneath reality. Like if I squint right, look through the light just right, I'll be able to see them again. I can still close my eyes and imagine the house the way it was the whole time I was growing up. Me, standing at the kitchen counter where there's now just open space, mixing up cookie dough. The crowd of us gathered there at Thanksgiving, food steaming up the windows, the old table laden with platters of turkey and potatoes and candied sweet potatoes and peas and salads and rolls and everything else. Now the kitchen is beautiful, functional, with counter room to spare, but in some ways it feels somehow wrong. The main bathroom has been expanded; they knocked out the exterior wall, so now it's huge. I love the new bathroom. It's like a spa. I would have loved it growing up, and it's gorgeous, perfect. But it feels like something is missing. Maybe it's the illusion of being able to return. Of course I can't go back to my childhood, but with the rooms all redone and mixed around it feels more permanent, more certain. As though back when the rooms were all the same as they used to be, maybe I could have slipped through time somehow and gone back to those moments, those days, but now that chance is gone.

In contrast, driving to Mom and Dad's I took the long route, past my old grade school and all the roads surrounding the area. So many ghosts haunt those paths, Gran. Did anyone love grade school? I know I didn't. Being back on those roads felt like driving through a time warp. It made me sad, made all my inner demons from childhood come swelling to the surface. I had to shake that all off, remind myself I've gotten past all that.

Time changes everything, but at the same time, every moment still lives inside us.

Well. In other news, I'm happy or sad to report that Erin is in love. Her last night in Hawaii, Roone – the object of her crush – convinced her to take off with him to spend the day and night at Haleakala, the mountain on Maui. They stargazed, "just cuddled," watched the sunrise. She fell in love. I'm conflicted. If the love is mutual I might lose her to another, bigger, warmer island. To a bigger, warmer man. If it's not she'll be sad. Life is too complex sometimes.

Whoops, I wrote too long – I have fifteen minutes to get ready! I have to go. Merry Christmas, Gran, and all my love to everyone over there with you. May your day be filled with all the love and warmth that I feel in my heart for you. I love you!

Ruby

December 26, 2010
Wishing Rock News
Millie Adler, editor
Letter from the Editor

Dear Rockers,

I hope those who celebrate Christmas all survived and are ready to walk off the Christmas goose (or whatever your dinner consisted of) – it's time for the 12th Annual Boxing Day Wishing Rock to Moon Bay Almost 6K Fun Run and Walk! I'm just about to head out the door, as soon as I get this sent off. I was going to drive along behind everyone with water bottles and first aid kits, but Walter has convinced me to take on the romantic walk in the rain with him. I have my walking shoes and my waterproof coat, and my camera in my pocket in case the sun breaks through and I need proof it exists! Now we'll see how long it takes two old fogies to walk 6K. If we're not back by dark, send a rescue team; please be sure to bring along some of Ed's Wishing Rock Brose, from the distillery. Like those old rescue dogs with the barrels of brandy around their necks. Were they Saint Bernards? I remember the brandy. Not the breed of dog.

A decision has been made regarding National Wishing Rock Day! By grand majority of vote as well as Millie's Executive Decree, we have chosen March 9, the day in 1976 on which Wishing Rock was officially incorporated. 2011 will be the 35th anniversary of the incorporation, so it'll be a good year to start celebrating. Not that we ever need a good reason to start celebrating!

Another good reason for selecting March 9, of course, is the Day's juxtaposition to the Idiotarod. I was talking with Alexandra and David about this happy coincidence, and they lit on the idea of putting together some Wishing Rock Olympics to coincide with the whole celebration as well. It could be a great marketing tool (look at me, just a few days out from the Open House and now you all have created a marketing monster!). We can advertise the week as a great time to visit Wishing Rock. Ed and Michael, please put your minds and money to work on creating a giant umbrella to cover the town. We know there will be rain! If only our dear Meriwether had thought to incorporate the town in July instead.

At any rate, Alexandra and David are the ones to talk to if you have ideas for Wishing Rock Olympics events or celebrations. I'm assuming they'll be looking for indoor events. Office chair races for sure. Potato sack races. You name it. If it's odd, it's perfect for Wishing Rock.

I've had a few requests to publish the beautiful little blessing Alexandra gave at the bonfire last night. I'm including it below.

Now we're off! Good luck with your walks and runs today, folks, or if you read this after, I hope you did well! I'm guessing you'll find me and Walter downstairs at the bar at Mac's tonight, feet up, glasses full, so come join us!

Millie

Alexandra's Bonfire Blessing

Welcome, everyone! Family and friends, new and old, we come together in a spirit of joyful celebration.

I saw a sign the other day: "We began as strangers." It was meant for lovers but it touched me as a sentiment representative of everyone we meet. The people we know and love most today were once strangers to us. The people we will know and love the most ten years from now could well be strangers too at this moment. Wishing Rock, my home and your home, regardless of whether you live here, is where we all began as strangers, but where strangers become family.

In this time of year, in the depths of winter, people have been gathering together for millennia to celebrate the turn of the seasons, the almost imperceptible return of the light as the days so slowly start to get longer. Even though the cold, dreary winter is really just beginning and the days will not warm up again for months, for much of the history of humanity, people around the world have set aside this time of year for special, sacred celebrations. It is the time of year when we are almost resigned to the possibility that the darkness will win, but every year, without fail, light once again triumphs. Some rejoice in the miracle of a new born child sent to save us. Others celebrate a different kind of miracle in the festival of lights. Some commemorate the lengthening of days, while still others celebrate the yin and yang, the balance and harmony of the cosmos.

Whatever it is that each person celebrates, there is a common theme: rejoicing, and the triumph of a new dawn. The light. The return of the light. The power of hope and the new day.

Tonight, I look around this bonfire and, brighter than the fire itself, I see the light in each of you. Some of us were born here, whereas some moved here long ago. Others have only recently joined our family, and some of you are just visiting for a short time. What draws us together? What draws people to this isolated island? I would suggest that it's not the solitude that calls out to people, but rather the community. That we see the light in each other, as individuals and, even more, as a whole. We see that together this light is brighter than anything we could create on our own. Like moths to the flame, we are drawn. Unlike moths, however, the light doesn't extinguish us, but rather, the light of our community nourishes us, empowers us, makes us greater than we would be alone.

And so, as we gather today, let us remind ourselves and each other that even in our darkest hours, whether literal or metaphorical, there is hope for a new tomorrow and a new day. That even when our own light goes out, we have each other to reignite the fire and hope within us. To remind us that even when we are discouraged, we are not alone. Just as the seasons always cycle and the tides always turn, when we are at our lowest, we can have faith that joy will find its way back to us. We need only to hold on.

In this gathering together around this bonfire, on these darkest of nights, these shortest of days, we find comfort and love. Together, we know light will always return and triumph.

Whatever you celebrate, with whomever you celebrate, I wish you all the greatest blessings. As the new dawn brings a new day, as the darkness returns once again to light, may your coming year be filled with love, laughter, and joy.

~

Text from Erin to Ruby
Sent: December 27, 2010

I was just taking out the trash and I saw a woman slip into Jake's apartment! Do you know who that is?

~

Text from Ruby to Erin
Sent: December 27, 2010

!! No! Claire mentioned Jake has a girlfriend, but he didn't say anything to me about her at all the other night. Maybe it's her? Who else would it be?

~

Text from Erin to Ruby
Sent: December 27, 2010

Must be. People don't just show up in Wishing Rock by accident. Generally. I'll see if I can do some reconnaissance. I'm sly and clever, you know. Stealthy is my middle name!

~

Text from Ruby to Erin
Sent: December 27, 2010

You go, Erin Stealthy Anderson! I'm trying to think if I have anything I need to drop by his apartment. I don't think I do! Darn it! Maybe I should make him some post-Christmas cookies or something. Keep me informed!

~

From: Ruby
To: Pip
Sent: December 28, 2010
Subject: Jake

Where did the year go? It's almost over! Did you all have a good Christmas? How is Liam doing? I can't imagine a bruised tailbone. I think about it all the time now when I'm walking or sitting. It's hard to do anything without in some way moving or impacting the tailbone, I've decided! Give him a very gentle hug for me next time you see him.

Can you believe it'll soon be 2011, the year your child will be born? It seems like yesterday we were in the backyard digging tunnels in the garden, that I was forcing you to eat grass and trying to get you to taste those questionable berries along the trail to the yard, that we were putting weeds in the spokes of our bikes and pretending it was gasoline. As though that made sense! And now here you are, about to bring one of your own into the world. I don't know where the time went. I don't feel old, and yet I know that when I was fifteen, thirty-five – no, thirty-six now – seemed ancient! I wish I hadn't made all those stupid mistakes along the way. I wish I hadn't worried so much. I wish I'd believed in myself more. I wish I'd been kinder. I wish, I wish. I know I had to go through all that to get here, but time seems so precious now and I want it back. I want that time, those carefree days making mud pies and building log houses and playing tag in the front yard, I want it back. The things we lose to time.

Speaking of gone: Jake's girlfriend. Gone! Gone before we hardly knew she was even here. She appeared yesterday, unannounced; Erin saw her in the hallway on her (the girlfriend's) way into his home. This morning I went to the commons room to read the paper (someone always leaves one there) (okay, maybe I was looking for excuses to peek down the hall; so sue me!), and saw her slipping quite unceremoniously out of his door and into the day. No lingering goodbye kisses in the hallway. I'm not even sure he was there. So, because of my kind heart and desire to do good, I went down about forty minutes later to deliver fresh-baked muffins to Jake. If Jake used that time to tell me all about what happened between him and this woman, who am I to blame?

"I was getting the paper this morning and saw a woman come out of your room. Who was that?" asked I, carefree and breezy as the summer wind as I handed over the muffins. Erin says her middle name is Stealthy – mine is Nonchalant! I am innocence personified!

"Ha. You saw her?" Jake's middle name is, sometimes, Evasive.

"Just by chance," I said. Nonchalant! "I was getting the paper."

"That was my girlfriend. Well, ex-girlfriend."

Aha! So much information afforded in two little letters. E-x. Ex as of this morning, to be exact. Ex-act. Ha! I'm so clever. Clever is my middle name!

"Ex? What happened?" The concerned also-ex-girlfriend, that's me, full of comfort and compassion. Is there a Nobel Prize for Best Ex-Girlfriend? I think I'd win.

And so I went inside, sat down with him at the kitchen table Carolyn and I had picked out for this room, and Jake brought out little plates Ed and I had laboriously washed and loaded into the cupboards along with all the cups and utensils and pots and pans, and Jake made me hot chocolate, and we talked. The woman, beautiful, but in want of a trophy husband not a life partner. She frequented the medical students' favorite hangouts, flirting with various men until she found one she fancied: e.g., Jake. At first he was charmed by her understanding of his schedule, the way she'd have dinner ready for him when he got home, even if he got home late, her quick offers of massage on his weary shoulders. But then he realized that as with so many people, she came with a price. She wasn't offering her self and her services out of love. She didn't quite understand that being a med student isn't the same as being a doctor, and he doesn't yet have the means to treat her to the dinners and jewelry and presents she felt she deserved for her troubles. What seemed at first to be selfless turned out, in fact, to be most selfish. She was giving, but with strings. He doesn't have time for strings. He cut her free.

If a man isn't totally into a woman, I'd say, he can feel smothered so easily. I think Jake just wasn't that into her. She could be a completely lovely woman, for all we know, but from his perspective, at this time, he just doesn't need that.

Anyway, then, in the most off-handed way, he said: "Besides, she doesn't want kids."

Wait, what?

The reason we broke up was that he didn't want kids. Has he changed his mind?

"Maybe," he said. He was quiet for a bit, then said, "Ruby, if it turns out that I want kids, and I lost you because I said I didn't, that would be the worst mistake of my life."

What does one say to that?

I went with my standard response: awkward silence. Then asked for a refill on my drink. When he came back, I changed the subject.

It's been nice having the chance to spend some time with him again while he's been home. I didn't even realize I've missed him.

And this brings us to Erin. She seems so happy with Roone – "with" being a relative term, seeing as she is here and he is on Maui. She's different. I mean, she never even used to start dating anyone between Labor Day and her birthday, remember, to avoid all the holiday entanglements. Erin is feeling liberated and emancipated and unrestrained, free from old rules and supposed-tos. So she says. I think there's a slight edge of clinging to her when she talks about him; trying to be breezy but unfortunately breezy is not something that can be forced or faked. Men can sense desperation like a pregnant woman can smell sugar (am I right?). I wish I knew him; knew things from his side, his perspective. He'd better not be playing her. She keeps talking about moving back to Hawaii to be with him. No – not to be with him, she insists it's not that. To be in the warm Maui sunshine, surrounded by the fragrant plumeria blooms, watching for humpback tails in the ocean, living on sultry "island time." I've tried to remind her we're on an island, too; we have our own "island time," but she says it's not the same. And maybe it's not.

I suppose I just don't want to lose her, too.

Well, I'd better get going. We have our Formal New Year's Eve Ball on Friday night and I need to fix the hem on my dress – I was flitting around with my full outfit on, and caught the hem on my heel. Smart move, Ruby! Grace is my middle name! So now I have to see if I can repair the damage. This could mean trying to bribe Carolyn into doing it for me; naturally she's a far better seamstress. The trouble is, there's nothing I can bribe her with! She makes better cookies, cakes, jams, home accessories, decorations, everything. Maybe I'll just practice looking sad and helpless.

Hello to Captain Gavin! All my love to the whole clan.

xxxxx

Ruby

From: Erin
To: Roone
Sent: December 29, 2010
Subject: Snow

Roone, it's snowing here! This snow is not romantic; it's cold. Do you know how cold snow is?! It's freezing. Freezing and wet and very un-Maui. Not the aloha spirit at all. I miss the sunset view from my balcony, the bright red-oranges and yellows and watching for the green flash. I miss going on adventures with you. I miss the fresh mangoes at the farmers market and the banana tree outside my window. I miss you! Tell me all about Maui. Tell me about the monk seals and the angle of the sun and the sweltering heat and the sudden wet-but-warm downpours that leave everything glistening, the sound of the waves crashing all night. Tell me about you.

I keep waking up each morning with that disoriented feeling, you know, when you wake up and have to think really hard for a while before you can figure out where you are? I keep waking up to cold and silence, find myself listening for the waves. The air is crisp here, not the soft, full air of Maui. My morning runs are cold and dreary. I miss running with the sunrise along the beach.

Some days it feels like reality is the dream, and I just need to wake myself up.

Alexandra gave all us poker gals the most beautiful gift for Christmas. She calls them "Wisdom Rocks." We each got a pack of about a hundred small, smooth rocks, with inspiring, positive, feel-good words written on each rock. Alexandra has her own pack of Wisdom Rocks and she said she likes to pull out rocks when she's feeling unfocused to see what the universe wants her to know or think about.

I just did so, and these are the words I drew: Awaken, Possibilities, Insight, Bliss, Destiny.

Write soon. x

~

From: Roone
To: Erin
Sent: December 29, 2010
Subject: RE: Snow

Good to hear from you. Weird to think you were here for such a short time. You're already in me.

I like Alexandra's Wisdom Rocks. Rocks, grounded, solid, of the earth, messengers of the wisdom of eternity for those who will listen.

At your request: Monk seals continue to lumber up on the beach to the delight of the tourists and horror of the volunteers who have to keep those rogue tourists away from the monsters. The green flash, it's just a myth. I don't believe it's real. You are not missing that. The mangoes are delicious. I am eating one now, its juices dripping down my chin and on my fingers getting my keyboard sticky. The sun is fierce today, unyielding. The rain is always a blessing. I am well.

I am working on the start of a poem that may become a song. I want to share it with you. It's just a few random thoughts right now, and it's not done, but I feel it, it's going to be more.

What if I
Didn't care
About the way the wind blows in your hair

What if I
Didn't see
The look in your eyes when you look at me

What if you
Didn't fear
I'd run away, not always be here

What if we
Didn't love
Our future weren't what our dreams were made of

I would still know
We would still be
Without the signs
It still would be
You and me

Although you're far from me
I hope that you can see
Our love is growing strong
Something that rhymes with strong

Have you ever noticed that every song ever written is about love? Finding it. Losing it. Wishing for it. Love of life. Love of God. Love of clapping your hands if you know you're happy. Love of bopping field mice on the head. Love of sunshine on one's shoulders and of piña coladas. I hypothesize that every song is in some way about love. I've challenged people to prove me wrong but no one has yet.

Will you come back soon? Hawaii has many great people but seems one short these days.

x

December 30, 2010
Wishing Rock News
Millie Adler, editor
Letter from the Editor

Dear Rockers,

Friends, here it is, the end of 2010. I think of all the wonderful people I've met over the last year, all the old friends I've spent time with, all the fun we've had and challenges we've faced together, and it hardly seems possible it all took place in just three-hundred-sixty-five little days. The measure of a year to be marked by the moments with people we love. For better or for worse, for richer or for poorer,

2010 is the year that was. Onward to 2011 and all that it will bring! Hopefully less of this rain. I heard this may well be the seventh wettest December on record. We'll know by the end of tomorrow!

For now, some quick reminders:

New Year's Eve Ball starts downstairs in the gym at 8:00. Turns out our visitor Amy Renee Nelson is an amateur professional photographer – that is, she's an amateur, but she has a monster of a camera! She has offered to take photos of individuals, couples, or groups, whatever you like, so be sure to clean up and look pretty to get your picture taken! Amy Renee will post her fees at the ball.

Don't forget, Saturday night Moon Bay is having its second annual Holiday Hangover Comic Relief performance, a fundraising event for the island's volunteer firefighters and rescue services. I hope you'll all go and support these wonderful men and women who do such an important service for us. We would be in trouble without them! So go, have a laugh, donate what you can. There's a silent auction beforehand at 6:00, and the comedy begins at 8:00.

And with that, I wish you all a very happy new year! I'll see you at the ball!

Millie

~

From: Ruby
To: Gran
Sent: December 30, 2010
Subject: Happy New Year!

Gran! Happy New Year! Happy almost new year, anyway. You'll get there a few hours before us – let me know how the future looks, will you? I'm feeling hopeful for twenty-eleven. Probably just coincidence but I've been noticing elevens everywhere lately, so much so that I looked it up to see what the number eleven is supposed to mean. It's all about intuition and balance. Learning to pay attention to things you know but aren't paying attention to. I suppose we all could use a lesson in that, right? Or many of us. Or at least me. Even if it really means nothing, it's good to think about. I would love to finally find some balance in the new year.

I'm just back from dinner with Ed, Alexandra and David, and Erin. Note that Alexandra and David are one item between the commas there, like peanut butter and jelly, shave and a haircut, hide and seek. They are a unit. They are a surprisingly good unit, actually. Two puzzle pieces that I would not have expected to fit together, and yet they do. It's nice to see.

And tonight's dinner was called to order for a topic just along those very lines. Erin received a poem (potentially to be song lyrics one day) from Roone, her friend from Hawaii, so naturally we had to gather to discuss what exactly this meant, line by line. I've never been good at interpreting song lyrics. I always feel there's a key somewhere and I'm missing it. Words missing from the song that would help me understand, help me get inside the songwriter's head. And it seems Roone once told Erin that he likes to make sure there are at least three layers of meaning to each of his songs, which complicates matters, I'd say. So many songs these days seem so convoluted. I would never be a good songwriter. I'd be too inclined to get to the point: "I love you. Lalala." Or "I hate you. Lalala." Or "You are confusing the hell out of me right now. Lalala." Okay so maybe I wouldn't get right to the point. Relationships are confusing. Friendships are confusing. Spending time with ex-boyfriends is confusing.

At any rate, the conclusion of our collective minds, three female (studiously studying the evidence) and two male (unconcerned and just wanting dinner) was that the song could mean anything. It could mean, as Erin hopes but is afraid to hope, that Roone is thinking of her and can't stand to be away from her. It could mean, as Alexandra pointed out, that he simply wrote a song about a man pining for a girl. Writers, she insisted, sometimes write about things that are simply a part of the human experience, but not necessarily about their own personal experience. I don't know. Do you believe that? I'd say you'd almost have to have lived through something to be able to fully understand all the nuances and write about it, but

Alexandra says our brains are amazing things and capable of great empathy in our quest to understand our world and each other. Ed and David said "pass the rolls." Such are men.

I'll be thinking of you at four in the afternoon tomorrow, our time, wishing you another year of happiness and love and laughter! Who knows what the year will bring. Life is nothing if not full of surprises.

Love,
Ruby

From: Gran
To: Ruby
Sent: December 31, 2010
Subject: RE: Happy New Year!

Hello, Ruby! Hello, Wishing Rock! We've four hours left of 2010 here in Oban, and then it's on to another year. Celebrations are about to begin here at our house. Liam is getting along but still feels a good bit of pain so once again the kids are all coming over to help set up, party, and clean up – next year! In the wee hours of the morning. Gavin and Pip came over on a late morning ferry to make sure they'd get here without incident, and will stay the night. I suspect they're not the only ones who will end up staying, but they're the only ones who have planned it at this point! Pip has been toiling away in the kitchen, baking fantastic treats for us for tonight though I told her she needn't, that she should rest, but she said she's not tired, is feeling great, and wanted to take advantage of it while she could.

Will and Rory came over early to help push all the furniture to the sides of the rooms so we have lots of floor open for dancing and general carrying on. Will's wife Aileen, Rory's wife Charlotte, Colin, Kenna and her husband James, and all the various local MacAlpine and O'Neill children have been trickling in; I think all the family are here now. Friends from all around the neighborhood have been invited too, and will likely be showing up in an hour or two. The Liam MacAlpine household is full of frolicking and frenzy and food, love and laughter and light hearts. We are ready to ring in the new year and all its possibilities.

While I was helping Pip slice apples for a pie, she filled me in on your date with Jake, to which you alluded. It sounds very much like a date, that is, Ruby. Where is your heart? Are you running scared from Ed? Don't make a mistake here, my darling. Think before you act. Don't lose what you have for what you think you used to have. The good old days were not always good. You broke up with him because he didn't want kids, but there was more to it than that. Don't run back before you take a good look at what you'd be running from.

Well, I'd better get back to the family before they send a search party for me. Wishing you the happiest of new years, Ruby. Hopefully one or the other or both of us will be able to visit the other in the new year. I miss you very much.

All my love,
Gran

January

From: Ruby
To: Gran
Sent: January 1, 2011
Subject: RE: Happy New Year!

Gran! Happy New Year! I feel like I haven't talked to you all year! Ha, that joke just never gets old, does it?

What a great night last night was. We started off the evening by throwing wishing rocks into Puget Sound. For the last few weeks people have been gathering rocks and making wishes on them, then piling them into a huge bowl in the lobby. Last night, each of us took a handful of rocks and tossed them in, saying (or thinking) "I wish that this wish comes true" as we threw each one. Sort of a nice way of saying we support each other in our hopes and dreams.

That was early in the evening, then we all went to our rooms to get gussied up for the much-anticipated Ball. Dancing commenced at eight, with a swing band we'd brought in all the way from Moon Bay, and a few Wishing Rock residents joining in on occasion (now that Walter has created a town full of musicians!). Just as happened at the MacAlpine home, we too frolicked and had fun and ate heaps of food. None of Pip's baking though, poor us! You are quite lucky!

The clock struck midnight, champagne was served and the new year was toasted, and then we all wrapped up tight and headed back out to the beach. Most of the ladies changed shoes; high heels and sand just don't mix, I have learned! We clutched at dress hems in the cool of the night and headed to the shore.

Ed had this idea for the new year, he wanted all of us to send up those giant lanterns they release in Buddhist ceremonies in Thailand at those huge festivals with thousands of people. Months ago he ordered the lanterns and all the works for us to use last night. I was sure it would rain (this having been the wettest December since Noah, after all) and we'd have to put it all back into storage, and/or the display just wouldn't be as impressive. Even if every one of Wishing Rock's residents released a lantern, that would still be barely one hundred. That would be impractical, too, since each lantern is huge and unwieldy, and takes at least two people to manhandle.

But, I was wrong on all accounts. The night remained clear and crisp, and the spectacle was spectacular. About fifty lanterns, all told, were released up into the sky with our hopes and dreams. Small but beautiful, just like home. Ed had also bought hundreds of little lanterns on tiny rafts, to be released into the ocean in case the giant lantern idea was rained out. Because we could, we did both: enormous lanterns into the sky, and tiny lanterns into the water. Watching the big lanterns float into the dark night, and the little fires as they flickered and bobbed in the waves while we on shore stood silent, savoring the moment and our wishes, felt like peace. I held Ed's hand deep in his wool coat pocket and thought about the future, and wondered where I'll find myself in a year. Where he and I will find ourselves in a year. More and more, I picture those thoughts together. Not even side-by-side, but overlapped. One.

I turned to Ed. "It's like watching stars float up into the sky," I said, mesmerized. "If I were creating the myth of the origin of stars, I'd say they were started with lanterns filled with wishes."

Ed smiled and took a picture of the lights lifting themselves into the universe. Later that night I found he'd emailed that picture to me in that moment: "If stars are filled with wishes, then every star in the sky holds my wishes of love for you. Ed."

After the lanterns and floats, we scuttled back inside and away from the damp midnight chill. The party dispersed, but after changing into more comfortable clothes, many of our crowd found our way up to the fifth floor commons room. Soon Michael had a roaring fire going, Carolyn served up molasses cookies and cups of hot chocolate and cider, and we snuggled together in the cozy couches and reflected on the feeling the new year brings of fresh chances, of possibilities, of starting over. There's no real difference, obviously, between December 31 and January 1; it's just one cold dark day seeping into the next. And yet it feels somehow different. Like anything could happen. Like the old year was a picture drawn in the sand, and midnight was a wave that swept in and washed it all away, leaving a clean slate. A brand new day.

So. Pip told you about Jake, did she? Gran, I know what you're saying. I hear you, I do. My heart, though, it recognizes Jake. You know what they say about amputees, that they often have phantom pain in the limb that is gone? They feel the limb as though it's still there. They're not idiots. They know the limb is gone. But they still feel it. My relationship with Pete was like that for a long time, but now that's gone. Last night, though, I realized my relationship with Jake is a little bit that. I know we're not getting back together, but he feels so familiar when he's around.

He was Erin's date, but we danced a few dances together, Jake and I, mostly faster ones but one slow song.

"I wish I could say I made a mistake," he said, "but I'm not the one who left."

He tears at my heart sometimes. I never meant to hurt him. And I never stopped loving him. That's the hard part. I never stopped.

"You stepped on my foot," I said, by way of reply. He had indeed, but I used it as an excuse not to say what I was really feeling.

Maybe it's because he's in the past that he feels safe. I don't know. But I'll be careful, Gran. I'm not going to do anything stupid. I love Ed. With my whole heart. My whole, stupid, vulnerable, scared, hopeful heart.

I can only imagine the level of sore heads going on in Oban today. Take care of yourselves! And yes, I will definitely try to get back over there, as soon as I can. I miss you, too.

Happy New Year to all the MacAlpines, O'Neills, and you, my favorite Parker,

Love,

Ruby

~

Text from Ruby to Ed
Sent: January 2, 2011

Where are you?

~

Text from Ed to Ruby
Sent: January 2, 2011

At my office. Distillery. A quick bit of work. Where are you?

~

Text from Ruby to Ed
Sent: January 2, 2011

At your house. Just walked up from my house. Past the fourth floor. Where David and Alexandra are racing down the hallway in potato sacks, screaming and laughing like screaming, laughing banshees.

~

Text from Ed to Ruby
Sent: January 2, 2011

Potato sacks? Do banshees laugh? I thought banshees were fore-tellers of death.

⁓

Text from Ruby to Ed
Sent: January 2, 2011

Potato sacks. Testing out games for the Wishing Rock Olympics. Yes, banshees, totally misunderstood. Life of the party, if you have earplugs.

⁓

Text from Ed to Ruby
Sent: January 2, 2011

Got it. Party banshees. Misunderstood. So very sad.

⁓

Text from Ruby to Ed
Sent: January 2, 2011

I'm back down at the fourth floor. Quite the spectacle going on here. Michael and Jake have joined in.

⁓

Text from Ed to Ruby
Sent: January 2, 2011

As they should. Spectacles are not there for us to watch in amusement from the sidelines. Spectacles are there for our participation. I'm on my way. Save me a potato sack. Get one for yourself while you're at it. Loser makes dinner.

Text from Ruby to Ed
Sent: January 2, 2011

Bring it.

From: Erin
To: Roone
Sent: January 3, 2011
Subject: New Year

Heyyyy. I tried calling you a while ago but you didn't pick up. Out in the sunshine? Playing the slack key guitar? Dancing in the waves? I admire your refusal to be tethered to your phone, your tablet, your computer, all of it. I need to try to do that more.

I've been reading that poem, those lyrics, since you sent them a few days ago (last year!). Words themselves become music through you. It's beautiful. I'm sort of stunned by the beauty of those words. Absolutely, they must become a complete song. A love song. A lovely love song.

Being back home has been interesting. I felt like in Hawaii I was starting to figure out who I was and where I'm going; almost like my inner self was starting to thaw and dry out. I'm afraid … I'm afraid of showing myself, I suppose. Afraid people will figure out I'm a fraud.

Afraid they'll figure out how boring and dull I am. Which is ridiculous – as though I can even hide those things! I'm sure they all know and I'm just in denial. But in Hawaii, I made that conscious choice to lose the inhibitions, and it felt so great. That comedy improv night – was that me on stage? How did that happen! But it was fantastic. That's what I want, to be alive like that. To be a part of it. I'm always the sidekick. I'm tired of being the sidekick. I want a little spotlight. At the very least, I want to be in my own spotlight. Is that selfish?

Every song is a love song? Every song? I challenge that. Itsy bitsy spider. Not a love song.

Miss you. Come visit? We have rain, and it's cold, but I have a fireplace, and it's warm.

x

~

From: Roone
To: Erin
Sent: January 3, 2011
Subject: RE: New Year

Well Ms. Anderson you caught me, I'm here at my computer right now, writing more love songs.

You, girl, are being silly. You have this story about yourself, who you think you are and who you think everyone else thinks you are. Have you ever thought that you could be wrong? What if the only one who doesn't see who you are, is you? You're telling yourself a story about yourself, who you are, because you don't have the courage yet to be who you really are. What if that funny, gregarious woman at the improv was the real you and everything else has just been a mask? What if the real you isn't boring at all? What if how you see yourself isn't how the world sees you? Are you wrong or is every other person on Earth wrong?

We make up stories about ourselves in order to get by. We make up stories about other people to justify our actions toward or against them. It's so easy to believe those stories. They seem so real. The trick, my friend, is to step back and see reality. Step away from your fiction. Who are you?

Out on a friend's boat yesterday, we saw a pure white humpback whale. Imagine that. Wish you could have seen it. Just gliding along, its back a cloud breaching the surface, its tail a sailboat sail. Incredible. We drank a toast to it when we got home. It wasn't a baby so it's been in the world a while. Made me think about all the unique and awesome things that exist in the world that we don't even know. Like people, people we're just about to meet. People we've just met.

Itsy bitsy spider: love song. Love of running up and down faucets. Love of living in the moment. Hypothesis stands. Try again.

~

From: Erin
To: Roone
Sent: January 3, 2011
Subject: RE: RE: New Year

I can't believe I missed the white humpback. What an amazing experience that must have been. Did you have your camera with you? I'll bet you didn't, did you? Sigh.

That is a weak weak link to love with the itsy bitsy spider, my dear, but I'll concede, barely. I'll get you on this one, though. Just give me time.

Who am I: Just an average Jane. Not exceptional in any way. Safe. Reliable. The one who's always there for everyone. The one who doesn't jump but instead stands ready to take others to the hospital when they fall.

That fish heads song, you know the one? Not a love song.

~

From: Roone
To: Erin
Sent: January 3, 2011
Subject: RE: RE: RE: New Year

Geez, girl, I only play guitar and uke, but here I'm gonna need me a violin for this pity party you're throwing yourself. No one said you have to stand on the sidelines when everyone else is jumping. The only one holding you back from jumping is you.

Safe and boring isn't who I saw. I don't know who you are when you're at home but if it's different from who you were here, and you don't like it, change it. There's wild in you. Do something crazy. How do you feel about the woman you were with me? What do you tell yourself about her?

No, I didn't have any electronic devices with me at the time of the sighting of the great white whale. Imprinted forever in my mind, worth a thousand words and more. We'll do a mind meld sometime and I'll show you.

Fish head song: love of fish heads. "Yum!" Love song. Try again.

From: Erin
To: Roone
Sent: January 3, 2011
Subject: RE: RE: RE: RE: New Year

What I tell myself about the wild woman you met: She was on vacation; she was allowed some leeway far from home. Okay to visit but shouldn't want to live there. Irresponsible.

I'm afraid to let people in, Roone. I'm scared to be that vulnerable. I don't want to be hurt.

From: Roone
To: Erin
Sent: January 3, 2011
Subject: RE: RE: RE: RE: RE: New Year

I've got news for you, pumpkin: everyone's afraid to let people in. You're not special. Stop wallowing. Stop thinking there's some glory in your pain. We all have pain. Sometimes you have to remind yourself you're not the only one who's broken.

~

From: Erin
To: Roone
Sent: January 3, 2011
Subject: RE: RE: RE: RE: RE: RE: New Year

Ouch. Harsh.

~

From: Roone
To: Erin
Sent: January 3, 2011
Subject: RE: RE: RE: RE: RE: RE: RE: New Year

I'm not trying to be harsh, baby. I'm trying to help you set you free. I'm trying to shake you free to live this life. It's the only life we know we have for sure, baby. That woman I met, she was full of life. Now that you're back in Wishing Rock you seem like a different person. What did you do with that spicy woman? Bring her back. You were so much happier in that skin. That's the woman I care about. You're being not you.

~

From: Erin
To: Roone
Sent: January 3, 2011
Subject: RE: RE: RE: RE: RE: RE: RE: RE: New Year

What if the me you met was a lie? What if I'm being me now? Could you love me as I am now? You should come visit and see who I am here.

~

From: Roone
To: Erin
Sent: January 3, 2011
Subject: RE: RE: RE: RE: RE: RE: RE: RE: New Year

You are you, Erin. You can't be someone one place and someone else another place. The you I met was the real you. You can't fake that abandon. You weren't afraid here, I know that. Maybe it was all new and fresh and exciting, being your wild self, but it was you. Erin Anderson, you are a passionate, electric woman. This I know. This I witnessed. This I experienced. This I love. Just try it out at home too, see if people don't accept you as you really are, or who you think you are, or who you think you want to be. You might be surprised.

I'm running late, got a gig tonight with some friends. I'll call you later. Don't get so down, girl! Just be! Remember? Plan BE. Stop thinking so much. BE.

Luv ya,
R.

~

Text from Ed to Michael
Sent: January 4, 2011

Are you near a TV? Turn it on! Channel 39!

~

Text from Michael to Ed
Sent: January 4, 2011

What's up?

~

Text from Ed to Michael
Sent: January 4, 2011

It's Aunt Meredith! I swear it is! Haven't seen a picture of her in ages but I just know. Turn it on!

~

Text from Michael to Ed
Sent: January 4, 2011

Channel 39? I don't see her.

~

Text from Ed to Michael
Sent: January 4, 2011

Keep watching. Short gray hair, dark blue suit.

~

Text from Michael to Ed
Sent: January 4, 2011

There! I saw! Was that her?

~

Text from Ed to Michael
Sent: January 4, 2011

It looks like her, right? It's been a while, but I swear that's her.

~

Text from Michael to Ed
Sent: January 4, 2011

Well, I'll be darned.

~

From: Ruby
To: Pip
Sent: January 5, 2011
Subject: Brooks family intrigue

Hey, Pip! How are you? How were the New Year festivities with the MacAlpine clan? How is my buddy, ol' Colin? Has he found himself a woman yet? He was such fun to travel with when he drove us around Glasgow and Edinburgh after your wedding. Tell him I said hello, will you?

We're doing well here; survived the holiday frenzy and are now just settling in for the long wet winter. Ed's still working on plans for his rooftop deck, and it's fun to fantasize about it, but for the time being there's not much that can be done. Still, he seems to be on the phone with the contractors all the time!

In other Brooks family news, yesterday Ed was half-watching some show – a spinoff – remember that show in the nineties about aliens, there was the guy who Believed, and the short redhead who was a Skeptic, and despite being abducted in like the second episode of the whole series, she still didn't Believe until like the eighteenth season when the actor who played the Guy who Believed left the show so they needed someone who Believed so then she … I don't even remember, had an alien baby or something? Anyway, there was a spinoff or something of this show on a cable channel, and he saw someone he thought looked familiar. He got Michael in on it, and they determined it looked like their aunt. When the credits ran by, they weren't so sure – their aunt is Meredith, but the actress listed in the role was Barbara Brooks. A quick call to their dad revealed that's Meredith's middle name, so she must either go by Barbara or use it for her stage name for some reason, but apparently ol' Aunt Meredith is an actress! Interestingly, Ed's dad didn't have Meredith/Barbara's phone number. Ed had to email his mom to get his aunt's contact info. (Which, incidentally, is why I now know the time zone difference between here and Iceland, which, for your edification, is eight hours, meaning I think Iceland must be in your time zone?)

So as I write this, Ed's on the phone with Meredith/Barbara, who lives and works in Vancouver, B.C., and they're having a hoot of a time getting caught up, from the sounds of things. I've gathered that she's a regular on that spinoff/parody/whatever show, but that's about all I can tell you at this point. Maybe this will spur on a family reunion! You may remember that ol' Grandpa Meriwether, Meredith's dad and Ed's grandfather, mostly skipped his son and daughter when doling out the goods in his will. I don't know if we even know whether she was upset about the whole thing. Mitchell (brother to Meredith) wasn't, since his sons were the primary beneficiaries, but I'd say Meredith has reason to be a wee bit peeved. From the sound of the laughing I'm hearing, though, can't be too big of a grudge being held there. I'll keep you updated.

In other news, Erin is desperately trying not to look too desperate as far as her tropical lover is concerned. Roone seems to have the "two day rule" down – putting plenty of space between her calls and messages to him, and his replies to her. It's hard to say whether that's an intentional slight, a calculated flirtation, or simply the fact that he's a busy guy who has made the choice not to carry his phone and life around with him, so he's just harder to get a hold of. What is it with guys and these relationship games? If she likes him and he likes her then what's the point in pretending to be coy? But it's not mine to judge (which doesn't mean I won't). She cannot stop talking about Hawaii. I won't be at all surprised if she goes back to visit him again soon. Long distance relationships – as you well know, they are difficult! Plus, I'm sitting here with a blanket over my shoulders, another wrapped around me, and down slippers on my feet, and it's eighty degrees in Lahaina. Maybe I'll move to Hawaii, too! This guy has definitely had an affect on Erin. I can see her brain churning but I'm not sure what all is going on in there. It seems to be good, but it's a mystery as of yet.

And, on a side note, I remain fascinated by the amount of time we women put into thinking about the right timing in communicating with men. We analyze the perfect moment for conversations: not while he's on vacation because he won't want to think about it or he won't remember. Not during sports or he won't know he's even had the discussion. And on and on. And meanwhile, do men even bother with such acrobatics? No, they say what they think when they think it. I suppose that's the benefit of not thinking about it all so much.

This coming weekend, Jake is heading back to Seattle for the next quarter of school. It's been fun having him around again, without all the angst and drama there used to be. I think he's on good terms with Ed again. They were in great form the other night, running potato sack races up and down the hall, shoving and joking with each other like good friends again. Warms a gal's heart, to see how resilient true friendship is.

Well, that's about it here. 2011! So weird, we're into the second decade of the twenty-first century, for reals. And according to those

Mayans we only have, what, less than twenty-four months left to live. We'd better make the most of it!

Stay healthy over there, watch over that little bun in the oven and give her a pat from Auntie Ruby! Love to you, love to Gavin, and I'll talk to you all again soon.

R.

From: Alexandra
To: Adele
Sent: January 6, 2011
Subject: Congratulations!!!

Adele,

Ruby just got off the phone with you and came running down the hall telling us all the news! Congratulations! When is the wedding? Will it be over there in Scotland, or will you bring your groom-to-be back here? I am just delighted for you both. News of nuptials is such a great way to brighten our dull gray days here! You will make a beautiful blushing bride. If you need anyone to tell you the facts of life before your wedding day, just say the word.

I have been terribly negligent in writing and I do apologize. However cliché it may be, David and I have been making a very concerted effort to live our lives In The Moment. I think a side effect of that is less time spent in our heads – which is a good thing – but wherein letters to loved ones are a very in-one's-head activity, I'm afraid my correspondence has suffered somewhat. What time I do spend in communication with people outside Wishing Rock has largely been spent getting to know the older half-sister I just found out about, who lives over in Bellingham. She's a nice enough woman. It's strange to sometimes feel her to be so familiar and such a stranger at the same time, knowing we share genes and DNA but have no shared memories. Odd mental gymnastics in all that. I haven't been to visit her yet, nor has she come here, but we're planning to do so.

Sometime next month, maybe. I would like to meet her. Despite the fact that her genes come from my father, who beat me and is therefore not the most pleasant of memories. I have to remind myself that she isn't a perpetrator or predator herself; nor is she at fault for having unwittingly escaped what I endured. She was simply a girl whose father left her, and any harm done to me had nothing to do with her.

It's funny, you think you're an adult and then something like this hits you and you realize, some wounds have just barely healed over.

But enough of that, that's neither here nor there. Dwelling on it will not increase my happiness! I believe you know that this summer, when my psychic powers all went "poof" for a while, I decided to go back to school to study the brain. Though the spirits did finally return to me, the idea of furthering my education continues to appeal to me. Now, I'm taking online courses about the brain and neuroscience and all that, and it's simply fascinating stuff. I especially enjoy that David enjoys it as much as I do, and we spend a good amount of time sharing and discussing what each of us learns. He takes the articles and books I share with him and is spurred on to research of his own out of sheer curiosity and joy of learning. One thing we recently learned that we (we being humans, not just David and me) are never as happy when we let our minds wander as we are when we are present in the moment. Wandering minds are the kryptonite of happiness, as it were. Even if we let our mind wander to pleasant thoughts, the scientists say, we are still happier if we live In The Now. And so, as I mentioned earlier, we are quite consciously living in the now, on a crusade to be happier, slapping ourselves mentally if we stray too far into the what was or what will be. It's been an interesting exercise, especially for two people whose mental lives have been, to this point, extraordinarily active. It is, I should say, quite nice. A challenge to maintain sometimes; there's a bit of pleasure to be had in reveries and idle ponderings. But finding ways to live in the now is forcing us to be more active, get out and do more, see more, and that has been most rewarding indeed. As a bonus, it has really bonded us together as a couple. As unlikely as we may have seemed at first, I think we were meant to meet at this time in our lives.

Well then, again, congratulations to you, and please give my warmest regards to Liam. Tell him I think he made a very wise choice. Now with your granddaughter married to his son, what does that then make you? Step-mother to your granddaughter's husband? Family trees sometimes are more like the old cotoneaster I had to pull out of my yard at a house I once lived at; branches winding all around, re-rooting, no way to know find the origin, just one big ball of connections. And perhaps there's nothing wrong with that.

Happy new year to you all,

Love,

Alexandra

From: Adele
To: Alexandra
Sent: January 7, 2011
Subject: RE: Congratulations!!!

Dear Alexandra,

What a treat to hear from you. It's been far too long. Yes, you heard right, this old hen is giving married life another go. Liam and I have been talking about it since July, but life and weddings and grandchildren and great grandchildren and travel and bruised tail-bones got in the way and I'd all but forgotten the topic. Until two days ago, when Liam got up off his donut pillow, got down on one knee (not wise; about killed him getting back up), and proposed.

"I've only done this once before and never imagined I'd be doing it again, but Adele, you were a surprise I never saw coming. Will you do me the honor of marrying me and making an honest man out of me?" He winked and said the neighbors are starting to gossip about us living together in sin. Silly old man. The neighbors gossip about everything and are not just starting to gossip about us, but I am delighted to marry him and make an honest man out of him, if that will make him happy.

The wedding will be here, in Scotland. We don't want a long engagement as we realize neither of us is a spring chicken and we don't trust time. Liam wants to get married on Valentine's Day so he has a better chance of remembering our anniversary. Who am I to argue? We don't need a big wedding, certainly. We'll probably just get married at the courthouse with a few witnesses and then have a reception for family and friends. I doubt we'll have any attendants. Just sign the papers and then get on to the celebration, as it should be.

Pip keeps insisting that she will make the wedding cake, but the poor girl has swollen ankles and a belly that's starting to grow, as well. By the wedding she'll be at seven months, and I can't imagine baking in a hot kitchen will be at the top of her list by the time the actual date comes around. Everyone else wants to make a bigger fuss about this than we do.

To be honest, I thought a lot about whether we even need to get married. The gossip of the neighbors is hardly enough to deter me. No, what finally pushed us in the end was knowing that if we make our arrangement legal, we have more rights when either of us is in the hospital, and at our age, that's certainly a concern. Ruby asked me whether I'll take Liam's last name, the unspoken thought being I'm far too old to change. Yes, I'm old but also old-fashioned, in some ways, and a MacAlpine I shall be. The kids have already fitted me with a lovely MacAlpine tartan scarf to keep me warm.

Speaking of warm, we do know that Scotland in February is far from it. If people choose not to come to chilly Scotland to attend the wedding, we understand. Love and celebration are not bound by geographical proximity.

But, that said, you are of course more than welcome to join us, and we would be delighted if you could come. Bring David if you like, or don't if you're far enough along in your relationship that a break from him sounds like a wee little blessing. Official invitations will be sent soon, but international mail being what it is, and the wedding being so near, consider yourself officially invited with this note.

All my best to you; I hope you can come. It was a joy getting to know you last summer at Pip's wedding. I hope we see you soon.

Love,

Adele (and Liam)

~

From: Adele

To: Millie

Sent: January 8, 2011

Subject: Invitation

Dear Millie,

You see how determined I am to meet you and your Walter? I have become engaged to Liam simply so we may have a wedding and you must travel to join in the celebration. I will go to any lengths!

You will, of course, have heard by now that I am to don the white gown once again at this, the sunset of my years. As I told Alexandra, invitations are going out soon but as the mail might not get to you in time, please consider yourself invited. And do bring Walter. I must meet both of you. You have the travel bug now after your cruise, I know you do; your young Ben seems well able to staff the store for you while you're gone. Please come.

The wedding will be February 14, here in Oban. I wish I could offer you a place to stay again but it seems we're to be full up with family in all the MacAlpine homes. Attached is a list of nearby inns and hotels. This area is gorgeous. You will love it. If you can, take some extra time off and travel around. February not being the peak tourist season, you're bound to get some good deals (along with some rain, but we are hearty folk, are we not?).

Hoping to see you soon,

Adele

~

From: Millie
To: Adele
Sent: January 9, 2011
Subject: RE: Invitation

Dear Adele,

Well I'll be a monkey's aunt! Congratulations in colossal abundance. Now that you mention it, I do remember your talking months ago about the possibility of getting married, but that slipped out of my brain along with half of everything else I once knew. I am just pleased as punch for you and Liam. I think at the time you first brought up the idea, Walter was just starting to court me, and getting married was the farthest thing from my mind. But, maybe I would like to get married just once in my life. I'd pretty well given up on the idea, after the passing of Clive and of time. Walter has changed my mind about a lot of things, though. Perhaps we'll follow in your footsteps, sooner or later.

As for the wedding, we officially RSVP in the affirmative. Walter and I are thrilled to hop on a plane and come visit. We've looked through the inns you mentioned and found one at the top of the hill, Dun-something-or-other, with a room with an expansive view, overlooking all of Oban and the harbor. Is it a harbor? Whatever it is, we have Room 4 reserved and we are more than excited.

We then plan to take your advice and travel around a bit, soggy though Great Britain may be at the time. Walter tells me he was in England around our Thanksgiving once (of course they didn't celebrate it there), and it was cold and dark but beautiful. Not having to worry about conflicting holidays, the whole place, he said, was done up early for Christmas, lit up like a Charles Dickens tale. Well, maybe not Charles Dickens, since he was about poor hungry orphans, not really the stuff of Christmas cheer, but you know what I mean. At any rate, we're quickly researching our options and making an itinerary. We are both planners, Walter more so than I am, which makes us a good match. We're looking into the south of Scotland, the north of England and perhaps a bit of London. If you have suggestions or ideas, let us know. I almost invited you along but I suppose the two of you will want a little uninterrupted honeymoon time? Will you be honeymooning? Where will you go? It seems you've been all over lately, what could possibly be next? I can't wait to find out.

Walter is in charge of flights and reservations. As soon as we have it all settled, I'll send it along to you.

What a change of plans for my winter into spring! Adele, I am so excited. We will meet at last, my friend, a wonderful thing.

See you soon,
Millie (and Walter)

~

From: Ruby
To: Pip
Sent: January 10, 2011
Subject: Ex

So. Guess who just showed up in Wishing Rock?

Ed's ex-girlfriend. No, seriously. What the heck!

Remember last year when we cleaned out the basement of the building, to prevent the firemen from fining us? And Ed had a whole box full of stuff that he'd kept from some ex, because she'd left without a forwarding address or some such thing?

You wouldn't think word would get around so fast in Alaska – I mean, it's a huge, huge state! I thought it was remote! I thought people were one per fifty square miles! But apparently you would be wrong. Laurel, you remember her, the woman who said she was Ed and Michael's long-lost half-sister but turned out not to be, well, Laurel was talking to someone at a bar in Anchorage, and this woman, this ex, overheard. Julianna. Julianna heard Ed's name and heard that he owns a town and what do you know, next thing she does is book a flight down to Wishing Rock. Okay, technically she took a flight to Seattle and a boat to Wishing Rock but that's details. She said "Alaska is freaking freezing" and that she had to come here to get warm, but you and I know she's here for more than that.

Ed got her set up at the Inn, but has invited her to dinner tonight. Me, Ed, Alexandra, David, and this woman. I'm not terribly pleased about this. I'm no green-eyed monster, Pip, but you should have seen the woman's cleavage. Shirt with a neckline down to her navel. In January. She can't be up to anything good.

I will report back after dinner.

In more pleasant news, Ed and I are making plans for Scotland. We may take a side trip to Ireland after the festivities, while we're over there. Ed has been talking to a colleague at the Old Bushmills Distillery up in Northern Ireland, and wants to visit that and a few other distilleries and the like while we're in the general area. Do you think Gavin's sister – is Katie the one living in Ireland? – would she and her husband put us up for a bit? We would love to spend some time with them if they are open to it. Toss the idea out to her and make sure she knows she can refuse if it's inconvenient.

I'm so excited to see you again! I know it hasn't been that long, but it feels like forever. It's going to be so much worse once that baby of yours is born and growing bigger every day, and I'm not there to see him or her. I tell you, scientists need to get on that transporter idea. If I could have one superpower, that would be it.

All right, more news to come after the dinner party tonight. I'll write tonight if it's not too late, otherwise tomorrow.

Love to all,
Ruby

~

Text from Alexandra to Ed
Sent: January 11, 2011

Are you alone? Can you talk?

~

Text from Ed to Alexandra
Sent: January 11, 2011

Good morning to you too! No, Ruby's here, why?

~

Text from Alexandra to Ed
Sent: January 11, 2011

I saw the way she was watching you and Julianna last night. Just be careful. Be sensitive.

~

Text from Ed to Alexandra
Sent: January 11, 2011

What do you mean? Julianna's an ex, nothing more! Ruby knows that. Nothing for her to worry about.

~

Text from Alexandra to Ed
Sent: January 11, 2011

Maybe one day man will learn to read woman body language. I'm just saying, be careful. We can talk about it later.

~

Text from Ed to Alexandra
Sent: January 11, 2011

You women, you're all impossible to understand. Add that to your Wishing Rock Olympics, will you: Overanalyzing. You and Ruby and half the women I know can compete for the gold. Okay, Lexalicious, I'll be careful. See ya later, Lexaroo!

~

From: Ruby
To: Pip
Sent: January 11, 2011
Subject: Ex, again

Pip, I'm so angry at Ed! That ex! At dinner last night in her low-cut curve-clinging shirt, her long curly dark hair (dyed too dark for her age if you ask me), her weathered and leathered face, like she's been out in the wind too much. She's a professional poker player, of all things. Who plays professional poker? And she drinks old fashioneds. Who drinks old fashioneds? Old dead actors in black and white movies, that's who. No one else but this Julianna. She's trying too hard to be chill, if you ask me.

She made sure to be the center of attention all evening, telling stories and making everyone laugh. Pity laughs! Hahaha. You are so funny, Julianna! You know what else is funny? The way the door would hit you on the ass on the way out.

And, she was all over Ed. Expertly maneuvered herself so she was sitting next to him at the table, then spent the whole night touching his arm and flipping her hair at him. And he didn't seem to mind, either, I'll tell you. He says he was just being nice and that he felt awkward the whole time, but it sure didn't show.

Alexandra and David left before Julianna did, to go watch some PBS documentary they wanted to see, and you wouldn't believe how mean she was about Alexandra.

"She's a psychic?" she asked, with a look like "Are you kidding me? Is she kidding you?" She went on: "Do you believe in that stuff? You don't believe in that stuff, Ed. I know you better than that." She lifted her right eyebrow at him, playfully, challenging him.

"You're the one with the tarot cards," he teased, catching her challenge, tossing it back. They'd danced that dance before. They knew each other's moves.

"Yes, but I only read them right side up, the positive stuff," she laughed.

"Why is that?" I asked, trying to be a part of a conversation I was most definitely not invited to. She looked surprised to see me still in the room.

Ed jumped in, because he knew the answer, you see. "She only believes the good things," he said. "Ignores the warnings about death and poverty and disease and danger. She only wants to hear it if it's to her advantage." His words scolded but there was a twinkle in his eye.

"You can't just pick and choose like that," I said, "What's the point? Why bother?"

"Who says I can't just pick and choose?" She asked. "It's all made up anyway; why can't I make my own rules? There's no harm in believing good things are going to happen, but there's potentially harm in believing that bad things will. If I go around thinking positive thoughts, I feel better. If I go around thinking death is around the corner or someone is out to get me, I feel awful. What's the harm in choosing to be happy about it? My tarot, my rules."

And with that she leaned over to pick up her drink, and there, right there, in my face, those boobs. Those boobs, the sixth (and seventh) person in the room last night. Plastic surgeons wanting to see what their porn star clients aspire to should come study Julianna. Editors of women's magazines wanting to tell their readers how to flirt should come study Julianna.

Ed seemed to be studying Julianna, anyway. I'm telling you.

We had a little fight about it, Pip, and I feel a little bad about it but I also don't feel bad about it. He should have made it clear to this woman that he was with me. He shouldn't have invited her to dinner. Am I right?

Tell me I'm right. I don't like feeling this jealous and I don't like Ed seeing me this jealous but I can't help but feel jealous. She picked the wrong time of the month to show up. Why couldn't she have showed up next week? My mood would have been much better. As it is, I can't stop crying. Ed wanted me to stay at his house tonight but I was too upset.

Why can I never figure out how to be a normal person in a relationship? Why can't Ed wear blinders to all the pretty women in the world?

Love you,

R.

From: Alexandra
To: Pip
Sent: January 12, 2011
Subject: Ex

Hi, Pip –

Ruby tells me she wrote you about Julianna. Don't worry, I'm working on mitigating the meltdown. I'm not quite sure what happened, but certainly jealousy and a gorgeous, funny, ex-girlfriend, blended together with hormones, is a bit like mixing alcohol with one's anti-depressants. Not the best outcome.

Despite what you may have heard, Julianna is a very nice young woman. I've tried to remind Ruby that this is a sign of Ed's good taste. I know she gets it but it'll be more obvious to her in a couple of days.

Don't tell Ruby I said this, but we really did all have a nice time, everyone except Ruby, I suppose. Julianna is a lovely young woman. She's complex. She goes against the grain, I'd say. Julianna is an artist, quite a good one in fact from the pictures she showed us of her paintings, and has dabbled in interior design and architecture, but she mostly works as a professional poker player. Her cleavage, which Ruby so despises, is one of her tools. Even when bluffing for high stakes, men are still men, she said. If it gives her the slightest moment of distraction, that's to her advantage. She said she once even thought about going undercover at a brothel, out of sheer curiosity, but couldn't figure out how to do it without engaging in the "work" of a brothel, if you will. At which I pondered: why is it there have never been brothels full of men, which women frequent? What would be inside if there were? Men who would sit and listen and cuddle? Men who would take out the trash without being asked? Not that we women don't like intimacy. But that's easier to find, it seems, than a man who will clean the bathroom of his own volition.

Anyway, if Ed was nice to Julianna and didn't throw her out on the street, well, that's part of what Ruby loves about Ed. I think she's just feeling a little emotional. Hearing about your grandmother's wedding has thrown her into an odd space. Wanting to be married herself; sad about being so far from all of you; plus, the speed of the nuptials is a reminder to her that she doesn't know how much time Adele has left. She's healthy and fit as can be, your Gran, but life doesn't always care about healthy and fit. Sometimes life has other plans, and Ruby hates that uncertainty while she's so far away from all of you. She's worried about you and the baby. She's worried about Liam and his bruised behind. She's worried about Erin moving to Hawaii. She's worried about everything she has no control over, and she's also stressed out trying to hide her worry from everyone, and it's getting to a breaking point.

We'll see what we can do.

Perhaps more Wishing Rock Olympics will be just what she needs! David and I are having a fantastic time coming up with off-beat events perfectly suited for the mishmash of mongrels and strays who call Wishing Rock home. (I mean the humans, of course.) So far our match-ups are limited: potato sack races, office chair races, a tug-of-war and, of course, cup stacking. Most residents are on board with the idea of cordoning off our hallways as needed for the

Games; they'll still be able to get around via stairwells at the ends of the floors, and the elevators. Still, Old Henry is overjoyed at having something new to grump about, and is determined to find a way in which the whole escapade goes against regulations or permits. This means David is perpetually perusing permits for permissions needed, but he likes that sort of thing so it's not too much of a problem.

And, I have to say, the permits are a good distraction for David. He's determined to bring ziplining to Dogwinkle. I'm not sure how I feel about that – it would be such a huge undertaking – but my reservations aside, it's unlikely we could have a zipline up before March (when the Games will be held). The line would almost have to be offsite; the only place around here we could set up a line would be between the Inn on the roof, and the distillery about a quarter mile away. Even so, we'd have to either clear away a series of old trees or get creative with a zigzag trail. And call me morbid but if someone is going to drop to their death from a zipline (hopefully not the case, especially if we're liable), I'd rather it not be right at my doorstep. No, out by our little not-quite-a-mountain mountain, I think that would be better. But, figuring out all the logistics, that's David's domain. I am happily ignorant for now, offering sage advice when requested but otherwise keeping my nose out of the whole thing. More or less.

I believe I'll be able to come out for Adele's wedding, but only briefly. Millie found a lovely little B&B in Oban, and I'll be getting a room there as well. David won't be able to come this time. I've been in contact with my newly discovered older half-sister, who lives in Bellingham, and we'd planned for me to come visit that next weekend, Presidents' Day weekend. So I'll be over and back, just long enough to give out hugs and well wishes, have a chat with your baby in utero, spend some time with all the delightful MacAlpines, and head on home. It'll be good to see you again.

So with that, I'm off. I think maybe I'll invite Ruby to do some meditation with me. This long wet winter has everyone getting cabin fever, I think; she's not the only one I've seen who has been quicker to anger or irritate. I mentioned Old Henry – he's in rare form these days himself! He lives next door to one of the units in the building that Ed and Michael have staged for rental use on the second floor, and even though it hasn't even been rented out yet, Henry already has oodles of complaints. Noise when they were setting up the rooms and painting. Future noise when people rent the space. Comings and goings and bedlam! If Old Henry didn't have something to complain about I suppose he'd have to find another hobby, so I guess at least it keeps him busy.

I'll see you soon! All my best to the family.

Alexandra

From: Erin
To: Roone
Sent: January 13, 2011
Subject: Salsa

Hey, babe!

Ruby's having all the poker gals over tomorrow night, since Ed (her boyfriend; I've mentioned him, right?) will be in Seattle overnight. I want to make that mango salsa your friend served at that pupu party I went to. Did you ever get the recipe? Can you send it over? Thank you very much! I had so many mangoes and pineapples while I was there; now I've been craving them since I got home. I hope I can find a mango at the store, come to think of it; it's not the right season. If I were in Seattle I could, but the Moon Bay store might not have any. I'm sure Millie (who runs the little store in the first floor of our building) doesn't have any. Does it come in cans? It wouldn't be the same but I could try. If nothing else, there's canned peaches. I will make do!

It'll be interesting to see where the conversation goes tomorrow night at Ruby's. Ed's ex-girlfriend came down from Alaska, totally a surprise as he hasn't seen her in ages, and the visit hasn't set quite right with Ruby. She seems nice enough, actually, if a little manic. I was down in the lobby this morning, stretching after my run, just as

Julianna was coming out to go on her own run. We sat and chatted for a few minutes. I can see why Ed liked her, and also why, if he liked her, he and I didn't work out. She's unreserved, candid, outspoken. Bold. That's what she is. Bold. Present. Unapologetic. Not the kind of person who is going to hold back her opinions. In our brief chat she talked about "kids today" (massively entitled; self-absorbed; tied to their phones; incapable of living their own lives; dependent on their parents for everything and unable to make their own decisions); road rage (again with the entitlement; people thinking the rules don't apply to them; no one looking out for anyone else; people nowadays like to bully the bully and that's no better, that's just an eye for an eye); and laundry (laundry is a personal thing and you have to have a certain level of intimacy with someone before you can mix your underwear and theirs, of course!). All this in five minutes! And then she was off on a run to get some more energy.

Maybe that's why Ed likes Ruby. She's sort of a blend of me and Julianna – she thinks but she also acts. Sometimes an overthinker but she'll also get right into the action, where Ed is. But she's not so gung-ho that a conversation with her leaves you exhausted. I did like Julianna but keeping up with her would be a chore!

How have you been? I've been good but still can't get over the chill creeping into my bones. I miss that Hawaii heat desperately! The afternoons of chi chis and pupus. And I miss you too. I probably haven't managed to convince you to come visit our cold rainy town?

I'm reading up on Maui. Finding out about everything I missed when I was there last month. Making plans for when I return. Soon, I hope. Soon.

xxx
Erin

From: Roone
To: Erin
Sent: January 13, 2011
Subject: RE: Salsa

Mango salsa recipe below. Good to hear from you, babe. Had enough of that rain yet? Come on back here, sun every day, can you handle it again? Once you have a taste of Laule'a – "peaceful happiness" – you want it all the time. I get it. That's why I moved here. You could. Always small jobs around, enough to keep a girl in mangoes and pineapple, at least. See if you can learn to relax. Challenge yourself to be the Erin you want to be. Free spirit, risk taker, dreamer, believer. Is it in you, babe? I know it is.

I'm great. A friend who does construction has a new house he's working on, needs some labor, so I've been there a few days earning my keep. Work hard during the day, come home and down to my ocean at night, that park where we met, there with my guitar and the waves and the moon. Sweet life.

My birthday's coming up, did you know that? February 3. My gal Ava is planning a big shindig at her place, she and her roommate. I'm supposed to go scouting around the neighbors for tables to borrow. I'll do it after a nap. It's a good day for a nap.

Your description of Julianna made me laugh. She's right about the laundry. Can't have my knickers mixing with your knickers if we haven't even touched skin yet. I guess you and I don't have to worry about that then?

Luv ya,
Roone

Mango Salsa
Ingredients
2 ripe mangoes, peeled, seeded, and diced
1 small red onion, chopped
1 1/2 Tbsp seeded, minced, fresh jalapeno pepper (1 medium)
1/4 cup coarsely chopped fresh cilantro

2 Tbsp fresh lime juice
1/2 tsp salt
1/4 tsp freshly ground black pepper
Directions
Combine, toss, serve. Live, love, laugh.

From: Ruby
To: Erin, Millie, Carolyn, Claire, Alexandra
Sent: January 14, 2011
Subject: Tonight

Ladies!

I am so excited to have you over tonight. Let's just cross our fingers that the bathroom pipes stay clear. The plumber from Moon Bay just left. Plumbing issues: what a pain! But can I tell you, this plumber! He must be new. How have I not seen him before? Where did he come from?

First of all, he was adorable. I'd say he was in his late twenties, or early thirties at absolute oldest. I didn't catch his name; something with five letters, starting with an S. Steve? Shane? Scott? He seemed so shy at first, reserved, sweet, but the things that came out of his mouth made me so curious to know more! I took him to the bathroom, where the problem lay: the shower drain. (Sort of an odd thing, really, to be in your bathroom with a complete stranger, isn't it? I mean, half the time I'm in there I'm either naked or pantsless. That's a weird aura to share with someone you don't know.) Showed him the bathtub, in case he couldn't tell the bathtub from the toilet from the sink. "So, here's the bathroom, and ... uh, there's the bathtub. It is plugged up." I'd already explained the situation before we got into the bathroom. "Anything else you need?" I asked, not knowing what to say.

"I could use a massage," he said.

Um, excuse me, what?

No seriously, did he just say that? This adorable, seemingly sweet shy and sensitive young man, did he just come on to me? Was that a come on? Could that be anything other than a come on? Do people really say things like that to strangers? What was that?

And what did I say? Well, what would you say? I, ever clever and quick-witted, said, "Well, er, I don't have any of those."

Smooooooth Ruby. That's why they call me Smooth Ruby. Smooth is my middle name. Well, I guess if I'm Smooth Ruby then Smooth is my first name and Ruby is my middle name. But you get my point.

I left the bathroom. Surely blushing as red as my name. The Ruby part.

Then later, we were sitting together at the dining room table (and again, it felt strangely intimate; this being where I eat, which is done with the mouth, and I was staring at his mouth, those pale smooth luscious lips that gave no clue to his thoughts), and he was explaining the bill to me, the rest of the plumbing process. "That's it," he said, "unless something strange happens," and I (remember me, Smooth Ruby, Clever Ruby?) said: "Like aliens?" He, without a beat: "Well, we could talk about that." Deadpan. Totally serious.

Where did this man come from?!

Now I want to stage another plumbing incident to see if I can bring him back. I am so curious.

Oh, I mentioned that I didn't catch his name, right? So as he left, I said "Thanks Steve – Shane – Scott." Thinking, of course, that he'd help me out with the correct answer. No, no, of course not. "You're welcome," he said, and turned to leave, without a massage or a conversation about aliens. Surely wanting more, having come so close.

I have to say, and I think I can say this with some certainty, that was the most bizarre home repair situation I've ever encountered.

But, the pipes seem to be clear, so come on over at 6! Can't wait to see you all!

R.

From: Claire
To: Ruby, Erin, Millie, Carolyn, Alexandra
Sent: January 14, 2011
Subject: RE: Tonight

My, my, Ruby! Your Steve/Shane/Scott is quite intriguing! You know, one of the sinks in one of the Inn's bathrooms has been acting up lately, and Tom has not gotten around to fixing it ... maybe it's time for me to call in the man from Moon Bay! I could use a little eye candy around here; I love Tom but a little bow chicky bow bow is fun to think about! Spice things up!
Do you need us to bring anything tonight?

~

From: Erin
To: Claire, Ruby, Millie, Carolyn, Alexandra
Sent: January 14, 2011
Subject: RE: RE: Tonight

Holy cow! I can't believe he said he needed a massage. What a random thing to say to a stranger. I thought that sort of thing only happened in a certain kind of movie – the kind with no plot! Have you ever noticed, plumbing is the kind of thing where it's almost impossible to talk about it without it sounding dirty? Having someone come snake your pipes, for example. Can you even say that in polite company? Totally innocent but still it sounds wrong.
I'm bringing mango salsa tonight, if I can find a mango at the Moon Bay grocery. Say, maybe I'll run into Shane-Scott-Steve!

~

From: Claire
To: Erin, Ruby, Millie, Carolyn, Alexandra
Sent: January 14, 2011
Subject: RE: RE: RE: Tonight

You're right, Erin – you can't talk about plumbing without it sounding like innuendo. That reminds me of another such thing, from back before I was married and I rented a house on the corner with a drainage ditch. I couldn't talk about my ditch without feeling like I was saying something naughty! Especially when it came to mowing my ditch!

~

From: Ruby
To: Claire, Erin, Millie, Carolyn, Alexandra
Sent: January 14, 2011
Subject: RE: RE: RE: RE: Tonight

Mowing your ditch! Now that sounds like there's a story there!
Erin, if you find the plumber in Moon Bay, get his name! I mean, I'm attached and dedicated to Ed but one never knows when one will have an emergency need to have one's pipes snaked.
Wow, you really can't say that without it sounding dirty!

~

From: Claire
To: Ruby, Erin, Millie, Carolyn, Alexandra
Sent: January 14, 2011
Subject: RE: RE: RE: RE: RE: Tonight

There absolutely is a ditch-mowing story. Let's see if I can remember how it happened. As I said, I lived on a corner house. On one side, it had a culvert, or ditch, with grass growing in it, and it was the responsibility of the person living in the home to maintain that ditch. Actually, come to think of it, it may have been the city's responsibility to maintain my ditch, but they never did, so the task fell to me.

Now, my ditch had very steep sides. Mowing my ditch by myself was really difficult. I didn't like having to mow my ditch by myself but I was a young woman, not dating anyone at the time, hadn't met Tom yet, and there was no one else to do it.

I was explaining this very plight one day to a lovely young co-worker, a man whom we shall call Robert. I was telling him how hard it was to mow my own ditch, what with the steep sides and all. Now, Robert was a strong, strapping, handsome young man, tall and muscular and as kind as a person can be, so he offered to mow my ditch for me. And he wasn't kidding! He was totally willing to mow my ditch. For free, even!

So we agreed on a time and date – a Saturday. I called and left a message on his answering machine with my address and my home phone number.

Saturday came. No Robert. No phone call. Well, as it turns out, there was an accident near his neighborhood that knocked out his power, erased everything off his answering machine, and he never got my message. He had my work phone number and had tried calling that, but of course I wasn't there.

But the end result was that I had to mow my own ditch. And I'll tell you, when a woman who always has to mow her own ditch thinks that for once she's going to have an attractive young man mowing her ditch, and then she has to mow her own ditch again – oh, the disappointment!!

I'm giggling and blushing here as I tell this to you – it was all completely innocent. Just yard work, pure and simple. And yet!

~

From: Alexandra
To: Claire, Ruby, Erin, Millie, Carolyn
Sent: January 14, 2011
Subject: RE: RE: RE: RE: RE: RE: Tonight

Well, hello, ladies! What a story to come in on! I'm just back from Moon Bay myself. 1) I wish I'd known you were heading in, Erin, and we could have carpooled! And 2) I saw no randy plumber but had I known I would have been on the alert! Yes, he must be new. I had a plumber in not too long ago and it was that man Owen who's been there for years. I wonder if he has an apprentice? Or even a son?

Claire, I would never have guessed you would be the type to invite a man to come mow your ditch! I'm so sorry it didn't work out. You're right, it's much nicer if you can get someone else to do it for you.

From: Claire
To: Alexandra, Ruby, Erin, Millie, Carolyn
Sent: January 14, 2011
Subject: RE: RE: RE: RE: RE: RE: RE: Tonight

Oh, but wait, I'm just remembering there's more. Flash forward in time a few months or a year, I can't remember. The weather forecast was for a gorgeous spring day, and I had much yard work to do. Some hay seeds had gotten into my ditch, and so I had three-foot-tall grass growing in my ditch – not pretty. It was in desperate need of a good mow. So I decided to use a vacation day and just stay home on this beautiful mid-week day, and get out in the garden.

I was weeding the rose bushes by the ditch, and I began to figure out why I never saw my neighbors out working on their yards, yet their yards were well maintained: They hired people to come do the work in the middle of the work day! The neighbor across the street, for example, had three rugged men working on her yard, all at once.

Oh, how I envied her! Here I was weeding my ditch by myself, and she had three men doing all the work for her while she just lay back and watched.

I looked at my ditch, its vast expanse of overgrown grass. I looked at the men and their power tools. I looked at my tiny hand-tools.

I called one of the men over.

"What would you charge to mow my ditch?"

He assessed the situation with a glint in his eye.

"Twenty dollars."

Knowing I only had $13 in cash, and knowing that this man would want cash for this under-the-table transaction, I went to get my purse. I came back, holding my wallet so he could see.

"I only have $13."

"$13 will be fine."

So he called over his two buddies, with their powerful churning weed-whackers, and honey, my ditch, they mowed it and they mowed it fast and they mowed it good. Three complete strangers mowed my ditch for $13 and it was the best $13 I ever spent.

And that story is about yard work, and nothing else.

~

From: Erin
To: Claire, Alexandra, Ruby, Millie, Carolyn
Sent: January 14, 2011
Subject: RE: RE: RE: RE: RE: RE: RE: RE: Tonight

Claire! Oh my gosh, Claire! That is hysterical. I can't believe that. You're so bad. Does Tom know?!

~

From: Claire
To: Erin, Alexandra, Ruby, Millie, Carolyn
Sent: January 14, 2011
Subject: RE: RE: RE: RE: RE: RE: RE: RE: RE: Tonight

I haven't a clue what you mean. It's a completely true and innocent tale of yard work. If you have read something more into it than that, I'll have to suggest that you are the one who needs a little soap to clean out your mind! I'm just telling a tale about my ditch!

~

From: Ruby
To: Claire, Erin, Alexandra, Millie, Carolyn
Sent: January 14, 2011
Subject: RE: RE: RE: RE: RE: RE: RE: RE: RE: RE: Tonight

Claire, that's the best yard work story I ever heard. I think Shane-Scott-Steve should look into hiring himself out for yard work; I think he'd be mighty good at it!

As for your earlier question, I have the mixings for all the favorite cocktails, plus bacon-wrapped asparagus and that gorgonzola fruit torte I've made before. Erin is bringing mango salsa. If you want to bring something, you are more than welcome to grace us with your culinary skills; if not, no worries, we'll make do.

See you all soon!

R.

~

From: Pip
To: Ruby
Sent: January 15, 2011
Subject: RE: Ex, again

Rubes,

Sorry it took me so long to get back to you. It just took me that long to get over your saying Ed's ex was "trying too hard to be chill." Was that what you said? You are so hip with the way the young kids talk. Been hanging around Jake a lot, have you? Is he still there? I missed that notice. Does he come back a lot?

Look, you're just anxious about love and that's fine. But don't be. Ed's awesome, you're awesome, you're awesome together. He's not into that Julianna or he would be with her. Men are like that. They don't really hang around women they're not into. Have you not noticed that? Men can pretty much find any excuse to not be near a woman they're not interested in. I know this gal who keeps trying to convince herself that this guy she likes, likes her; that he's just busy or he'd call more often, etc. Well, fact is, if guys are into you they make time for you. Is he going out of his way to make time for Julianna? Then don't worry about it. He's into you, not her. Trust me.

In other news, I don't know if this is what is meant by the "nesting instinct" I've heard about regarding pregnant women, but I suddenly have this obsession with the idea of getting chickens. I wouldn't want to take care of them, of course – I still remember that high school biology class where we had to care for those baby chicks. What was the point of that? I can't even remember. We must have done some experiments on them. Had I known then what I know now I would have said something about that. What the heck did they have us do to the chicks? But what I do remember is that while newborn chicks are cute, there is very little that is cute about them after the first day or two. Then they're mean and poopy and annoying. No, Gavin can be the one to take care of them. I just want the fresh eggs. I bought farm fresh eggs from an island woman a few times last year, and they were gorgeous, the yolks almost orange, and I swear my baking was better with them. Now I want my own fresh eggs. Gavin can handle it. He's still in the I'd-do-anything-for-you stage so now's a good time to start with the chickens.

Still cold here but not as bad as it was. I can't believe Gran is getting married. Good for her. I can't figure out if that makes my relationship with Gavin incestuous or not but I'm going with "not." And I'm excited to see you! I'll be big as a house by then, I think. This baby is determined to prove it's related to the hearty MacAlpines. I am lumbering. I try not to waddle but it's getting worse, not better. Can't wait to get my ankles back. It's the little things.

Here's Katie's brown bread recipe. Make it to get yourself in the Irish mood. I adapted it for you from UK measurements to American measurements. Hopefully I got it right.

See you soon! x Pip

Katie's Irish Brown Bread
Ingredients
>3 cups organic stoneground whole wheat flour
>4 1/2 cups all purpose flour
>3/4 cup steel cut oats
>1 Tbsp salt
>1 Tbsp baking soda
>2 1/4 cups wheat bran
>3/4 cup wheat germ
>1 Tbsp demerara sugar
>2 large eggs
>1 quart buttermilk
>Melted butter for top of loaves

Directions
- Pre-heat oven to 400°.
- Mix all dry ingredients. Beat eggs and add to dry ingredients. Note, this won't make the dry ingredients wet so don't be surprised when it doesn't. Add buttermilk, and knead to smoothness – not for too long. Every time I make it, it's sort of sticky, so there's that. I do cakes, not breads. Anyway, di-

vide the mixture into three greased loaf pans. (Katie's recipe says four pans but I feel like that makes such short loaves.) Bake 40 to 50 minutes or until bottom of bread sounds hollow. Remove from oven and spread butter on tops, if desired. Let cool 10 minutes, then release from pans. Cool completely. Slice and freeze any bread you will not be using in the next two or three days.

~

From: Erin
To: Roone
Sent: January 16, 2011
Subject: RE: RE: Salsa

Babe,

Thanks so much for the mango salsa recipe. I ended up having to use peaches, which wasn't as great, but still not awful. Next time I'll have to plan ahead and/or put in a special order. Such is life on a tiny little island in the Pacific Northwest!

I didn't know your birthday is coming up! So soon! I wish I could be there with you. Have a chi chi on my behalf, will you? Toast yourself as you do. Let's see, what will the toast be: "Here's to Roone, who opened my heart to Plan BE."

How is that song coming along? Hey, I'm a poet and I didn't know it! If you need my help with lyrics just say the word. They come to me like ... um, wings on a bird? Okay, needs some work yet.

Julianna, you remember her, Ruby's boyfriend's ex, was in town for a few days. It's always interesting to see people's exes. They tell you a lot about a person but sometimes it's hard to tell just what they say. Maybe they tell about their insecurities? What they needed at the time they were dating that person? What they believed and didn't believe about themselves? Who they thought they deserved, or didn't?

What would I learn about you if I knew your exes?

~

From: Roone
To: Erin
Sent: January 17, 2011
Subject: RE: RE: RE: Salsa

Erin, the thing is, part of Plan BE is that you don't worry so much about people's exes. All an ex is, is someone a person used to date. It's not a secret code to a hidden inner self. It's a person. I date all sorts of people, just because I find them interesting at the time, or I wonder if they might be interesting. All that says about me is I'm interested in women and I'm interested in a variety of women. Don't read too much into these things. BE, babe, BE. Being is now. Not the past.

But: what would I learn about you if I knew your exes?

~

From: Erin
To: Roone
Sent: January 17, 2011
Subject: RE: RE: RE: RE: Salsa

If you met my exes I think you'd think I've been very confused. They're a rather random conglomeration. More about men who liked me than men I liked. People who weren't a threat to me, I guess. You'd learn that I held my heart too close, that I didn't let anyone in. You'd learn that I'm a bundle of insecurities that I pass off as indifference.

~

From: Roone
To: Erin
Sent: January 17, 2011
Subject: RE: RE: RE: RE: RE: Salsa

Life motto: No one can embrace you if you keep everyone at arm's length. Time to let people in, babe. You win through love, not through having the toughest exterior.

I gotta go, Monday pupus at Ava's. Chat later, babe. Stay open.

From: Millie
To: Adele
Sent: January 18, 2011
Subject: The blushing bride

Dear Adele,

Well, hello, again! I thought I should check in on the bride. How are wedding preparations, and how is your fine young gentleman groom? I'm hoping he's healing up well from his injury. And you, do you have the cake and the banquet hall and everything planned? Have you decided all the details of the reception? Alexandra tells me you're looking at doing the whole affair rather small. Don't worry about inviting us to all the events if you don't want to. We are honored to be a part of whatever you'd like to include us in.

Walter has been researching up a British storm and has determined the day after your wedding we're going to head on up to York, England, for a few days. There's an Abbey in the area, Fountains Abbey, I think, that he says he must see. We're renting a car, so I'm hoping he remembers how to drive on the left side of the road as well as he thinks he does. It's been a few dozen years or so. He has confidence but as we know our mental synapses aren't as quick as they used to be. I certainly don't plan to drive on the other side of the road, but as far as I can tell if we want to go anywhere special we need to rent a car. The public transportation seems wonderful within London but outside of London, I'm not so sure. At any rate, we'll give it a try and see how it goes.

We've booked our flights, direct to London, train up to Glasgow, if I remember right, and then we'll pick up our car. The travel part of travel is so wearying, but we will do it for our dear friend! I am excited to travel again. Memories from my recent cruise have me eager to pack up my suitcase again and see the world before either I or it gets too old.

Let me know if there's anything I can do to help with the preparations or plans. We are so eager to meet you!

See you soon! Millie

~

From: Ruby
To: Jake
Sent: January 20, 2011
Subject: Howdy

Hey, Jake –

Just wanted to say how nice it was to get see you over your break. Thanks for being open to spending time with me. I know it's hard sometimes, to be friends with exes, but you mean a lot to me. Thanks.

~

From: Jake
To: Ruby
Sent: January 20, 2011
Subject: RE: Howdy

No problem, it was good to see you. Maybe I'll be back again soon, we can do dinner again.

~

From: Ruby
To: Jake
Sent: January 20, 2011
Subject: RE: RE: Howdy

You're on. Dinner would be nice, especially if you're cooking. One of these days I'll learn! Let me know when you're around.

You know, it's funny. Time is funny. Our perception of the future is so funny. So dependent on the moment. Back in our days together, I was so sure we'd stand the test of time.

From: Jake
To: Ruby
Sent: January 21, 2011
Subject: RE: RE: RE: Howdy

I thought we'd stand the test of time, too. But you never know. Time isn't over yet.

Looking at my calendar and classes and tests. Will let you know when I can come home.

January 22, 2011
Wishing Rock News
Millie Adler, editor
Letter from the Editor

Dear Rockers,

Ladies and gentlemen, boys and girls, can you believe it's that time again? It's time to start thinking about the Idiotarod!

For the uninitiated – is that anyone? I can't recall anymore who was here at this time last year and who wasn't – for the uninitiated, the Idiotarod is Wishing Rock's own twisted version of the Great Alaskan Race, the Iditarod, held the same day as the start of that much more dignified race, which will be March 5 this year. This is an event in which the residents of Wishing Rock cart around other residents dressed up as dogs, in homemade sled-like contraptions, up and down stairs and around halls and throughout the entire building, while the rest of us cheer on the madness. Ed invented this. Need I say more? The time has come to register your teams and start building your sleds! See Ed for more information if you don't already know everything you need to know.

At the same time, as if that weren't enough, this year we're initiating National Wishing Rock Day on March 9, and Alexandra and David are hosting the First Annual Wishing Rock Olympics. To explain further, I bring you the words of the Chair of the Olympics Committee, Our Perpetual Lady of Spirits, Alexandra herself:

"The Wishing Rock Olympics will commence Wednesday, March 2, and run through Sunday, March 13. We bumped the opening ceremonies back a couple days so as not to interfere with the sacred Idiotarod traditions. (This spurred a discussion amongst the Olympics Chairs as to whether moving a date two days earlier, from March 4 to March 2, was considered moving it back or moving it forward. After long debate, no agreement was reached. However, as I'm the one writing this up, we shall consider the date moved back, as in backwards in time. Discussion closed.)

"Our Olympics will consist of a wide variety of events, from the usual to the unusual. Weather-dependent, we may have some outdoor games, but most of our activities will be inside. It is spring in the Pacific Northwest, after all. Soon we'll have the full list available so everyone can begin training as appropriate. We will definitely have a short walk/run of some sort, so if you plan to participate start training now, if need be. Other events will include speed whittling, a line dance marathon, leg wrestling, and more. We are trying to figure out how to incorporate the element of competition into a potluck event. We scoured the internet and discovered there are in this world competitions for wife carrying, pea shooting, cheese rolling, and even extreme ironing. Yes, extreme ironing; you heard me right. We think perhaps if we all pool our infinite wisdom we may be able to come up with a quintessential Wishing Rock competition. We only recently discovered there are other places in the world which have their own version of an Idiotarod, and we believe Wishing Rock deserves something unique. If you have any ideas for the Games, let us know! We aim to have all events decided and scheduled by the end of this month."

And, this is Millie again. I don't know about you, but to me, "speed whittling" sounds like an accident waiting to happen. Hopefully our resident doctor-in-training (Jake) will be home for the weekend to sew back on any appendages that might get speed whittled off. Note: Do not try this at home! I am also pleased to report that the idea of nighttime lawn darts has been nixed, though daytime lawn darts is, apparently, still on the list of possibilities. Stand clear!

Carolyn is working with Ben on a design for the Olympics logo and uniforms, should anyone want to have an official team uniform. Speak to them if you need more information.

As a final note, all went well at our quarterly fire drill yesterday. Nice job, everyone! Next time I'll try to send out an earlier reminder so no one has to run to the lawn in their underwear again. Sorry.

That's it for now. Back to your regularly scheduled cold wet weather. Bundle up!

Millie

From: Ruby
To: Gran
Sent: January 23, 2011
Subject: Hey

Hi, Gran,

How is everything coming along? I wish I could help more. I talked with Pip for her birthday yesterday – she sounds a bit tired!

Make sure she doesn't work too hard. Make sure you don't work too hard! Make all those MacAlpines do all the work. There are more than enough of them. They owe it to you for your honoring them by agreeing to be a part of their family! Save me some things to do and I'll do them as soon as I get there. We're flying over on the 10th, and we get there on the 11th. I can't wait to see you again!

Ed has been mysterious lately, Gran. Making lots of calls and then being vague about who he's talking with. He says he's talking to the people who are doing work on his rooftop deck, but when he says it he doesn't look me in they eye. And he's been making more "distributer runs" lately, too. Alexandra keeps telling me to trust him but how do I know which signals I should pay attention to? My gut says he is up to something and I don't like it. It's just a matter of what. Why won't he tell me? If it's not something bad why wouldn't he tell me? Why would he keep lying?

How do I know?

R.

From: Gran
To: Ruby
Sent: January 24, 2011
Subject: RE: Hey

Hi, darling,

Sweetheart, don't worry about helping out here. The numerous MacAlpines are barely letting either me or Liam raise a finger, and besides which our wedding will hardly be the event of the year. We're not making a fuss at all. The children are insisting on far more fuss than we'd ever ask for, so they're doing every bit of work to make it happen. Don't worry at all. We are well taken care of.

As far as Ed, darling, don't jump to conclusions. You know you have an active imagination. Don't let it overtake you. Ed may have his reasons for not telling you – IF he is up to something. It's my guess that you're just worrying too much. You do that, you know. You get it from your father. He always worried too much, too. That's one thing your mother did, or I suppose I should say does, she helps him not to worry so much. Tap into your mother's genes; they're in you. Be calm and think about your trip, distract yourself, and this worry will pass.

If you are determined to help, there is one thing you can do. I didn't bring all my pictures with me when I came over here. I didn't realize I'd be here for the long haul. Would you pack up my albums and ship them over? I'd ask you to bring them with you in your luggage but they may take up too much space. You can decide. I've been wanting to share those old memories with Liam. If you have the time, that would be lovely.

We will see you soon.

Love,

Gran

From: Erin
To: Roone
Sent: January 25, 2011
Subject: Fun

Heyyyyyy,

What are you doing in March? You should totally come to Wishing Rock. Alexandra and David have created this whole Wishing Rock Olympics thing, and I've had a peek at the competitions – crazy fun. You'd love it.

It's weird, I used to date David, you know, but I never ever ever would have described him or anything he did as crazy fun. Something about him and Alexandra just works, or maybe they made that choice together at the same time to be that kind of person. I've never been the fun one among my friends. Funny, sure, but never really fun, not the one anyone calls when they think of a crazy night out. I'm too reserved, I suppose. Do you think that's ingrained, or learned? Could I become the fun one if I really wanted to? Because maybe I want to. Maybe I want to be the life of the party from now on. Maybe I want people to think of me first when they think they want to head out for a good time.

You asked about my exes. (Well, I asked you and you asked back.) When I was with David I totally had my protective instincts going. Full force. That was my old pattern, all my relationships, all my life. As soon as someone would get close, I'd turn away. Reject before being rejected. Keep my heart safe. Problem is, I always kept my heart safe – from heartbreak but also from real love.

I'm turning over a new leaf. I'm scared, but I'm opening up.

With you?

Actually, you may not need to come up for the Wishing Rock Olympics – or rather, if you come up, I may not be here. I'm thinking of coming back to Maui. Temporarily or permanently? I don't know.

What do you think?

~

From: Roone
To: Erin
Sent: January 25, 2011
Subject: RE: Fun

Heyyyyy back,

Funny you should write. I've just finished another song. Can't stop writing these days, songs flowing out of me day and night, middle of the night, in the shower, in the car, everywhere I go. Drawing on emotions old and new. The muses are filling me up.

Reject before being rejected. Makes a safe boring life, that's for sure. Hurts everyone who dares to love you along the way.

Can't be up for the Wishing Rock Olympics but thanks for the invite. I'm heading out now to give out free hugs. Friend gave me a

T-Shirt, says "FREE HUGS" on it. I'm going to put it on, head out, and see what happens.

Open up, babe.

Here's the song. Working title: "Nearly Gone."

Echoes of memories
From when our love was new
Your lips on my heart
Rush of joy, me and you

Love is faded but not gone
So many words left unsaid
We asked too much, or not enough
Fears linger and loom instead

It's now or never
Show me that you care
'Cause I'm nearly gone, moving on
Nearly gone
Moving on

This love is lost, buried deep
Don't know if we can find it
If you made the effort
Could I rally one more time

We never stopped caring
We just stopped trying
Our walls grew strong
Now our love is dying

It's now or never
Show me that you care
'Cause I'm nearly gone, moving on

We've nothing left to lose
But I can't try for two
Oh I'm nearly gone, moving on
Nearly gone
Moving on

~

From: Ruby
To: Gran
Sent: January 26, 2011
Subject: RE: RE: Hey

Hi, Gran,

Absolutely, no problem about the albums. I'll go over this weekend and find them. And I'll make room in my luggage. That just means I'll create plenty of empty room in my bags to shop and bring things back on the way home! Sounds good to me! One of those Aran Island sweaters from Ireland, maybe, or a kilt or something from Scotland. Or both!

I know you're right that I worry too much but sometimes I worry about what would happen if I didn't worry when I should have. Maybe I could prevent something if I worried at the right time. Right? Is that not good logic?

I was talking with Erin this morning about Roone, speaking of jumping to conclusions. Roone sent her some new song lyrics he wrote, and she's trying to figure out if he's sending her a message. Actually, she's convinced he's sending her a message. "Why would he send me this if it wasn't intended for me?" she asked.

"Because he wanted to share it with you?" I suggested.

"Yes, but he told me to open up. He's saying I need to make an effort with him, that this long distance thing isn't enough."

She's certain she's reading it right, though, and is deciding to trust her instincts, let herself "undergo a metamorphosis," she said.

Time to change, she said. Time to be more like Julianna, she said. Ha! Like the world needs more Juliannas.

Time is going too fast, there's too much going on, I need it all to slow down.

Better get myself to work! No time to waste.

Love you,

R.

~

From: Erin
To: Ruby, Millie, Alexandra, Claire, Carolyn
Sent: January 27, 2011
Subject: Moving

Hey everyone,

I know, this is sudden. Don't hurt me. Don't lecture me. I'm too young not to take risks and too old not to take risks. I gotta go where my heart tells me I gotta go.

I'm going back to Hawaii. Maybe moving there. I'm going to give it a try for a few months, and then if it works out, I'll move there. I just feel like I have to do this. I don't want to live with regrets.

~

From: Claire
To: Erin, Ruby, Millie, Alexandra, Carolyn
Sent: January 27, 2011
Subject: RE: Moving

What? What? Did I miss something? What??

~

From: Ruby
To: Claire, Erin, Millie, Alexandra, Carolyn
Sent: January 27, 2011
Subject: RE: RE: Moving

Whaaattt?? Are you serious? Erin. Seriously. Have you thought this through?

Claire: She's moving to be with a guy.

~

From: Erin
To: Ruby, Claire, Millie, Alexandra, Carolyn
Sent: January 27, 2011
Subject: RE: RE: RE: Moving

Ruby: Yes, I'm serious.

Claire: No, I'm not moving to be with a guy. Yes, there's a guy, but he's not the reason I'm moving. I'm moving because I think now is just a time where I have to open up and be vulnerable. I want to go somewhere new, somewhere where I can reinvent myself a little. I know you think I could do that here, we all can just change at anytime, but it's harder when people know you, when they have expectations of who you're supposed to be. I don't want people staring at me every time I do something that's out of character for who I am but totally in character for who I want to be. Like, Roone was going to go out and give free hugs the other day. What if I wanted to give free hugs? First of all, this island is too damn small. Second of all, you all would look at me as if I'd grown two heads. I need a fresh start, free of expectations. Free of other people's opinions about who I am and who I'm supposed to be. I want to go somewhere where people don't know me, so I can try out new skin. Maybe I'll come back to the skin I'm already in, but I want to at least have the chance to try it out.

So maybe it's a mistake, right? If it's a mistake, I'll learn from it. But I don't think it's a mistake. I moved to Wishing Rock on a whim years ago, and that worked out pretty well, didn't it? You guys have to trust me on this. I have to trust myself on this. If it doesn't work out, nothing is set in stone. Planes fly both ways. And if it works out, well, you all have somewhere to stay on Maui. Is that not a win-win-win-win-win?

~

From: Alexandra
To: Erin, Ruby, Claire, Millie, Carolyn
Sent: January 27, 2011
Subject: RE: RE: RE: RE: Moving

Erin, I'm a firm believer in both following your gut and following your heart. As you said, planes go both ways. You can always come back and we will welcome you with open arms and no "Told-you-so"s. Right, ladies?

When are you going?

~

From: Erin
To: Alexandra, Ruby, Claire, Millie, Carolyn
Sent: January 27, 2011
Subject: RE: RE: RE: RE: RE: Moving

Well, let me be clear, I AM NOT MOVING FOR A MAN. However, Roone's birthday is next week. I want to be there to surprise him.

~

From: Ruby
To: Erin, Alexandra, Claire, Millie, Carolyn
Sent: January 27, 2011
Subject: RE: RE: RE: RE: RE: RE: Moving

Whaaaaaaaattt?? Next week?? Erin! You are being ridiculous. This is all for Roone, don't try to pretend it's not. You can go visit again but hold off on moving, won't you? Stop being irrational and listen to yourself. Of course you can change who you are here. You don't have to move for that. We won't judge. I promise we won't judge. You can give away free hugs here! You can!

I just think you're making a mistake.

From: Erin
To: Ruby, Alexandra, Claire, Millie, Carolyn
Sent: January 27, 2011
Subject: RE: RE: RE: RE: RE: RE: RE: Moving

Come on, Ruby. As if you've never made any rash decisions. And this isn't a rash decision. Just because I don't verbalize everything I'm thinking about doesn't mean I'm not thinking it over. I have thought this over a lot. I've been restless for a long time. I've been trying to find … something, for a long time. When something presents itself, it's not like I haven't given it all the thought it needs. From the outside it may look sudden, but on the inside, I've thought it all through for a really long time. This is the right decision for me. Just trust me on this. Support me on this.

From: Alexandra
To: Erin, Ruby, Claire, Millie, Carolyn
Sent: January 27, 2011
Subject: RE: RE: RE: RE: RE: RE: RE: RE: Moving

We all support you, Erin. It's just a bit of a shock to the rest of us who haven't been inside your head while you've been working this all through. But we all support you. Whoever that "you" turns out to be.

That said, it looks like we'll be needing a goodbye party. My house, tomorrow night, six o'clock. I'll do the main dish. Carolyn, can you bring a dessert? Claire, salad? Ruby and Millie, side dishes? Erin, you're the guest of honor so just bring yourself.

We will miss you, Erin. I will miss you. I hope you find what you are looking for. Sometimes the path takes us far afield for a reason. I trust this is part of yours.

I'll see you all tomorrow night.

~

From: Ruby
To: Jake
Sent: January 28, 2011
Subject: Erin

Have you heard the news? Erin is moving to Hawaii. She says. Moving for a guy. She doesn't say that part. We all just know.

She's leaving Tuesday. If you want to say your goodbyes you'll have to come home this weekend. The poker gals are having a gathering tonight for her. Let me know if you're here.

~

From: Ruby
To: Pip
Sent: January 29, 2011
Subject: Erin

Hey, Pip –

So last night we had a goodbye party – a goodbye party! – for Erin. Who is moving to Hawaii. Do I smell bad or something? Why does everyone move away?

She wants to go become someone else, give out free hugs and stuff. And love on her new lover, Roone, whom we don't know at all.

Ruby is not happy.

So you want to have chickens now? Is that even sanitary? It can't be sanitary. I mean, I guess babies have been raised on farms since the beginning of farming but still it sounds like a lot of chicken poop. Fresh eggs, though, that'll be nice. Looking on the bright side?

Can't wait to get away from Wishing Rock and come see you. Everything is crazy here.

Ed told me Julianna is moving to Seattle. Why does she need to move to Seattle? Why does he know that she's moving to Seattle?

I've got to start meditating or something. Gotta buy me some yoga pants, first, and then I'm definitely going to start meditating. I tried it once at an experimental college and they told me to focus on an imaginary candle floating in front of my eyes, but I couldn't get past trying to decide what kind of candle it was. What color was it? What size? Was it drip-free? Floating in a holder or just floating in the air? Was it floating on a cloud or just sort of hanging there? And by the time I settled on what my candle looked like, class was over.

Love you,
Ruby

~

January 30, 2011
Wishing Rock News
Millie Adler, editor
Letter from the Editor

Dear Rockers,

Ladies and gentlemen, may I present to you the Official Wishing Rock Olympics schedule! Note that events happening on weekdays will take place in the evenings; weekend events will be spread throughout the day. Full schedule, including times and locations, will be posted in the lobby soon. That's also where you'll find sign-up information for the various events. As you probably guessed we are not having timed trials or any sort of preliminary qualifying events. First come, first served. Everyone who wants to enter can enter up until the maximum number of entrants is reached. If you have questions, you know who to contact: Alexandra and David. Officiants will attempt to match up competitors in the fairest way possible to account for strength and size, as dictated by who enters the contests. Let the games begin! In about a month. And yes, we will have three potlucks over the course of these twelve days. That's what this community is about, people! Stretch your potluck muscles, we're in for a marathon!

March 2, Wednesday: Opening ceremonies

March 3, Thursday: office chair races – individual; speed whittling – individual

March 4, Friday: Idiotarod Route Laying Parade; potluck competition – individual

March 5, Saturday: Idiotarod – teams

March 6, Sunday: walk/run – individual; rock skipping – individual

March 7, Monday: potato sack races – pair; bowling – individual

March 8, Tuesday: leg wrestling – individual by gender; arm wrestling – individual by gender; thumb wrestling – individual by gender

March 9, Wednesday: National Wishing Rock Day / Founder's
  Day Potluck
March 10, Thursday: cup stacking – individual
March 11, Friday: line dance marathon + dance night – indi-
  vidual
March 12, Saturday: tennis (if weather holds) – individual; toilet
  paper / plunger race – teams of 4
March 13, Sunday: lawn darts (if weather holds) (keep your children inside!); closing ceremonies; non-competitive potluck
In much sadder news, we are saying goodbye to our dear friend
Erin, though we don't know for how long. We're all torn, both hoping she finds her bliss on Maui, and hoping she comes back. Maybe
she'll find a way to do both. Ruby is taking Erin to Seattle tomorrow,
and then she flies to Hawaii on Tuesday. Erin, my love, we all wish
you all the best. Stay in touch. Whether or not Wishing Rock is
your home, you will always have a home in Wishing Rock and in
our hearts.
Millie

~

Text from Ruby to Ed
Sent: January 31, 2011

Just got to Mom and Dad's. Out to dinner in a bit. Looking for
Gran's photo albums first. Do you need anything in Seattle while
I'm here?

~

Text from Ed to Ruby
Sent: January 31, 2011

Hey, beautiful! Nope, I'm good, plus I'll be there next weekend.

~

Text from Ruby to Ed
Sent: January 31, 2011

You're in Seattle next weekend? What's up?

～

Text from Ed to Ruby
Sent: January 31, 2011

Rooftop construction stuff, work stuff, some stuff I gotta do before the trip, just stuff, nothing exciting. Is Erin all ready to go?

～

Text from Ruby to Ed
Sent: January 31, 2011

She is. Very excited. Still hasn't told Roone; she's just going to surprise him. I hope he likes surprises. So just "stuff"?

～

Text from Ed to Ruby
Sent: January 31, 2011

Just stuff, boring stuff. I hope he likes surprises too. Doesn't everyone like surprises?

～

Text from Ruby to Ed
Sent: January 31, 2011

Depends on the surprise, I guess. Okay well if you need anything let me know. I'll check in later. Love you.

Text from Ed to Ruby
Sent: January 31, 2011

Love you too, sweet stuff. xxx

February

From: Erin
To: Ruby
Sent: February 2, 2011
Subject: Searching for home

Oh my gosh, Ruby. The sun. The sun!! How we live so long without the sun up there. This sun, I can't get enough of it. Did I mention the sun! Got to go on my morning sunrise run again this morning. In the early morning even the waves, slow and sleepy, seem like they're just waking up. The dew and the remnants of the overnight rain, the squawking of the myna birds, the call of the rooster that lives across the road, the world fresh and new. It feels like home.

I'm back at the condo unit I rented in December, while I look for a more permanent place to stay. Lucky for me they had a last-minute cancellation, but I have to be out in eight days. The condo manager says she might have some leads for me. Her sister manages some cottages that rent month-to-month, and she has friends who might know of other possibilities, so I'm feeling good that I'll find something quickly.

Thanks so much, Ruby, for taking care of my house while I'm gone. For however long that is. I'll come back and pack it all up, once I figure out where I'm going to be for the next few months or years. If you could just make sure Carolyn came and got the plants, that would be great. Millie is going to store my mail for me and send on anything important every few weeks, and pay bills from my account as they come in. Hopefully I've thought of everything but if something comes up, let me know. Did I mention that this all happened rather suddenly?

Tomorrow is Roone's birthday. The official party is Friday, at a local restaurant. I'm going to go and surprise him. I can't wait. I'm so excited to see him again! The way I left him left me wanting so much more.

And thanks again for the ride to the airport.

So what's going on there? Are you ready for Scotland? You'll be heading to Ireland and staying with Pip's sister-in-law, right? Beautiful Ireland! I envy you that part of the trip! How do we always end up on islands?

Keep me updated. Miss you already. Here goes everything.

Love you,

Erin

From: Ruby
To: Erin
Sent: February 3, 2011
Subject: RE: Searching for home

I have to admit, the sunshine sounds good. Having grown up here I think I'm immune to too much seasonal affective disorder, but sunshine does sound awful nice sometimes.

Yes, we're just about ready for the trip. Ed's heading to Seattle tomorrow to take care of "stuff." Work stuff, mostly, he says. He'll be back Monday, and we head to Scotland on Thursday. Wedding on the 14th, of course. I've been putting things I need to pack on the bed in the guest bedroom as I've thought of them, so it shouldn't take too long to pack it all once I'm ready. I've given in on checked luggage. I was going to try to fit everything into a carry-on but I decided the $25 is worth it to save having to lug everything through the airport and all the connections. We get there a few days in advance of the wedding so if my luggage is lost that gives it time to be found, right? Why in the world must air travel be so difficult! All for the sake of love.

So Ed talked with his Aunt Meredith again last night and got some interesting info about her life and times. Did I ever fill you in on her? I can't remember what I told you. I think I mentioned she's living and working in Vancouver, B.C., as an actress. She was married for a short while, then divorced, and is now dating a famous actor but she won't say who. Anyway, I think I'm making headway on the Brooks family reunion I've been trying to get Ed to arrange, or at the very least on getting Aunt Meredith down here. Ed told her about Wishing Rock and Dogwinkle Island, and she's all charmed to pieces. She's trying to get the writers to write our wee little home into an episode of the show she's on. I guess that means if she comes here with cast and crew we might end up with aliens on the island? Or something? That would be awesome, to be an alien extra. If there's a chance, you know I'm going for it. Especially if you get to keep the costumes! Fingers crossed! A TV show filming in Wishing Rock would give us something to talk about for the next ten years!

I'm eager to hear about your reunion with Roone! Or as the poker ladies might say, a reRoonion? Haha, I still got it. Eager to hear how it goes. Tell him hello from me and all the other people he doesn't know. Ha. Hopefully we'll all meet one day soon.

Miss you already, stay in constant touch, I want to know your every movement, your every breath! I'm going to start stalking you. You need to start a blog and put up pictures of your adventures and travels so I can visit every day and think of you and miss you all the more.

Tons of love.

R.

From: Ed
To: Alexandra
Sent: February 4, 2011
Subject: Travel

Hello my lovely Lex!

In Seattle, totally forgot to check with you whether you need anything while I'm here. Anything?

What day are you heading to Scotland? David's not going, right?

From: Alexandra
To: Ed
Sent: February 4, 2011
Subject: RE: Travel

Hello my lovely Ed!

I have no need of anything in Seattle, thank you for asking. I'm traveling pretty light this trip. I'm not even there a week. Barely a half a week. I promised my half-sister I'd come up and visit her over Presidents' Day weekend, so I need to come home right after the wedding. No, David's not going. It didn't seem worth it for him to go through the agony of international flights for just a few days. I do want to travel with him, though, somewhere, sometime soon. Travel will give you the measure of a person, or at least the measure of how well you travel together. Which is not to say it is the measure of a relationship, I suppose. The strength of relationships sometimes lies in knowing – and managing – the weaknesses. I suppose if he doesn't like travel or we don't travel well together, then we just won't travel together. One does not need to be joined at the hip, especially if one doesn't find one's soul mate until one's hips are as old as David's and mine are. He won't be going to Bellingham (where the half-sister is) either, but that's a given, I'd say. It would be rather awkward. I'm a bit nervous about meeting her, to tell the truth. I haven't a clue what she's going to be like. Sometimes I even forget, for a while, that she exists. Funny, isn't it, all the people in the world who exist, with whom you'll one day cross paths, but for now their lives are as good as invisible to you? We're all such self-centered creatures. Forgetting that every other person on the planet is, at every moment, at the center of his or her universe. I suppose that's the way it is. Our centers cannot, by definition, be anywhere other than right where we are. Still, it stretches the heart and mind in a good way to try.

All of which is to say that no, I need nothing.

What are you doing on this mysterious trip of yours? Ruby says you are there doing "stuff." What kind of "stuff," darling Ed?

From: Ed
To: Alexandra
Sent: February 5, 2011
Subject: RE: RE: Travel

You ladies sure are curious. Can't a guy just have stuff to do? I'm heading to some distilleries while I'm in Scotland and Ireland, so I wanted to meet up with some people here first to discuss business. Also, I'm still working on plans for the rooftop deck, so I'm meeting up with my architect and my peeps. Good enough? I'm off to meet with one of them now. See you when I get home, sweetcheeks!

Text from Millie to Alexandra
Sent: February 6, 2011

Alexandra. Trouble. Remember Julianna? She just called the store trying to figure out how to find Ed. Said he left his phone at her place in Seattle. Please advise?

Text from Alexandra to Millie
Sent: February 6, 2011

What??

~

Text from Millie to Alexandra
Sent: February 6, 2011

Do you know what hotel he's staying at?

~

Text from Alexandra to Millie
Sent: February 6, 2011

Yes. I'll get a hold of him. Why did she call you?

~

Text from Millie to Alexandra
Sent: February 6, 2011

She called the store. Ed was the only person whose number she had, and she had his phone. Looked up Wishing Rock, found me.

~

Text from Alexandra to Millie
Sent: February 6, 2011

Okay. Don't say anything to Ruby yet. Oh, Ed.

~

From: Erin
To: Ruby
Sent: February 7, 2011
Subject: Things fall apart

Hey Ruby –

Sorry I fell off the radar for a bit there. Not much has gone according to plan the last few days. I did find myself a place to stay – one of those cottages I mentioned – but other than that, well, life likes to keep us on our toes.

Friday, the day after Roone's birthday and the day of his party, started out as planned. Morning sunshine run (a little rainy but it's warm rain, and I don't mind); some time writing in my journal as I watched my ubiquitous whales migrate by. Farmer's market to pick up fresh fruit for lunch. An appointment to go check out the cottages, and subsequent signing of papers and exchange of checks and keys once I saw one and deemed it perfect. It was vacant and furnished so I could move in right away. Having only two suitcases full of belongings to my name, it didn't take long. I found an ironing board in the cottage, pulled out my party dress and ironed it, showered the sweat of a hot moving day off me, and got ready to surprise Roone at the restaurant.

He'd told me the party was going to begin at six, just before sunset, and carry on through the night. I decided not to show up right at the beginning, knowing people would be late and not wanting to be there before everyone. Seven-thirty seemed about right. At my chosen time I hopped into my rental car (must find a cheap car to buy; renting is not cheap!), and meandered over. Excitement and nervousness growing in me like a thirsty gazelle approaching fresh water in the desert. Smoothed my hair a million times. Looked through the restaurant windows to see if I could see him first. I wanted to be the one to see him first. Didn't want to chance his seeing me walk through the restaurant before I'd seen him. I don't know why. Maybe because I felt so like that gazelle – vulnerable, a little scared. Should I have called first? Should I have told him I was coming? Why was I worried? I knew this was the right thing to do, I knew it. I pulled my shoulders back and strode in purposely.

And I did see him first. Because he was otherwise occupied, off in a corner, lost in a deep kiss with some woman I'd never met.

He looked up and saw me.

I turned and speed-walked out.

He didn't chase me.

I raced back to my cottage, as much as a non-local can race on the island's unfamiliar winding roads, flopped onto my unfamiliar bed with its unfamiliar bedspread in my unfamiliar room filled with belongings that were not mine, and cried. Cried, and wondered if there are any beds on all of planet Earth that have never been cried on. My first day with this bed and already it was drenched in my tears. I felt lost. Stupid. What the heck had I been thinking? Surely there was always a part of me that hadn't been sure. Surely I should have listened to it. To you. But I didn't, or wouldn't, or couldn't. I had it in my mind somehow that moving to Maui would solve all my problems. Nothing was going to deter me.

When I woke up, on top of the covers and still in my dress, makeup smeared across my face and sheets (great, now I have to do laundry, on top of everything), I saw I had a text. From Roone.

"Did not know you were coming? Call me?"

Call him? Was there something to be said?

I emailed him instead. Said I'd meant to surprise him and thought it would be a good surprise. Thought we were building something.

He wrote back.

"Erin. Look, I never lied to you. That woman you saw me with, that was Ava. We date, we break up, we date, we break up, we date other people while we're dating and we date other people while we're broken up. That's what we do."

I wrote: "I thought those songs you sent me were about us? I thought you were telling me you loved me, that you were saying I had to come give you a chance? What happened?"

He replied: "Erin, you should have asked. You assumed. I might have fallen in love with you if I thought you loved me, but I'm not as dense as you think I am. You don't love me. I know that. You love the idea of me. You made up a story about me, and that's who you love. You love the wild, the unexpected, the unpredictable. You love the parts of me that you want to make part of yourself. As for me, though, you want to fit me to your needs, too. You want me wild but not too wild; unpredictable but reliable. You want to keep me in your pocket as a reminder of who you want to be. You want the parts you love and you want to change the parts you don't. I wasn't leading you on when I went on dates with you while dating Ava. Ava and I do that. That's who I am, who we are. If you don't like that part of who I am then you don't love me. Those songs were about Ava. I like you too, but you don't love me, never would. Those songs were about Ava."

I wrote: "What makes you think I want to change you? I never said that. I want to change myself, not you. How do you know? How could you know?"

He said: "It starts out wanting to change yourself but ends with wanting someone else to change to fit who you've always been. That's the way it works. None of us ever changes. We're set from birth, Erin. Who we are, who we're going to be, it's all in that tiny one cell from the very start. Your personality is in your DNA. Just accept who you are and find someone to love you for that. I do care about you but I'm not the one you're looking for. Close, but no cigar."

I told him I'd moved here and he said to keep in touch and we should hang out. And that was that.

Do you think things happen for a reason, Ruby? Sometimes I think they do, and sometimes I just think we're good at giving reasons to things that happen.

Either way, though, the next day, Sunday, yesterday, things changed again.

I got back into my little gray rental-that-could, a tiny chugging force of nature that sputters grumpily when asked to go speeds over 40 mph. (Luckily, there are few roads on which one gets over 40 mph on Maui.) You know how, when your mind is wandering, your subconscious takes over the steering and you end up somewhere familiar? That's how I found myself down in that little village again, at the end of the road at the tiny beach park where I met Roone.

I sat on a log at the edge of the park for the longest time, watching the waves crash against the rocks, finding peace in the study of their patterns. Watching the waves roll along the rocks and trying to predict the timing of the biggest sprays. Twenty minutes, half an hour, I don't know.

Then, somewhere behind me, someone coughed.

I jumped up, heart racing. Not that it's a particularly dangerous place – a would-be rapist would have to wait a long time before a would-be victim would appear, generally, but some dangerous people are opportunists as well. In an instant I calculated the distance from myself to my car, which I'd left unlocked; bemoaned my non-running-friendly flip-flops; decided if I ran fast, I had a chance.

Then I saw the source of the cough.

There, deep in the shadows, on the hammock where I first met him, was Roone. Looking, as best I could tell from the darkness, a bit less disheveled than usual. Would that be more sheveled? More put together. More ironed and sharp.

I stared.

"Hello," he said.

I wanted to say "What are you doing here?" but I knew that question was rightfully his, not mine. I wanted to have some excuse for being there, like "Oh, I was just passing by and thought I'd stop" but one does not find this spot without intending to. Not once you know it's there, anyway.

So I stared.

"Everything okay?" he said.

I shook my head. "No. Of course not," I said. "I wish you'd told me," I said. "I feel like a fool."

He looked at me for a second, then tossed his head back slowly, like he'd just had a realization. A smile, and a nod, and he got up out of the hammock, into the sun, where I could see him better.

I stared some more.

"Roone?" I asked. Rather uncertainly.

He smiled, Roone's smile, but with a different look behind his eyes. His face, not so tan and weathered. His hair, cut shorter, darker, not lightened by the sun. "So you know my brother," he said. He held out his hand. "Twin brother. I'm Raine."

Twin brother Raine. Had I known so little about Roone that I had no idea he had a twin brother? Apparently so. Apparently we see what we want to see and so easily forget there's more to the story.

And that is how I met Raine. He was at the party (a shared party, of course, for their shared birthday) but didn't see me, and I wasn't there long enough to see him. We chatted at the park for an hour or so before he said he had to be getting back to Roone's. He's on Maui indefinitely, arrived for the birthday party and staying for work. He's a journalist and writer, he said, though I'm not sure yet of the distinction. I sense that he's quite different from Roone, too, though I'm not sure yet in what ways.

I'll have my chance to find out all this and more tonight, at dinner with him.

So maybe things do happen for a reason, after all. Just not always the reason we're expecting.

I'll talk to you soon. Sending along my new address at my cute new cottage as well; pass it on to the others, will you?

Love,

Erin.

~

Text from Alexandra to Ed
Sent: February 8, 2011

So Millie mentioned to me that you left your phone at Julianna's this weekend.

What's up, Ed?

~

Text from Ed to Alexandra
Sent: February 8, 2011

Come on, Alexandra. You know me. It's nothing.

~

Text from Alexandra to Ed
Sent: February 8, 2011

If it's so innocent, why didn't you tell me when we talked? What are you hiding? Are you going to tell Ruby?

~

Text from Ed to Alexandra
Sent: February 8, 2011

I love you, Lex, but I don't answer to you. I'll tell Ruby when the time is right.

~

Text from Alexandra to Ed
Sent: February 8, 2011

Tell her what?

~

Text from Ed to Alexandra
Sent: February 8, 2011

Maybe use your psychic powers and figure it out?

~

Text from Alexandra to Ed
Sent: February 8, 2011

Okay, Ed. You know, sometimes it's better not to shut out the very people most likely to forgive you.

~

Text from Ed to Alexandra
Sent: February 8, 2011

Maybe the people who are so willing to forgive me should think about the fact that they trust me and know me better than that.

~

Text from Alexandra to Ed
Sent: February 8, 2011

This is going nowhere. I love you and I'm here if you want to talk about it.

~

Text from Ed to Alexandra
Sent: February 8, 2011

Good to know, champ.

~

From: Ruby
To: Gran, Pip
Sent: February 9, 2011
Subject: On our way!

Hello my loves! Just a quick note, Ed and I are getting in the car and heading to Seattle. Non-stop flight from Seattle to London tomorrow arriving the next day, then a hop from London to Glasgow, pick up our car, and we'll be there in less than 48 hours. Oh, how I hate travel! Thank goodness Ed got us business class tickets; it'll make up somewhat for the fact that there's no wifi on the international leg. I get so fidgety. Can't sit still that long. I hope I sleep! Who am I kidding. I never sleep on planes.

If you need anything else from Seattle, speak now or forever hold your peace! (See what I did there, incorporating wedding talk into my missive? And is it peace or piece? What piece would I hold, vs. how does one hold on to peace? Some idioms make no sense.) Gran, I got all your albums into my suitcases, so I'm ready to shop and refill my bags once I get there. What a girl has to do!

Love you both, can't wait to see you very very soon!

xxx

Ruby

From: Erin
To: Ed
Sent: February 10, 2011
Subject: Julianna

Julianna? Dude. Millie told me. Are you going to tell Ruby why Julianna had your phone? Or even that she had your phone? Why did Julianna have your phone?

Don't be hurting my friend, buddy.

I know you're on the plane right now. I'm just saying, Ruby is a gem. Don't hurt her. If you're going to hurt her, just rip off the bandage, dude. Make it fast.

Just your bad luck, Julianna called Millie. If she'd called Carolyn, no one else would have known. Carolyn would have dealt with it quietly. But Millie, well, she writes the town newsletter for a reason. You're just lucky Millie hasn't told Ruby's Gran.

~

From: Millie
To: Adele
Sent: February 11, 2011
Subject: Wedding of the season

Adele, Adele, Adele! Walter and I are packed and ready to go! Heading in to Seattle tonight, flying out tomorrow. It would certainly be nice, sometimes, to have an international airport on Dogwinkle Island, so much more convenient than timing ferries and shuttles and planes. But we are excited as can be! Can't wait to see you and the family, and then take a little trip of our own.

Say, I have a question for you. What would you say if I told you your granddaughter's boyfriend somehow happened to leave his phone at his ex-girlfriend's house? Recently, that is. Would you say we should tell her?

See you soon!

Love,

Millie

~

From: Ed
To: Erin
Sent: February 12, 2011
Subject: RE: Julianna

Hey, we got here safe.

Look, just don't say anything to Ruby, okay? You guys gotta trust me. My middle name is "Trustworthy"! Right?

~

From: Erin
To: Millie, Alexandra
Sent: February 13, 2011
Subject: Ed

Okay, I think we should just trust Ed. I don't like that he's running around with Julianna but you never know, it could be innocent. So until further evidence arises … That's my opinion. Give the kid a chance.

~

From: Ed
To: Ruby
Sent: February 14, 2011
Subject: Anniversary

Hello, my love,

If I could have, but for this jetlag and lack of a kitchen, I'd have gotten up early to make you heart-shaped pancakes for breakfast. Valentine's Day, and one year from the day I met you. Do you remember meeting me that day? Do you remember what you thought of me? I know what I thought of you. You looked like hope. You were in pain, that was clear, vulnerable and cautious, but as you carried all your worldly belongings up to your new home in Box 315, your shoulders were square and your eyes were determined. I don't know if you saw it in yourself then, but I knew: this is a strong woman. This is a woman who won't let life get her down, not for long. This is a woman I want to know. This may just be the woman for me.

Took a while, didn't it? But I was right. I'm always right, you know. I was right about you, anyway.

Your Gran and Liam, they were just glowing last night at dinner. What an event. Busy day ahead. Save a dance for me.

All my love,
Ed

From: Erin
To: Ruby
Sent: February 14, 2011
Subject: Catch-up

Hey, Ruby!

You're probably dancing the last dance by now as I write this. Scotland and Hawaii have almost no daylight hours in common, do they? It's 3:30 in the afternoon here, and you're ten hours ahead, what time is that? 1:30 a.m.? I hope the day was as wonderful as all the people involved. You'll have to tell me all about it.

I'm doing so well here, Ruby, which is quite surprising considering how everything fell apart almost the moment I got here.

I know it's not always obvious, but the fact is, I'm a hopeless optimist sometimes. The fact is, there's a part of me that believes in the fairy tales and the happy endings. I believed so completely with Roone. I listened to the love songs about finally finding the right one, about falling in love for real, and I thought, "That's it. This is it. This is Roone." I knew! Just like Pip knew with Gavin, I knew! Roone was the one. I listened to one of those songs again yesterday and shook my head at myself. I would call it naïveté, but is it? Or just ... hope? I don't want to be without hope, but sometimes, in retrospect, it seems so ridiculous. He was right. I loved him for the person I thought he was, the person I wanted him to be, the person I thought I needed in my life, even the person I wanted to be myself, but not the person he really was. That's all we ever have, though, isn't it? We can't ever know someone for sure. We just have to trust.

I hope he and I can be friends again one day but right now I'm keeping a bit of distance. Having Raine around makes the whole past with Roone weird enough.

Did I tell you Raine is a writer? We were out for Valentine's Day breakfast yesterday at this place that makes fantastic pancakes, a tiny little gazebo where people line up an hour ahead of the time it opens just to get in the first seating of the morning for pancakes. We'd just been served and were talking about my hopes of being friends again with Roone, and Raine had some interesting thoughts on it.

"There's much to be said for giving white space to your heart and your relationships," he said. "Almost everything is better with white space."

"White space?" I asked, pouring coconut syrup on my banana-macadamia nut pancakes. I am still new enough here that I cannot get enough coconut. I start the morning with coconut syrup on my pancakes, create fruity coconut cocktail concoctions to end the day, and am on the prowl for anything coconut I can add in between. Coconut, and mango, and pineapple, and everything fresh and juicy and tasting of sunshine.

"You know, white space, like on a printed page. It's a design layout term, I guess. A page that is all text, has no paragraph breaks, that has no white space. A page that has some short lines and some long lines and lots of paragraph breaks, that's said to have white space. The empty space. Except it's not empty. Even the white space has its purpose. It makes it easier to absorb everything else."

He looked at me to see if I got it, so I nodded. "White space," I confirmed.

"Some conversations need white space," he said, taking a bite from his eggs benedict, also delicious. "Time to think, time to reflect, time to absorb what's been said before any more is added to the fray. And some people need white space. Relationships, arguments, they both need white space. Sometimes, your heart needs white space. Too much gray space and you feel suffocated. It's exhausting. Some conversations need to linger between people for days, or months, or more. That time for the conversation to linger, that's white space."

"That makes sense," I said. It does. It's like that quote by that woman about the ocean or something, that no relationship is the same all the time. Things change. You have to leave space for that change, the tides of a relationship, that constant ebb and flow. "Interesting analogy." I said.

He shrugged as he sipped the last of his orange juice, fresh squeezed. "Life isn't so complex. Most things can be equated to some analogy. Things correlate. It's all the same, in one way or another. Just a matter of realizing it."

I think he and Alexandra would get along well. I remember asking her once about being psychic, about intuition. She said "Intuition is largely just a matter of recognizing patterns." She said that most things in life, most people, follow pretty regular patterns, whether we realize it or not. When something strays from those patterns, when something is off, amiss, not quite right, we get a gut feeling about it. That's just our intuition kicking in, telling us something is different, and we should be alert. Our monkey brains are still alert to the world in a way our logical brains aren't, she said. With our logical brains we talk ourselves out of our intuition, because we think there's no way our monkey brain can be a match against our logical brain. "But when the hairs on the back of my neck raise up," she said, "I have learned it's best to listen to that monkey."

Far too early to talk about Raine meeting everyone, given the distance and all, but you never know. Stranger things have happened, right? I'm taking it slow but I'm also trusting my gut.

Anyway, I'm giving Roone white space, and giving myself space from Roone.

"He means well," said Raine of Roone. "He meant well. Everyone means well, you know. We're all just doing the best we can."

"You sound just like him," I replied. Thought to myself what Roone had said of himself, of us, "Close, but no cigar." First, where the heck does that saying come from? And second, regardless, if Roone was close but no cigar, could his twin brother be ... the cigar? "Well, we are related. Can't help that." And we finished our breakfasts and left the little gazebo, hand in hand, as the waiter rushed to ready our table for another couple, perhaps more in love, perhaps less. Time will tell.

My brain keeps trying to fill up all that Roone space with endless clutter, but the peace of Maui helps calm it all down. As does Raine.

Sending warm waves of love to all of you over there. Please pass on my heartiest congratulations to the newlyweds.

x Erin

~

From: Ruby
To: Erin
Sent: February 15, 2011
Subject: RE: Catch-up

Hello! Oh my gosh, what a late night! The wedding was fabulous. If you wrote at 1:30 a.m. we weren't anywhere near our beds yet. Gran and Liam headed home around 2 a.m., I think, but the most determined of us didn't get to sleep until after 4. I thought the sun was going to come up before we got back to our rooms! This does not bode well for my jetlag, or for today. I'm up far earlier than I'd like, getting ready to head to the Emerald Isle. We have to drive south to where we'll catch the Scotland-to-Northern Ireland ferry, which will take a few hours. Then a couple hours on the ferry, then I think an hour or two drive to Gavin's sister's house (Katie, and her husband Stephen), and then I am going to be a very rude guest and go right to sleep!

Pip decided to join us. She wasn't sure she'd be up to it, and after all she was just there in September, but she decided to come along just so we can visit a little longer. Gavin is too busy with work, so he will be staying here.

I like this Raine person you have met. (And I like the sound of those pancakes! Now I'm craving pancakes.) I hope we get to meet him. I'm so glad you're doing well there. I was worried about you. He sounds like he has a good head on his shoulders. Be true to you.

Speaking of pancakes and of monkeys, did I ever tell you that Gran used to have a special breakfast she'd make for Grandpa a few days before their anniversary, as her way of reminding him not to forget? She'd make monkey bread and honey ham with scrambled eggs, a week or something before their anniversary, and it was her way of making sure he'd remember something special was coming up. Your talk of pancakes made me wonder if she'll do the same thing for Liam. Or maybe having a Valentine's Day anniversary will be enough of a reminder. Or maybe they've lived long enough that they know to appreciate every day rather than waiting for one day a year to come around.

So, tonight we get to Ireland. I don't know what all the plans are but I'm guessing they have some ideas for us. Ed will be spending time at distilleries in "meetings." Ha! Rough life. Maybe I'll get Pip to go on a road trip with me. As you said, time will tell.

Alexandra should be on her way home by now. Millie and Walter head out tomorrow on their adventures of this big island; I think Walter was planning to take them around Scotland a bit and then south into England.

And with that, my bus driver is calling – I have to shut down my computer, pack it up and go!

Love you!

Ruby

~

From: Ruby
To: Gran
Sent: February 16, 2011
Subject: Ireland

Hello, Mrs. MacAlpine! So funny that you're now Pip's step-mother! The Parker-MacAlpine family tree sure has some twiggy bits, I'd say. Maybe it did before, though, am I right? That's probably what has brought our families all together. When you find people who "get" you, it's best to hold them tight.

What a great wedding that was, Gran. I cried a river of joy, plus maybe a little of sadness that I don't get to be with you guys all the time. Being here has reminded me how very much I love and miss you and Pip. I'm so glad we were able to come over for this beautiful occasion, and so glad the weather cooperated, too. Thank you and Liam for everything!

Pip, Ed, and I are well and situated over in Ireland for the next few days now. We got in to Katie and Stephen's late last night and Pip made introductions. We tried to stay up to chat, but using Pip's pregnancy as my excuse, I said we really all should get to bed. I probably was more tired than she was! I slept straight through the night and woke up drooling in the same position I fell asleep in, I think – dead tired! But feeling much refreshed on waking. Finally over the jetlag, I hope. Katie served up a gorgeous breakfast, and then our day was our own. (Have you had Irish potato bread? Recipe attached.)

This, the Inishowen Peninsula, is amazing. You should come, Gran, soon! You haven't been here yet, have you? Come soon! Sometimes when I'm in yet another gorgeous place in the world I think, how many gorgeous places are there in the world that I will never see? It's this poignant but beautiful thought. The world is absolutely full of breathtaking beauty that I don't even know about. I want to see it all.

This is another of these spots. Katie and Stephen live not in the middle of nowhere but rather on its edge. I'm not even sure this town has a name. Town? Township? Village? Hamlet? What's the name for the smallest place a place can be and not just be someone's house?

Katie gave me a brief geography lesson, let's hope I get this right. You probably know all this by now, so correct me if I'm wrong. The island which is Ireland actually consists of two countries, the Republic of Ireland and Northern Ireland. Northern Ireland is part of the United Kingdom (along with England, Scotland, Wales, and a smattering of smaller islands). The Republic of Ireland is the rest of the island. To complicate matters, "Northern Ireland" doesn't encompass all of the northern part of Ireland. There's a tasty morsel of land in the northwestern-most part of the island that is actually part of the Republic of Ireland, and which therefore seems to be referred to as being "in the south" even though it's in the north. Am I right?

At any rate, if I have this right, the Inishowen Peninsula where Katie and Stephen live is "in the south" but in fact is one of the most northern parts of the island. It's dazzling in its pastoral, isolated, shaggy green beauty. Katie and Stephen are about as far out as they can get, out at the northeast tip of the peninsula. Their home is literally across the street from a secluded pocket-sized beach. When I say "secluded," it's not really; it's right off the "main" road. But the main road itself is secluded. Walking through the area, I had the strangest feeling that I was being watched. Spirits from the other realm, watching me while they party from beyond? Or just the dozens of sheep and cows?

To help wake myself up and walk off the delicious breakfast, I went out for a stroll this surprisingly warm and clear morning. (Surprising because I thought it rained in Ireland all the time, thus the "forty shades of green"?) (Ed and Pip stayed in to talk with Katie and Stephen, but I needed fresh air so they excused me.) I started my walk at the beach across from the house, shuffling my toes through the pristine sand and clambering over rough boulders to find another, even tinier bit of beach. The place felt undiscovered, like I was the first person ever to set eyes or feet on it, but a carelessly discarded water bottle (which I picked up and carried back to the trash) declared otherwise.

And, following the script of my life, wouldn't you know it, once I started looking, I found wishing rocks all over. At first I didn't see any, but once you find one, the rest all pop out as if they had been invisible but all started uncloaking themselves on cue. I started looking around this beach, and my beloved rocks were just everywhere, wishing rocks left and right. It made me feel so connected to the place. I could very well call this home, if Ed ever wanted to move out here. It felt like home. I soaked in the cool sunshine for a while and thought about you and Liam, and about family, and about love, and about home, and about Ed. And then, I dusted the sand from my toes, put my shoes and socks back on, and continued my exploration of this little village.

Leaving my Irish Wishing Rock beach, I headed up the road a ways and discovered another beach, this one maybe the size of two pockets rather than just the one, tucked beneath a black-and-white striped lighthouse. This beach was also pristine (but with a track of footprints to prove itself not unvisited). What is it about beaches that soothes the soul? You've talked before about water and rivers and how our cells recognize their brethren. I think you may be on to something. That, and the waves, the breath of life, the meeting of ocean and beach is like our bodies wrought large, made into earth. Or maybe the other way around. I sat for a while on a boulder, warmed ever so slightly from the valiant sun, socks and shoes doffed again, wriggling my toes in the sand, and stared out at the crashing and retreating water, and I could not have been more content. I felt that deep contentedness where you can't imagine ever not having felt that content, or ever not feeling that content again; where you feel completely at peace with your life and certain that you have within you the ability to take on anything that comes your way. The contentedness where you're able to look at the people who irritate the crap out of you and feel nothing but compassion and love for them.

A good day.

After a bit I headed farther up the road, which curved around through a "more populated" area and back out again. I took a fork in the road that looked like it would take me up a trail tracing the coastline, and sure enough it did. I ended up on a hilltop surrounded by sheep, every one of them watching me very carefully through the chain-link fences, as I looked back down over the black-and-white lighthouse and its tiny two-pocket beach, now so far below.

Peaceful, Gran. Some places, some days, define peace.

As I said, it was sunny (and even slightly warm, or at least not cold), but I feel like even if it were raining I would love it here. I love knowing that Katie and Stephen live here and I have some sort of de facto right to visit and stay with them. We haven't even left yet and already I want to come back.

So that was today. Ed is meeting with people at the Old Bushmills Distillery the next couple days, so Pip and I decided to go on an overnight road trip to Dublin tomorrow. (Katie and Stephen have to work.) Then on Saturday I think we're all going to the Giant's Causeway. Beyond that, we'll play it by ear.

I'm being called to dinner. All in all, we're off to a good start.

Love, Ruby

Irish Potato Bread
Ingredients
    1 large potato
    About 1 cup flour
    2 to 3 Tbsp butter
    1/2 to 1 tsp salt
Directions
- Bake potato, or microwave about 10 minutes, turning over once. Peel potato and mash thoroughly or press through ricer. Mix all ingredients while potato is hot. Press into a flat round about 1/4" thick. Cut into quarters or eighths. Grill in a hot, greased griddle until both sides are browned to perfection. Serve.

From: Alexandra
To: Ed
Sent: February 17, 2011
Subject: Sister

Edward,

Remind me next time I want to fly somewhere that the older I get, the less my body appreciates these cross-Atlantic trips lasting only a few days. I couldn't even tell you what day it is, or what time it is, aside from the fact that it is more or less daytime, more or less daylight outside. Water. My body needs water. And sleep.

But, I shall survive. It was lovely to witness the wedding of Adele and Liam. What is it about love late in life that gives us such a feeling of joy and hope? The idea, I suppose, that our hearts are always capable of loving more and even more, as long as we both shall live. The idea that lives can still be intertwined, even decades into the journey, only one or two dozen years from the end. The idea that it is never too late. The idea that even at Adele's age of eighty-one, love still matters. That love will always matter.

Worth the flight, I'd say.

Such as it is, I am home again, and packing up to head to Bellingham tomorrow to meet my half-sister, Cynthia. Cindy. She invited me to stay at her house but I declined. I thought it would be awkward enough just meeting, much less being a house guest, so I'm staying at a quaint Inn we passed by last year when I went to Bellingham with the poker gals. You were out of town, I think; where were you? I can't remember. Anyway, I'll be staying offsite, as it were, so if things get awkward I can make my excuses and leave.

I don't really know what to expect, and my spirit friends aren't helping me this time. I guess I'm on my own for this one.

David will be staying behind, working on the Wishing Rock Olympics. I have to say, I'm quite excited for all the events. I'm exhausted just thinking of it all but I'm going to participate in as many as I can. Is it wrong for the organizer to participate? I can recuse myself from any winnings. I just want to join in and have fun. David is having a great time with it, too. Clearly he has found his calling, and its name is adventure. Getting to know David is very much like the spelunking he so adores: you would never guess from the outside what the depths will reveal, but it is a journey most worthy of taking.

Tell me all about your Ireland. I was there years and years ago, did I ever tell you? But only the southern part, the Rock of Cashel, the adorable little Kinsale, some Kilkenny. Around that area. I'd love to get back and see it all again, and more.

Wish me luck this weekend!

With deep devotion,

Alexandra

From: Ed
To: Alexandra
Sent: February 18, 2011
Subject: RE: Sister

Darling Alexandra!

You did not tell me of your prior visit to this Emerald Isle! It's a beautiful country and I'm sorry we won't have time to explore farther south. Perhaps one day your spelunker in shining armor and you should join my sweet princess and myself and we should all come visit again. All these ruins, and Ruby's tale of having stayed in a haunted castle at Pip's wedding, have me wanting to stay in one myself. Haunted, for sure. Ruby says no, but she seems to be forgetting I am Ed, bearer of great testosterone. I believe the ancients said that excessive testosterone would ward off all ghosts, am I right? Or was that garlic? Six of one, half dozen of the other, details, details.

I'm assuming by now, having been away from me for a couple days now, you miss me desperately? Unable to get out of bed, I'm guessing, pining for me? We should have planned some video chat times. These eight hours of time zones separating us are a lot more inconvenient than I thought they'd be.

PAM STUCKY

We're having a grand old time here. Lots of driving around looking at green things and old things and rocks. Beaches up on this
north end are fantastic! I had no idea. They're Hawaii-like, more
than Washington-like. Well, maybe coast-like but not Puget-Sound-
like. I did not expect that. Funny how when you travel you look for
the similarities. The area keeps reminding me of the coast, actually.
Good stuff. Nice work, Nature!

Ruby and Pip are off on a sisterly road trip, so Stephen and Katie
took me out to an old site just outside Derry this afternoon. I can't
remember nor spell (Irish spelling) the name but to my uneducated
ears it sounded something like "granary." (The name, that is, not
the place.) It was a ring fort, at the very top of a hill, a ring inside a
ring inside a ring, with mossy steps leading up from each level to the
next. Driving out I was sure we were going nowhere. Stephen was
driving, and this being his home I assumed he must know where he
was going, but it sure felt like we were lost. But suddenly you round
the bend and: voila! The granary! Or whatever its name was. At the
top you could look out on a nice day (slightly nicer than today, that
would be) and see all of Derry, Donegal, all around, I suspect, probably as far as Greece and Greenland (or close). Not so much today. Bit
of a mist on the day. But it wasn't really raining, and we're all hearty
island folks. We walked around and around the top of the middle
ring (misty = a bit slippery, so Katie wouldn't let us run around the
top ring, spoilsport), then we men sat on the rim of the top ring facing out whilst (Irish word) Katie with her more cautious sensibilities
sat on the next ring, and Stephen and Katie taught me traditional
Irish drinking songs, which we sang at the top of our lungs until a
giant dark cloud cried out in its wrath on our sound, started dump-
ing water on us, and had us running (and slipping on the grass) for
our car. A good time.

The theory on this ring fort (built around three thousand years
ago or so) is that it was a royal fort, that there was a grave under it,
yada yada yada. Frankly, I think it was built by ancient teenagers
who had nothing better to do. Why is it that we always assume old
things were somehow sacred? These people didn't have TV, the inter-

net, cars, heck I don't even know if they had books back then? Or cell phones? I think all they had was dirt and rocks. Nothing to do. Nothing to do but build ring forts. Personally I'm of the opinion that there were giant opposing fort-building gangs. "Oh yeah? You think that's a fort? WE will show you a fort!" Or, someone told me recently about this cave in France somewhere, a mile and a half into the hillside, with paintings inside. Clearly a sacred site, right? Do archaeologists not have or know any teenagers? I can imagine myself in those ancient times as a kid, being told I had to spend more time inventing the wheel and less time with my ring fort gang or who knows what, and going off in a huff deep into the hillside, following a cave as far as it would go, and finding this spectacular little cave at the end of it. I'd claim it as my own, "ED'S CAVE" (if they had writing back then, I don't know; if not I'd invent the alphabet but not tell anyone, out of spite, being a teenager and all), and if I were a kid with any artistic skills I'd go there all the time and draw on the walls in my supreme disobedience. Right? I'm just saying. We don't know. Until we finish that damn time machine (really hoping someone in Wishing Rock has a dream of building a time machine, so I can fund it with an ED grant, and then I'll get to be the first, or maybe second, person to time travel, after they've done all the testing, you know), we don't know. That's what I'm saying.

Regardless, the ring fort was pretty rad, as the kids said back in our day, and all in all, this country is pretty groovy. I'd come back.

You will be fine with ol' Cindy. How could she not love you? If she doesn't, that's on her, not on you. Hopefully she's lovable, herself. This is your dad's daughter, right? I'll be curious to hear what you think. Let me know how it goes.

Miss you,

E.

~

From: Ruby
To: Erin
Sent: February 19, 2011
Subject: Friendly policemen

Hey, tropical lady! How are you? We're all fantastic – too much so, I'd say! I'm wishing we could stay longer than just a few days. We will most definitely have to come back. There's far too much to see and do, and we're trying to pack as much into our visit as we can. I love Ireland so far. After our Scotland trip and now this, I really feel I've more or less gotten the hang of driving on the left, and I'd even say Pip more or less agrees. I think what throws me off most is sitting in the right side of the car, but I'm getting used to it.

Pip and I are just back from our grand somewhat spontaneous road trip adventure. Ed has a lot of meetings (or, from the sounds of it, "meetings," since those meetings always seem to involve a lot of tasting of the products!) at the distillery and with distillery-related people while we're here, which leaves me and Pip with plenty of time to wander. So, we decided to take a whirlwind overnight trip down south. Parker sisters on the loose on the Emerald Isle! Watch out!

We started off very early Thursday morning by meandering down to Dublin. We wanted to take in a good bit of Dublin but didn't want to drive in the city (I'm confident in my driving, but neither of us is confident enough yet to drive in such a big city), so Katie (Gavin's sister) arranged for us to meet up with (and stay overnight with) a friend of hers who lives just outside Dublin. After getting to her house at about noon we left the car in her driveway, and she drove us into the city. She dropped us off a bit outside of town so we could tour Kilmainham Gaol, then we took a bus to the Guinness Warehouse (what a view from the top!). After that we went to Trinity College to view the Book of Kells exhibit, and then got some food at a store and had a picnic in St. Stephen's Green (a park) as the sun set. We wandered the shopping area called Grafton Street for a while after that, and then a taxi took us back to Katie's friend's house for the night.

The Book of Kells was amazing and really got me thinking. It's just a book, right? A pretty book, an "illuminated manuscript," but it's more than that. The exhibitors did a brilliant job of setting the scene so you're educated and ready to appreciate the moment you enter the dimly lit room where the book sits in a glass case, opened to a two-page spread. All you can do is look at the book, and yes, it's lovely, but if you didn't have the context of the book then it would be pretty boring. But the people who created this exhibit put some real work into explaining the process of book making as it existed about twelve hundred years ago, and that's what was awe-inspiring. Right now, I'm writing to you and all I have to do is open up my computer and type. I can add as much as I want, delete, move things around; there's nothing to it. The elements involved in the process of writing are so simple that they become part of the background, and my thoughts are able to come to the forefront. Even if I were writing to you on paper, though, I would barely have to think about it. I'd go to the store, buy some sort of stationery, pick up a pen, put it to the page, and voila! A letter is born. But for these monks more than a thousand years ago, to create a manuscript took weeks, or months. Or more. They had to kill the cow or sheep or goat and skin it and make the vellum or parchment, and trim it to the right size. (That is, after having raised the cows or sheep or goats first.) They had to find the berries, plants, roots, minerals, bugs, or whatever they could find to get the particular color of ink they wanted, and then grind it up and mix it with other elements depending on the base. They had to find feathers or reeds to write with. Writing was a labor of love, so the texts they chose to replicate had to be so sacred to them for them to put all that effort into it.

It got me thinking about language, and how amazing it is, really, and we don't even think about it. I write these lines, these dots on a screen, and because some people a really long time ago decided what lines represented what sounds, and what words are formed when you put those sounds together, and what those words mean, because of all that, I can communicate with you from the other side of the world. We're nowhere near each other and yet you know what's going on inside my mind. Or those monks from the year eight hundred, they're nowhere near me in time rather than space, but I can know what they were thinking too. And it all comes down to lines and dots on a flat surface. Which is really sort of incredible.

So! That was Thursday, a lovely day in fabulous Dublin. Friday we woke up and decided to head north to meet up with Ed at Bushmills (the distillery), so the north coast of Northern Ireland was our ultimate destination. We set out a route for ourselves, skirting the west side of Lough Neagh (a lake) so as to avoid the city traffic in and around Belfast, plugged that route into our GPS, and headed off.

We were driving along just fine when wouldn't you know it but suddenly, there's a notice that there's construction ahead, road closure, a detour. Panic set in. Looking at the map we couldn't tell if there were viable options on small roads. Being completely unfamiliar with the area and not equipped with a good local map, we were stymied and needed a moment to regroup and figure out a new path. I was the one driving as we headed out of Armagh, when we got to the point where the road ahead of us was closed. I maneuvered the car to the left shoulder, where a few other cars had parked as well, and stopped.

GPS console (a piece of s***, by the way) in one hand and a national map in the other, I swear not two minutes had passed before I looked into the rear view mirror and saw a police car pulling up behind us. And stopping. Police getting out of the car. Coming at us.

Now, I realize Northern Ireland today isn't the same bomb-ravaged place it used to be, but all the things I ever remember hearing about Northern Ireland growing up were about Troubles and danger and how it's a country best to be avoided. So far I'd seen none of that myself, but those old memories, they are ingrained. Being pulled over by the police in Northern Ireland was never on my bucket list.

This soon changed.

"Is there a problem?" the young policeman, a quite attractive policeman I might add, said when I'd rolled down the window. His partner stepped up behind him, another handsome young lad in uniform. Well, well!

"We're confused," I said, discreetly checking out these young gentlemen.

"That's obvious," said the first officer. Really? Was it that obvious? Did the map and GPS unit, now in my lap, give us away?

"Where are you going?" He asked.

"Bushmills," I said, "To the distillery."

The two officers looked at each other. The first turned back to me, suddenly seeming more on guard and distrusting. "This isn't the way to get to Bushmills."

A rush of fear swept over me and my heart skipped a beat. I thought, do they think I'm lying? Are they going to arrest me for … driving the long way around? Suddenly, I was scared.

Flustered, I stammered. "We were, so, uh, which is the right road? We are taking the A29 up, is that wrong?"

Clearly these gentlemen frowned upon our route choice but thank goodness they acknowledged that the A29 would, in fact, get us there, though not as quickly as if we went through Belfast. I explained that we were trying to skip around the big city, and that we had this crappy GPS that I was now going to try to reset to some new route that we had yet to figure out. I held up the GPS unit in frustration at the situation and at not knowing what I was doing. "Do you know how to program this thing?"

And what do you know, he did. Officer Colm (the darker haired officer who approached me first; the other was fairer-haired Officer Sean) gently took the GPS unit from my hands and proceeded to re-program it with the route he'd suggested. When he was done, he gave it back to me and asked if we knew our way back into Armagh, so we could get on the right track. I admitted we pretty much did not have a clue, and feeling bold and a bit flirty asked if they might give us an escort?

Officer Colm looked at Officer Sean. "We've nothing else to do," said Officer Sean, shrugging his shoulders.

Officer Colm turned back to me. "Sure, why not. Follow us until I flash our hazard lights, then you keep going and we'll turn off."

And so we followed them until they flashed their hazards, and we waved at them and went on our merry way up to Bushmills, where we had a tour while waiting for Ed to get out of his last meeting.

And that is how two Parker sisters got a police escort through a part of Northern Ireland by two very handsome young men in uniform. I must say, this country offers more to love every day. After Bushmills we meandered along the northern coast on our way back to our temporary home. What a beautiful place this is. I swear, though, in places the speed limits on the roads are more dares than laws. "Yes, go on then, give this curvy winding narrow road a go at 60 mph. We'll watch." It's a good thing there's not a lot of traffic because if there were they would be angry at us for driving so slowly!

We're off to the Giant's Causeway now, and then plan this evening on going on a walk, taking Ed and Pip (if she's up to it) on my favorite route past my secret beaches and the lighthouse, and along the path up the hill. Then some of Stephen and Katie's friends have invited us all over for dinner, so we'll make a dish to share and head on over. Wish you were here with us! Write soon.

All my love,
Ruby

From: Ed
To: Alexandra
Sent: February 20, 2011
Subject: Yo

Lex!

Another letter from me, so soon? I know, the gods are shining down on you today! Cherish this moment! I just have so much to report, I couldn't help myself.

We're doing great, my meetings all went well and I'm chock-full of new ideas and energy and contacts and people I gotta come back and visit again soon. Maybe in better weather, though!

Yesterday we went to the Giant's Causeway, and I'd say we left our mark on the place. At least, Ruby did! And some skin, too! She slipped, all but face-planted on the rocks, nearly tumbled down into the waters below. She's bruised up and down her right side. Stephen and I were climbing up another section of rock, and Pip didn't venture too far out since it was raining and the rocks looked slick. (She was right.) Katie stayed back with Pip, chatting. So Ruby was left unsupervised, and you know, generally that works out okay but it looks like yesterday she could have used a handler. Completely by chance I looked over at her just as she fell. She was carrying an umbrella, which I guess made her less able to balance herself, and she started to slip and just went down. It was awful, watching it happen in slow motion with no way to get over there in time to catch her. And there were these tourists right next to her, didn't even help her up. Ruby says they'd been telling her she shouldn't be carrying the umbrella as it would throw off her balance, and they were right, but who just stares at someone who has nearly fallen to her untimely and painful death by bouncing off slick rocks? I wanted to give them a piece of my mind but Ruby wouldn't let me. (No comments from the peanut gallery, if you please, about whether I can spare a piece of my mind!) Ruby was covered head to toe in Giant's Causeway but she was a trouper and we went on to have a great time. When we got back to the visitor center we heard another tourist had fallen and broken her pelvis just a couple days before, so we'll consider a few bruises to be very lucky! I guess I wouldn't want them to put "slippery when wet" signs all over, littering this natural wonder, but if you ever go be aware: it's slippery when wet. Plus, Ruby got extra pampering from me out of the whole deal. Probably her motive all along.

We are not ready to leave yet but leave we must. You start planning our double-date return trip here, I command thee! Gotta come back. Lots more old rocks and stuff to be seen.

Love,

Ed

From: Erin
To: Ruby
Sent: February 21, 2011
Subject: RE: Friendly policemen

Ruby –

Hey! What a lovely police encounter! I love that they escorted you back to town. You flirt! I didn't know you had it in you. I should say, that's the side of Northern Ireland the country should advertise, if they want to get tourists over. Women would flock! I'm on my way! Haha.

No, actually, I'm doing so great here. Raine is … hm, well, you know how everything looks clearer and brighter after a cleansing rain? Yes, it's cheesy, I see it, Raine – rain, but it's true. He's a breath of fresh air, so honest and open and real. I feel like I don't have to play games. I mean, I never thought I was playing games before (mind games, obviously, not talking about board games), but looking back, I know I was always … I don't know, it's like the me that I'd let people see was me inside another Erin, and I was manipulating the outer Erin to protect and … I hate to say manipulate, but I guess in a way it was benign manipulation, trying to get people to stay away, maybe? To push people away? But Raine, I don't know, who knows if it'll last, maybe he's here forever and maybe he's just here to teach me some lessons, but I feel good with him. I know I've said this, but I used to always think I was broken. I mean, in a way, we're all broken, right? We're all fragile, we're all wary, we all protect ourselves, all that stuff that Roone told me (though he could have said it more nicely!). But in a way I'm starting to think maybe I was never as broken as I thought I was. Actually, Raine put it beautifully: he said we're all broken, but we have to look at our broken parts from the perspective of Japanese kintsugi – that is, "golden joining," the practice of repairing broken pottery using gold, and thus making the thing that was once broken even more beautiful for having been broken. Honoring the history of the broken object, and the fact that it's whole again and even more valuable. I like to think of it that way.

The ways we've been broken enable us to grow and become even better than we were when we were "perfect" and whole. Our heart's scars are mended in gold, and they're nothing to be ashamed of. I actually was visualizing it the other day, my heart with ragged ripples of gold running through it. I pictured the hurts I remember, the people who slashed and dashed my soul, and I pictured me, melting gold and putting my heart's pieces back together, and it felt … beautiful.

My love to Ed, who once gave me a small creek of gold in my heart, if not quite a river, and to Pip, and all the rest. Miss you terribly. Will you come visit me? It's lovely and warm here.

Erin

From: Alexandra
To: Ed
Sent: February 22, 2011
Subject: RE: Yo

Darling Ed,

I'm so sorry for having been remiss about writing you, whilst you have been divine about writing me about your troubles and travels. Poor Ruby! Is she all right? You'd better be pampering her, the poor girl. You hear about people being hurt or even dying like that and you just always think it'll be someone else. That could have been a serious fall! I'm so glad she is okay.

Yes, you are correct that I miss you dreadfully. Aside from the travel to see Cindy, I haven't moved since you left, sitting here longing for you, bon bons, tissues, woe is me. Life without you has no meaning, my love.

Let's see, what else did you say in your missives. You are undoubtedly correct about the ring fort gangs. How archaeologists and historians who have spent their lives in this work have missed something so obvious is beyond me. Though I do agree with you about the cave drawings. Some of it surely was simply graffiti or something to do to while away a rainy day. It makes one wonder which of our oddities people will look back on with wonder and reverence. "And in this town, which historians speculate may have been called Wishing Rock, all the people lived in the same building. This may have been due to disease, or perhaps religious rites that prohibited mingling with people outside the walls of what seems to have been known as 'The Box.' Clearly a xenophobic society filled with separatists." When you get that time travel machine sorted, sign me up. I am most curious as well, about the future as well as the past.

My spelunker in shining armor is fine, by the way. Completely unrelated to my curiosity about the future. Ahem.

As for the half-sister. What is it about certain situations that takes us back to our insecure childhood years? I'd think we can all agree I'm a relatively confident, competent, together young woman (my peanut gallery will leave your "piece of your mind" comment alone if your peanut gallery will leave my "young" comment alone!). However, going to meet Cindy I was thirteen years old again, assuming the worst, assuming I'd be hurt and rejected, assuming she would hate me for having been a part of the family that our father chose, rather than her family, which he left (to which I would say: lucky her). I was tense and hyper-attuned to every nuance, every word, and I have to say, the whole meeting didn't go as well as I'd hoped, and I think part of that is my fault. My fault for not trusting her to take me at face value and acknowledge that I had no role in whatever tragedy our father wrought on her and her mother. My fault for being so tense that I couldn't relax and just be myself. I wouldn't say the whole meeting was a failure, but it wasn't the happy, poignant, beautiful family reunion of fairy tales and TV shows. It was awkward. I was awkward and perhaps overly odd. We did not particularly mesh.

But then on the other hand, the fact is, I simply am sometimes awkward and overly odd. Who among us isn't occasionally awkward and odd? If I didn't care for awkward and odd people, I would have no friends. We all face those times in friendships when someone's actions challenge the relationship, but it's then that we must decide what matters. Finding good people who share our values, people who are kind and who will fully share in our joys and support us through our sorrows, that's not easy. When we find these people, it behooves us to give them the benefit of the doubt in their awkwardness and oddity. I'd rather have friends who are a bit strange, but nonetheless kind and compassionate and fully in my corner, than people who never say the wrong thing but whom I feel I cannot trust.

All of which is a bit of a tangent. Anyhoo, as it were, Cindy was tense and a bit aloof, but so was I, so it's difficult to say if that's the real her or if it was simply a difficult situation. I'd say we both deserve another chance, and after a bit of time passes – "white space," as Erin's new beau would put it – I'll invite her down and we'll see if we can't try again. The encounter is stretching my compassion muscle. As Erin and I were discussing the other day (I miss that girl!), each of us is the protagonist in our own story. Cindy in hers, I in mine. Our goal, as humans seeking to live in a state of compassion, is to see the protagonist in each other.

Eagerly awaiting your return. All my love to you gaggle of jollies over there. I imagine you're either on the plane or nearly so, as we speak. Safe trip home, sweetheart.

x

⁓

From: Ruby
To: Erin, Alexandra, Carolyn, Claire, Millie
Sent: February 23, 2011
Subject: Catching up

Hello, ladies!

Thought it was time for a poker check-in since we've all been spread out across the globe. I know Millie doesn't have her computer with her while on her travels (what a concept! Being so unplugged!), but I'm including her so she can catch up when she's home.

Ed and I are home, tired, but had a wonderful time. Gran's wedding was beautiful and special, and seeing Pip with the bump of my growing niece/nephew was priceless. I could tell Mom is having a hard time being so far from Pip and cherished all that time with her. I see lots of trips to Scotland in Mom and Dad's future! They're going to be such great grandparents.

So I'll admit (don't tell him), there was a moment in Ireland when Ed and I were out on a walk where I thought he was going to propose, but alas, I was wrong. What would I have said?! I hadn't even thought much about it, not since the day he got down on one knee to invite me to the New Year's Ball, and then suddenly I thought I was going to be faced with it. Funny how one question can change the path of a life. Or rather, the answer to one question.

Alexandra, Ed told me a bit about your visit to see your half-sister. Sorry it didn't go better. I hate that, when for whatever reason things don't go as you'd hope on the first impression, and you're left kicking yourself with regrets. Well, we move on. Maybe a trip to Wishing Rock is what she needs. Sometimes, I think a trip to Wishing Rock is what most people need, really.

And, speaking of our dear wee town, are we all ready for the Wishing Rock Olympics? Does anyone need someone to fill out a team? I've been so focused on the wedding and Gran and Pip and our trip that I haven't signed up for a thing. Pretty sure Ed and I are going to join the cup stacking competition (WATCH OUT, CHARLOTTE ALEXANDRA DAY SPARKS and DAVID DuBOIS!), and possibly potato sack races. Lawn darts, for sure, if it's not raining. What are you all doing? Honestly, all the races sound fun. Can we do all of them?

Erin, how goes Maui and the second Mr. Solberg these days?

So good to be home. Those of us here must get together soon.

~

From: Claire
To: Ruby, Erin, Alexandra, Carolyn, Millie
Sent: February 23, 2011
Subject: RE: Catching up

As it stands right now, here are the Stewart household plans:

Tom and Ben are participating in speed whittling, heaven help us! Bring out your bandages!

I'm joining in on the office chair races.

If you have ever seen Tom and me bowl, you will know it is pointless for anyone else to sign up for that competition, now that we've signed up.

Ben is running the walk/run; Tom and I are going to walk. If Jake can make it, he'll do the run as well.

Ben is signing up for all the wrestling activities. Tom is signing up for the thumb wrestling. (I don't know if you've ever noticed Tom's thumbs, but they are quite large.)

And of course I'm doing the line dancing! Tom is a reluctant hold-out on this one but I'm trying to convince him.

We need to put together a poker gal team for the toilet plunger races! I've seen that online – that is a hoot!

~

From: Carolyn
To: Claire, Ruby, Erin, Alexandra, Millie
Sent: February 23, 2011
Subject: RE: RE: Catching up

Claire, you all are getting quite into these games! That's wonderful. It sounds like so much fun.

Welcome back, Ruby. Ed kept Michael up to date on all your activities. Are you still bruised from your fall at the Causeway? How frightening! And I can't believe those other tourists just scolded you, rather than rushing to help. On the other hand, it sounds like you made the most of it, and brought home a story to tell. One of many, that is. Your tale of meeting those policemen had me laughing so hard. The things that could only happen to you!

Michael and I will be running the run/walk; bowling; and tennis if the weather holds. Michael has been practicing his cup stacking while you guys have been gone, so don't rule him out. I'll be participating in the potluck activities, of course. (Claire, won't you be?) And I'm sure Michael will be in on the lawn darts, never one to pass up the opportunity to throw dangerous sharp objects.

I could be convinced to join a poker gal toilet plunger team. How many are on a team? Can it vary? We have six so if they're doing teams of four that wouldn't work. Maybe three of us on one team and three on another, and we pull in one more person for each team? I think if one of us is in, we all need to be in. Solidarity in humiliation.

From: Erin
To: Carolyn, Claire, Ruby, Alexandra, Millie
Sent: February 23, 2011
Subject: RE: RE: RE: Catching up

Hi, all! Well, Carolyn, I am so touched that you still count me in your numbers, but I'm not actually there for the games! I'm on Maui, remember? So only five of you need to figure out the toilet plunger team madness. Sounds like a lot of fun. Alexandra, you and David have done such a great job, from all accounts I've heard. What a great way to make dreary rainy March into an event, something people will really look forward to in the years to come. The beginning of a wonderful tradition.

I'm doing great. Raine and I have been touring all over the island and having a blast. Yesterday we went into Lahaina and wandered around. If you want a souvenir from Maui, Lahaina is the place to get it! Much of the town was actually too tourist-oriented, kitschy, t-shirts and tacky trinkets for my taste. But we did manage to find a photography studio with the most amazing photos, blown up to several feet wide and high, that left me salivating. (The prices, however, put a stop to that!) Waterfalls, forests, beaches, the most spectacular nature photography I've ever seen. I'm thinking maybe I should take up photography and see if I can't recreate some of these scenes myself. I guess I'd need something a little more powerful than my tiny camera phone. We shall see! Raine has a pretty good camera that he uses to take pictures to go along with his articles. Sometimes he'll be assigned a professional photographer to accompany him on a story, but that's rare, so he's learned to manage himself. He said he'd be happy to teach me what he can. And where better to learn than Hawaii, with a picturesque scene at every turn?

I'm not working tomorrow afternoon, so we're going to try our hands (and feet) at stand-up paddle surfing. Everywhere you look (in the water, anyway), people are stand-up paddle surfing. You have a surfboard (I don't know yet if it's a regular surfboard or one specially designed for the purpose, but I'd guess the latter) and a really long oar, and, just like it sounds, you stand on the surfboard and paddle around all over. I'm told this is the way people used to get from island to island long ago – can you imagine! I would be terrified of falling in and being eaten by sharks. But people seem to get the hang of it pretty quickly. It looks like fun, especially when the water is a bit calmer. Hopefully we'll have calm waters for our lesson!

So that's it here, every day an adventure as we try to explore every nook and cranny we can find. I'm taking hula dancing lessons from one of Roone's friends and loving that, too. I still don't know how long Raine is here, and I don't know that he knows either. Taking it a day at a time.

For the record, if I were there, I'd totally be in on the line dancing, lawn darts, the walk/run, and the leg wrestling. I don't think you all realize how very strong these legs are.

Miss you guys!!!

xxx

From: Alexandra
To: Erin, Carolyn, Claire, Ruby, Millie
Sent: February 23, 2011
Subject: RE: RE: RE: RE: Catching up

My beloved friends! I'm so pleased you're all so excited about our Games. Claire, I think that's a fantastic idea, a poker gal team for the toilet plunger race. Unfortunately, being in charge of the race, I don't think I'll have time to participate in most activities as I'll be too busy making sure they all run smoothly! So the four of you who are here – Carolyn, Claire, Ruby, Millie – why don't you all be a team. I can always act as a fourth if another team needs one at the last minute. Or I can stand with my video camera and watch you all. One for the memory book!

Erin, it sounds like you are getting out of Hawaii exactly what you needed, and I'm delighted for you, but we do miss you.

Yes, my visit with Cindy was not all I'd hoped. It's challenging when you've been anticipating something, some event, and then it happens, and then it's over, and you can't go back and re-do it. But, I have faith that things work out as they're meant to. I'll have Cindy down sometime and we'll chat more. Sometimes second meetings are much less stressful than first meetings, as they're not laden with so many hopes and fears and expectations and baggage.

David and I are heading out to the Skagit River this weekend for a bald eagle float trip. I'm quite excited but I do wish the eagles would be more prevalent in warmer weather rather than this cold rainy stuff! I hear, though, that you can see upwards of fifty bald eagles on one trip, so I'm very excited. Speaking of photography, David has a nice camera, so he'll capture the memories. I plan to just watch, enraptured, and absorb the magnificence. Is it possible to look at a bald eagle and not feel awe? I can't wait.

Ruby, you may join in on as many activities as you want. It's not like the real Olympics, which strain the body and soul. These are all just for fun. Sign up for everything!

From: Ruby
To: Alexandra, Erin, Carolyn, Claire, Millie
Sent: February 23, 2011
Subject: RE: RE: RE: RE: RE: Catching up

Oh, it's so good to be home! I love you guys. All right, I'm going to see what all Ed plans to do, but I think I'm going to try just about everything. Even speed whittling? Yes, I think even speed whittling. Do we have to actually make something or just whittle fast? Can I make a toothpick?

I hope the weather is good enough for lawn darts. I haven't played lawn darts since I was a little kid and we had no idea how dangerous the things were! Good old lawn darts. Nothing says fun like giant flying weaponry!

I'm off for a nap – can barely keep my eyes open. Millie gets home tomorrow. Alexandra, you're heading over to the mainland on Friday, right? Hm. Trying to figure out when we all can get together. Maybe we'll just have to wait until after the games.

xx R.

~

From: Erin
To: Ruby, Alexandra, Carolyn, Claire, Millie
Sent: February 23, 2011
Subject: RE: RE: RE: RE: RE: RE: Catching up

Wow do I miss you guys. Take care, ladies, and have an extra cocktail on my behalf at your party. xx

~

From: Ruby
To: Gran
Sent: February 24, 2011
Subject: Home

Hey, gorgeous!

We're home! I can't decide if going eight hours east or west is harder on the body, but I'll be glad when I feel like a normal human being again! It was worth it to see that bliss on your face and on Liam's as you said your quick vows. Thank you for sharing that moment with us, Gran. I know it would have been so easy just to go to the courthouse and get married without telling anyone, but since I couldn't be there for your first wedding I wouldn't have missed this one for the world!

It does make a girl lament a bit, though. I'd thought Ed was ready to propose in Ireland – there was this moment when he looked at me with this look, and I've not seen that look before, even when Pete proposed. But then, nothing. And now we're back and within an hour he was whispering on his phone with a funny – different – look in his eye. Maybe I'll start a spinster house and just get ready to live in it! Or maybe Pip and Gavin can have a room for me in the basement, and I'll be down there with fifteen cats and an overabundance of romance novels with pictures of bare-chested men on the covers, and I'll never get dressed or do my hair. Do you think?

It all makes me think too much about Jake, though, Gran. Like, I get scared and suddenly he feels like safety. What is that about?

Perhaps I'm still a little tired.

Anyway, thank you again for everything. I hope to be over again once the baby is born, but I've traveled so much lately that I don't know whether I'll be able to. Fingers crossed! Or bring Liam here! Wishing Rock would love him, and you still need to meet everyone, and the town.

Love love love you,
Ruby

From: Gran
To: Ruby
Sent: February 25, 2011
Subject: RE: Home

Hello, darling,

You know that phrase, the good old days weren't always good? That's what Jake's about. We look back on the past with rose-colored glasses. We forget the bad and idealize the good. Because it's familiar, because you know how bad that pain was and you know you can handle it because you already did, and it's less scary than the unknown and the potential for new, unknown hurts. It's normal to want something secure to hold on to. I had a chance to talk with Ed, though, and I really believe he loves you. You're right; you're tired. Trust, sweetheart. That's all you need.

Dinner tonight at Will's; Pip and Gavin are coming over along with a few others in the family. I'm told some of the grandkids have put together a play to celebrate our wedding! I can't wait. Lovely to be surrounded by so much love. I think maybe I had let myself get a little lonely before I met Liam. I'm glad that changed.

Love,
Gran

From: Millie
To: Adele
Sent: February 26, 2011
Subject: Thank you!

Adele! Walter and I wanted to thank you again for inviting us to your wedding. It was about time we met, I'd say, after writing all these letters for the last year! Couldn't have had a better time, and traveling with Walter was superb. I was a bit worried — you know how it is, you never know what traveling with someone will do to a relationship until you do it – but Walter came through with shining colors. He's a prince and so gallant, just a charmer, took care of everything. Carried my bags when he could. Dealt with the ATMs and exchanging money. Handled the bills. We split everything evenly but he took care of all that, too. And he did all the driving, though I'll say with both of us having such old eyes we kept our driving to daylight hours as much as possible. This meant we spent most of our evenings in or near our bed-and-breakfasts, but we made a point of going down to the lobby or shared area each night and striking up a conversation with whoever walked by, until inevitably other guests or the hosts would come in and join us in a game or chit chat about life. Somehow Walter even talked a good majority of the B&B owners into bringing out bottles of wine to warm us up on those cold English nights. He's good at that, I didn't even know it, but he's good at making connections like that when he wants to. Sometimes he likes to just sit and be quiet, but he was the life of the party on a few nights, especially in those cases where the common area had a piano for him to play and for the rest of us to gather around. We visited so many beautiful sites – Fountains Abbey, the York Minster and the quaint town of York, Hadrian's Wall, all sorts of places – but I'd say my favorite memories are those lively evenings in those living rooms, meeting people from around the world. Thank goodness for the long nights of winter that bring us all together! I didn't take my computer along, either, which meant I was out of touch with everyone back home, but completely in touch with the people I met. So many kids these days, wandering around with their eyes on their phones, not even talking to their companions but rather texting with people who aren't even there! Attached at the thumbs to their various devices. If you ask me, it makes for a generation of people who don't really know how to communicate. You have to wonder if they'll learn or if the world will adapt to them.

The area, the countryside was just spectacular. A lot like home, really. I commented on this fact to Walter and he told me of a friend of his, who lives in North Bend. The friend had gone off on a bicycling trip through the Pyrenees. He came back and said it was beautiful, but the others on the trip seemed to be oohing and ahhing more than he was. Then it occurred to him: out here, we're so used to nature, the exceptional beauty of our area. It doesn't get much prettier than home, I'd say, especially on a sparkling sunny day. We may have a lot of gray days but you can't beat our mountains, our islands, our evergreens, all of it. We live in a mighty fine place, Adele.

As do you, now, of course! Scotland impressed me. Those gentle hills covered in fuzzy purple heather and golden bracken, that magnificent image is how I will remember Scotland.

As it goes, we are back home now and the jetlag isn't as bad as I'd expected. Maybe because I don't sleep much these days anyway.

Alexandra and David are just heading off for the ferry to Seattle tonight, so they can get up early and go on a rafting trip to see eagles. Alexandra has invited me over for a cup of tea, so I'll be heading over soon. I'm supposed to bring an appetizer but I don't know if I even have any food in the house. Might be a chips and salsa kind of night.

All my best to you and Liam, and thank you again for including us in your beautiful day,

Millie

February 27, 2011
Wishing Rock News
Millie Adler, editor
Letter from the Editor

Dear Rockers,

Is everyone ready? Are we all ready for a couple weeks of non-stop fun and activity? I'm not sure my old heart can even handle the fun! But fun will be had, mark my words!

Sign-up sheets for all events can now be found in the lobby. Looks like spots are filling up so get your name on the lists! Alexandra tells me we're even going to have medal ceremonies. Well, that makes things interesting, doesn't it! Not just bragging rights but actual Wishing Rock Olympics medals at stake. I hope you all are practicing! I saw a team from the second floor working on their toilet plunger race technique. You people, be warned. This is some serious competition here.

As if that weren't enough, dear Ed tells me we have guests coming to our humble home! The prodigal daughter of our dear founding father – that is Meredith Brooks, daughter of Meriwether and Madeline – is coming to town! She holds a leading role in a ... let me see, how did Ed describe this ... a "paranormal mystery show," and after chatting with Ed as of late, she convinced her producers that Wishing Rock and Dogwinkle are the perfect setting for a future episode of their show. Cast and crew have booked up all the rooms at the Inn and several of those new apartments Ed and Michael are renting out, so we will have a full house! I'm told they'll be arriving on March 3, day after the Opening Games. To help make things easier on them, Meredith's producers have sent along release forms for us all to sign, giving permission so that if they catch us in the background of a shot, they can use the film, something like that. They'll also be looking for people who want non-speaking parts as aliens or creatures of some kind. Ed told Meredith about our multi-talented and extremely capable Ben, who as a result is now acting as our on-site liaison to the show, so if you have any questions see Ben!

Sounds like we're about to be nose-deep in wonderful chaos, people of Wishing Rock! Get ready!

Millie

~

Text from Ed to Ruby
Sent: February 28, 2011

Quick, what's a good name for a cove?

~

Text from Ruby to Ed
Sent: February 28, 2011

Quick? Why, is there some cove-naming emergency?

~

Text from Ed to Ruby
Sent: February 28, 2011

Nah, all right, just think about it. What's a good name for a cove? That little bay on my island needs a name.

~

Text from Ruby to Ed
Sent: February 28, 2011

I'll think about that. Why does it need a name?

~

Text from Ed to Ruby
Sent: February 28, 2011

Wouldn't you want a name if you were an unnamed cove?

~

Text from Ruby to Ed
Sent: February 28, 2011

I suppose I would, at that. I'll think about it. Are you making me dinner tonight?

~

Text from Ed to Ruby
Sent: February 28, 2011

You read my mind! Do it again: What am I planning to make you tonight?

~

Text from Ruby to Ed
Sent: February 28, 2011

You're making me Mongolian beef. I think you have most of the ingredients except for the beef itself, and maybe the onions. Check when you get home. I'll email you the recipe.

~

Text from Ed to Ruby
Sent: February 28, 2011

I'm such a great guy to have thought of this.

~

Text from Ruby to Ed
Sent: February 28, 2011

You are, indeed, a great guy, Mr. Brooks. Emailing you the recipe now. Hold on.

~

From: Ruby
To: Ed
Sent: February 28, 2011
Subject: salad and steak

Recipe below. Would you also pick up some leaf lettuce while you're at the store? I'm going to make this salad (also attached). I think we have everything but the lettuce, but check the ingredients for me, will you? Thanks, babe!

Perfect Almond Mandarin (PAM) Salad
Ingredients
   1 head romaine and/or red leaf lettuce, rinsed, dried and torn
       into bite-sized pieces
   1 (15 oz) can mandarin oranges, well drained
   6 green onions, thinly sliced
   2 Tbsp white sugar
   1/2 to 1 cup sliced almonds
   2 Tbsp white wine vinegar
   3 Tbsp honey
   1/2 tsp dry hot mustard
   1/2 tsp celery salt
   1/2 tsp ground paprika
   1/4 cup olive oil
Directions
   • Heat sugar with almonds in saucepan over medium heat.
     Cook and stir while sugar starts to melt and coat almonds.
     Stir constantly until almonds are light brown (about 10
     minutes total). Turn onto a plate, and cool for 10 minutes.
   • To make the dressing, thoroughly blend the vinegar, honey,
     dry mustard, celery salt, paprika, and olive oil.
   • In a large bowl, combine the lettuce, oranges, and onions.
   • Before serving, toss salad with salad dressing until coated.
     Transfer to a decorative serving bowl, and sprinkle with sug-
     ared almonds.

Mongolian Beef

Ingredients

 1 lb flank steak
 1/4 cup cornstarch
 1 Tbsp vegetable oil
 1 tsp ginger (minced)
 1 Tbsp garlic (minced)
 1/2 cup soy sauce
 1/2 cup water
 1/2 cup brown sugar
 2 Tbsp rice wine
 1 tsp red pepper flakes
 3 green onions (sliced)
 1 medium onion (sliced)
 Oil (for frying)

Directions

- Sauce: Heat oil. Add garlic and ginger and sauté briefly; do not burn (about 10 seconds). Add the soy sauce, wine and water. Add the brown sugar and mix until it dissolves. Mix in the red pepper flakes. Bring to a boil and boil for 2-3 minutes. Remove from heat.
- Steak: Slice the steak against the grain about 1/4" thick. (Cut at an angle, top to bottom, to get wider cuts.) Toss the slices with cornstarch and let sit for 10 minutes.
- Heat up about a cup of oil (preferably in a wok, but a frying pan will work) to about medium heat. Add the beef slices to the pan/wok and cook for about 3 minutes. (You could also use a deep fryer.)
- Drain the steak on paper towels. Remove or add enough oil to the pan/wok to make about a tablespoon of oil, and add the onions. Stir fry for a couple minutes, then add everything back into the wok/pan, and cook until it bubbles.
- Serve over rice. Serves two generously.

~

From: Ed
To: Ruby
Sent: February 28, 2011
Subject: RE: salad and steak

Your wish is my command. PAM salad? Where'd you get that?

~

From: Ruby
To: Ed
Sent: February 28, 2011
Subject: RE: RE: salad and steak

It's actually the salad Claire made for my Welcome-to-Wishing Rock potluck a year ago. She said she got it from a woman she used to work with, named Pam. Funny gal, Claire said. Liked to name things after herself. She used to make this salad for work potlucks all the time. She called it PAM Salad, and it just caught on. PAM Salad.

~

From: Ed
To: Ruby
Sent: February 28, 2011
Subject: RE: RE: RE: salad and steak

PAM Salad and Mongolian beef it is, then! See you soon! Don't forget to be thinking of a name for the cove! x

March

From: Ruby
To: Erin
Sent: March 1, 2011
Subject: Cove

Hey! What up, tropics girl?

So the exciting news is that it's cold and rainy here! Ha, just kidding. I mean, it is cold and rainy. It's just not all that exciting.

What is exciting is that Aunt Meredith is coming to town! I'm telling you, I'm going to make a Brooks Family Reunion happen this year if it's the last thing I do! Can't wait to meet Aunt Meredith. She sounds sassy. Plus, rumor has it I might have a chance to be an extra on the show. Oh, sure, I'll be covered in gray-green makeup with a bald-head wig with bumps all over it, and you might not be able to tell it's me, and I'm not even sure I'll get credited in the credits, but still, it'll be something to show my grandkids. Or my niece.

Did I tell you it's a niece? Yes! Pip and Gavin were more or less on the fence about whether they wanted to know in advance if he or she would be a he or she, but at the begging of people trying to buy baby clothes for them, they finally gave in and found out. Pip had been thinking she wanted a boy, but she is more than delighted about a girl. A girl! I'm going to be an aunt rather than an uncle! Haha, old joke. So now the push is on to get them to name her after me. Maybe a middle name? I mean, what little girl wouldn't want to be named after her favorite Auntie Ruby? Oh, Erin, it makes my heart ache to know I won't be able to see her but once or twice a year at most. I'm already certain Baby MacAlpine will be gorgeous. I can't wait to meet her.

Do you remember the island Ed owns? Yesterday he asked me to be thinking of a name for the cute little cove. I have no idea how to name a cove. Are there legal implications? Like, how does something officially get named anything? Any good cove name ideas?

~

From: Erin
To: Ruby
Sent: March 1, 2011
Subject: RE: Cove

A cove? I don't know, should it be marina-related? Related to something meaningful in Ed's life? Could he just go with Ruby Cove? You should suggest that and see what happens.

Hey, I've been trying to figure out whether to tell you this. Like, am I a good friend if I tell you, or a good friend if I don't tell you? I can't figure it out. I mean it's none of my business except that you're my business, right? Being friends isn't always about being comfortable. Sometimes it's awkward and weird and that's when the friend part kicks in, we forgive and understand intentions, right?

Anyway, apparently Ed's been in contact with Julianna in Seattle. I mean, it's no big deal except that he was hiding it from you. Which is weird. So, I just wanted you to know. I don't want you to be hurt, either way, but I also don't want to not tell you just because it's uncomfortable.

So, please don't hate me. That's all I know.

Love you, Ruby Cove

Erin

~

From: Ruby
To: Erin
Sent: March 2, 2011
Subject: RE: RE: Cove

I asked Ed about Julianna last night. Don't worry, I know you were just watching out for me. He said she's an artist and she's been helping him with conceptual plans for the deck.

The thing is, I made a resolution yesterday, a March 1 resolution rather than a January 1 resolution, to trust him. To be vulnerable with him. To be all in. Which scares the crap out of me, but I'm just going to do it. What's the worst that could happen? He could break my heart? Sure, but I've been there before and I survived. Worst case scenario, he breaks up with me and I run away to join you in Hawaii. Right? That wouldn't be so bad.

I found a "trust meditation" audio file that I'm going to listen to when I go on walks. In the rain. Maybe I'll just roam the halls. Sometimes Old Henry does that; maybe I'll run into him and we'll get into a good chat. What do you suppose he thinks about? He's a funny one. But he won't leave. For whatever reason, Wishing Rock is embedded in his heart as much as yours or mine. Well, except that you left. But you'll be back.

Opening Games tonight! I am so excited. David made a video of Wishing Rock and our island, and he's premiering it at the theater tonight, and then the Games will begin! And Meredith arrives tomorrow.

Dang, I wish you were here!

Ruby Cove. Hm, perhaps a little more ego-centric than even I am, but I'll think about it!

Trust is my middle name.

R.

From: Ed
To: Alexandra
Sent: March 3, 2011
Subject: Games, Meredith, etc.

Hey, Queen of Games Organization! Great show last night at the opening ceremonies! Loved the Wishing Rock video. Where did you guys find all those old pictures? That was fantastic. Send me a copy, would you? I want to keep that.

Can't wait to beat everyone at the Office Chair races. To see all those people in my five-wheeled wake. That medal is mine. May as well engrave it now. Are they engraved, by the way? I just want to know so I can design my Wishing Rock Games Medal Case.

Aunt Meredith should be arriving any minute now. I offered to pick her up, but since there's so many of them and they have shoots all over the island, they're getting a couple vans and driving themselves. Good thing, or I might have missed both the Chairs and the Speed Whittling. Should be good to see her, get to know her, really. She's never been part of the family, for some reason. I mean, obviously she's part of the family but she's never been around.

Dinner party with the Aunt tomorrow night at Michael and Carolyn's, after the Route Laying Parade. (We wouldn't want to deprive anyone of Michael's traditional bagpipe playing in the parade!) You and David are invited. I don't think you need to bring anything – Carolyn has it covered, will bring all the food out of her Magic Oven of Neverending Deliciousness – but you can ask her if you want.

Let me know if you need anything during the Games! Seriously, Lex, thanks so much for making this happen in our little town. It's people like you who make living here the greatest! Love ya!

Ed

~

Text from Erin to Ruby
Sent: March 4, 2011

I'm at the grocery store. Just passed Roone's favorite drink in the drinks aisle. I don't like the taste of it myself, but I stocked up on it when I was here in December, in case he might drop by unexpectedly. Tried too hard. Cared too much. Weird how one little thing brings a flood of emotions and memories so quickly.

~

Text from Ruby to Erin
Sent: March 4, 2011

True. Sometimes good, sometimes bad. Every time I see a parade float, I think of Ed. But you've moved on, that's good! Raine is good?

~

Text from Erin to Ruby
Sent: March 4, 2011

Raine is really good. Coming to dinner tonight. Wish you could see my little cottage. So quaint and sweet.

~

Text from Ruby to Erin
Sent: March 4, 2011

Wish I could too. Too many places to be all at once! Dinner party tonight with Aunt Meredith at Carolyn and Michael's. Can't believe we're missing the post-Idiotarod-route-laying parade potluck, but Aunt Meredith doesn't come around that often! Excitement!

~

Text from Erin to Ruby
Sent: March 4, 2011

How will the potluck survive without all of you? You must tell me how it goes, and any good scoop that is learned. I don't suppose we could do a dinner conference call?!

~

Text from Ruby to Erin
Sent: March 4, 2011

Probably not. Tell Raine hello! Almost said Roone. Why must parents of twins give them matching names?

~

Text from Erin to Ruby
Sent: March 4, 2011

It's a hardship we must bear. Have fun tonight! Chat soon! x

~

From: Millie
To: Adele
Sent: March 5, 2011
Subject: Idiotarod + Meredith

Hello, Adele!
Well, it's been a while, hasn't it, since I gave you a Brooks family history lesson? Three cheers, then, because last night I got a whole new lesson myself, which I'm now passing on to you.
I don't know if Ruby told you, but Ed and Michael's Aunt Meredith – a TV star who goes by the stage name of Barbara Brooks, if

you want to look her up – has come to Wishing Rock! The fact that she is special is proven by the fact that a handful of us skipped out on our traditional pre-Idiotarod potluck to have dinner with her.

I'll tell you, Adele, what struck me about Meredith's tales and stories is how different her perspective on her parents – Meriwether and Madeline – was from … well, from Meriwether's. Of course I never knew Maddie, and I only knew Meriwether later in his life, after Maddie's death changed him into the man I knew. Ed and Michael knew their grandparents mostly from afar. But Meredith, of course, had a front-row seat growing up with them, and she had a few things to say.

You may or may not know that in Meriwether's will, he skipped right over his children's generation to give almost everything to his grandsons, Michael and Ed. Meredith had a few thoughts on that, you can be sure. Apparently, her relationship with Meriwether was always strained.

"Dad only had space for one woman in his life," she said, "and that was Mom. Dear old perfect Madeline. There was never any room for anyone without a Y chromosome in the Brooks family, unless you were the Queen." Meredith and her parents clashed throughout her childhood, she said; Meriwether and Meredith butted heads, while, to hear Meredith's side of things, Maddie all but ignored her. "She didn't want any competition for the men's attention," said Meredith of her mother. "She was jealous of me from day one."

"I thought all the Brookses were perfect?" said your Ruby. "Never a bad word spoken about Madeline or Meriwether?"

"It's all in who you ask," said Meredith, but, honestly, believe it or not, I'd say she said all this without bitterness. From her matter-of-fact tone in the way she relayed her stories, I'd say she's forgiven and moved on.

Alexandra joined in. "It's as I always say, each of us is the protagonist in our own story, and most of us are antagonists to someone."

"Are you sure? Mother wasn't. Everyone liked her," said Meredith. "Everyone always seemed to, anyway. I admit it, I was as jealous of her as I thought she was of me. I felt so hurt for a very long time."

"Well, there you go then, as far as antagonists to Maddie, there's you," Alexandra pointed out. "And surely others. Not anymore, probably; time has a way of softening our memories of people, but somewhere in time, she was someone's foe, the pea under someone's mattress, the bee in someone's bonnet. A jilted lover, a petulant co-worker, an overprotective mother-in-law, someone. We are all both protagonist in our story and antagonist in someone else's. It's just a matter of our perspective, the angle of the light."

Despite being pretty open-minded, Meriwether and Madeline didn't like the path Meredith had chosen for herself. She wanted to act. "That wasn't okay with Mom and Dad," she said. "They were sure I'd end up whoring myself out, and never make it anyway." She laughed a bit at the memory. Those Brookses, Adele, they are stubborn and independent people, and when they want something they go for it. At eighteen, Meredith headed to Hollywood and didn't look back. "I didn't speak to my parents for years," she said. Meredith was two years younger than her brother Mitchell (Ed and Michael's father). (Mitchell and I are about the same age, as a point of reference – I'm just under a year his senior.) Meredith left home in 1963. She didn't come to the wedding when Mitchell got married in 1965, and was still angry at her parents when Madeline died in 1967. "I was at the funeral," she said, "but no one saw me. I snuck in, cried a little when Dad spoke, out of self-pity as much as sadness over losing my mother, then snuck out the back before anyone could notice. I blamed Dad for ruining my life – for making Mom the center of everything and ignoring me – and now, on top of it all, I blamed him for pushing me away so I wasn't there in Mom's last days. The rift between us was strong. It felt like he didn't even remember I existed."

So, out of both self-protection and anger, this wayward Brooks cut ties with her family to the extent that they all more or less forgot each other. This, of course, was back in our day, when long-distance phone calls were expensive and we monitored our minutes, and when writing someone meant taking out pen and paper and a postage stamp. It was easier to get lost then, easier to stay unfound.

Meredith's career began slowly, as so many in Hollywood do. She started dating a fellow actor, who was undiscovered at the time she met him, but then he got a bit part on a hit show and made it big. (Back then, before cable TV and the advent of five hundred channels available but nothing to watch, if you were on a show at all, people knew you.) She got pregnant; they married, she miscarried, and she never got pregnant again. After several years, they came to see the error in their ways, having married for the wrong reasons, and parted more or less amicably. An official divorce followed soon after.

"I learned a lot about love and about people from that relationship," she said, "even if it didn't work out. He was a good person, a good man, but people in the business – people who wanted what he had – loved him to his face but gossiped about him behind his back. They begrudged him his success. People envy those who have brilliant lives, but they envy them from the sidelines. They forget that having a brilliant life requires emotional bruises and isolation and a hell of a lot of hard work. Great success requires many failures, and it is, in fact, lonely at the top. 'If living an amazing life were easy, everyone would do it,' he'd say. It is those who are willing to step forward, take a chance, who can persevere through the losses, who eventually win. He showed me that, and that's a lesson I have kept with me."

To help you keep track with our timeline, at this time it was the mid-seventies. Meriwether had built our beloved Wishing Rock, people were moving in, I'd moved here, we were all a happy family on Dogwinkle but Meredith remained in California. By then she'd established herself enough that she had regular work, even if it was not terribly lucrative. No quitting her day job just yet. She worked retail in a wedding shop by day, did theater by night, with a TV guest spot or extra role or advertisement now and again. She felt occasional remorse over having disowned or having been disowned, but she was too busy working to do anything about it.

Time went on, passing quickly, as time does, as we assume there will always be more of it. Next thing she knew, she got notice from Mitchell that Meriwether had died.

That, of course, was 1995, when Meriwether went on his fateful skydiving trip.

Meredith came up for this funeral, no hiding from anyone this time. "I was in a bit of shock," she said. "I'd talked with Mitchell every few years, and somewhat randomly got to know and kept in touch with his ex-wife, Kathy, so I had a vague idea of what was going on. I'd say staying out of Dad's life was more habit than intention by this point. From what Mitchell said, Dad was in reasonably good health – he'd only just turned seventy-seven when he died. I knew that I'd intended to make amends at some point, but I'd just not gotten around to it yet. And suddenly, that chance was gone. I couldn't forgive or be forgiven. I couldn't hug Dad one more time. I couldn't chuck him on the shoulder and tell him with a laugh that he'd been a jerk, but that I understood, we all make mistakes. I couldn't ask him to tell me more about Mom, whom I'd never really gotten to know due to my own stubbornness. Any questions I had wanted to ask, would forever go unanswered."

Meredith said she started writing letters then, letters to her mother and father. "I couldn't mail them, obviously, but I needed to get out all the thoughts I had storming through my head." She laughed. "I only wrote them for about six months, but I still have them all. I'm not sure what to do with them. They're not for anyone else to read but I don't want to just recycle them."

"We have just the thing for that," said Ruby. "Beach bonfire. Or a fire in the fire pit outside the Inn upstairs. Either way, it's cathartic."

"I don't have them with me," said Meredith, "but I like that idea. Maybe I'll have to come back."

Ruby got a gleeful glint in her eye, because she has been working tooth and nail to try to get Ed to get his family together out here. She may get her wish yet!

Fast forward a bit. After years and years of actorly struggle, almost ready to retire on her lifetime of earnings plus the small bit that Meriwether did leave her, Meredith finally got a major acting role on this paranormal mystery something or other show she's on now that is filming at Wishing Rock this week. She's found not only work but also love, as she is dating, a co-star, but they're pretty private about it, so don't tell anyone. "Not that anyone cares about people as old as we are," she laughed. "They can't get enough gossip about the whippersnappers, with their taut necks and tight butts, but lucky for us old people they more or less leave us alone." Her gentleman friend couldn't come to dinner last night as he had a scene to film that Meredith wasn't in. I've met him, though, and he seems friendly and warm, a nice enough man.

Well, I'd intended to tell you more about the Idiotarod, which was today, but I've been writing so long that it's actually tomorrow already. This old lady needs her beauty rest. Suffice it to say we all had a grand old time, once again. Meredith did not participate in the Idiotarod, and of course her crew didn't have time to make their own entry, but the good people of Wishing Rock in their everlasting kindness found places amongst their own teams for all those on the TV crew who wanted to join in. The producers even filmed a bit of the action, though I can't imagine it's at all relevant to the show! On Monday, they want to do some filming down in my store, which is exciting. I will be playing the role of "shop keeper" so I'm studying up on that! Ben – who has become quite the production assistant – is gathering up a handful of people to be extras in that scene, walking around the store and buying things in the background while Meredith and a few other actors have some sort of confrontation. Wishing Rock is abuzz, Adele! We'll grow this town into something special yet, just you watch.

And with that, I'll sign off, hopefully before I fall asleep!

Goodnight,

Millie

~

From: Ruby
To: Erin
Sent: March 6, 2011
Subject: The latest

Hey, babe! How are you?

I'm good. Ed's out of town, in Seattle. Business something or other. Which sucks, because we were going to do the potato sack race together tomorrow, but he won't be back until tomorrow night! At least he was able to do the walk/run this morning, but darn it, I was so ready for that potato sack race. I'm not sure I ever told you, but I won a ribbon in grade school for the potato sack racing, on a field day one year, you know, the last day of school where they aren't going to even try to teach you anything but have to do something with you so they send everyone outside. Totally won a ribbon. And now, my partner for the Wishing Rock Potato Sack Race, surely to be the first in my string of Potato Sack Race medals, is gone. I'll forgive him, I suppose, but he owes me.

Wait: Aunt Meredith! Maybe Aunt Meredith can be my partner! No, I don't think she's really the potato sack race type. Maybe there's someone on the TV crew who would do it with me. Surely there's someone on the cast or crew who would do it with me. Now I need to find them wherever they're filming and find out. I'm a woman with a mission. I WILL be in the potato sack race and I WILL WIN.

But back to Aunt Meredith. It's been so great having her here. We had a big dinner with the whole gang a couple nights ago, and Ed and/or Michael along with me and/or Carolyn, in varying combinations, have joined her for dinner or occasional lunches for most of the time she's been here. She's great. She says what she thinks, especially about some of the pitfalls of fame, e.g.: "I hate gossip. People don't ask me as much as they used to, but back when I was young and married to my first husband, people were always trying to get 'scoop' out of me. If you want to know something, ask the source. If you don't have the balls to go to the source, maybe it's not yours to know," she said, and I have to say, she has a point.

We also got into a discussion about life, and death. Someone brought up the old saying that you should live each day as if it were your last.

"Bullhockey," said Meredith. (Incidentally, isn't the word "bullpucky"? Although I guess bull hockey would be something to see, too.) "Complete foolishness. Live your life as if what you do matters, yes, but there's no way anyone can live each day as if it were her last. Can you imagine? What would you do on your last day? Most of us certainly wouldn't go to work. You might spend all your money, or give it away on a street corner, pay for everyone behind you in line at the coffee shop – something wonderful but irresponsible. You might tell off your boss, tell him or her everything you've been thinking without a care for diplomacy or the need to keep the job. You might destroy the printer that never prints right. Things like that."

"I think, Aunt Meredith, people really mean that you have to make the most of each day. Not literally to live each day as if it were their last," said Ed, ever the philosopher, you know.

"I'm sure you're right," said Meredith, "but that points to another issue. People say things because they sound good without actually stopping to determine whether what is being said makes any sense at all. Like that guy on TV, the one who says that if you say 'but' in a sentence, you negate everything you've said up to the 'but.' Absolute nonsense. For example, if I say 'I love you, but I need you to clean up after yourself,' he'd say that the 'but' negates the first part. So stupid. He has his little catch phrase about saying 'but' and it makes a nice little sound byte, so people repeat it, but it's ridiculous. If I say 'I love you, but you need to clean up,' that 'but' doesn't negate the fact that I love you. That's the beauty of the human mind: we can hold conflicting ideas within our brains. And 'I love you' and 'you need to clean up, Sloppy Joe,' aren't even conflicting thoughts. They're just two different thoughts. People need to think before they go around repeating things just because they sound good or quotable or someone on TV said it. People need to use their brains. Practice critical thinking. We've lost the ability to practice critical thinking. In fact, I'd say, we've lost the ability to practice critical thinking, but on the whole I still think people are good. Do you see what I did there? I inserted a 'but' in the middle of that sentence but you can be sure I did not negate the first part. Our culture has deteriorated, people think in bits and bytes that will sound good if posted on their status updates, but they don't bother to think about whether any of it makes any sense. Noise. We're becoming a culture of noise, everyone shouting for attention, no one listening, no one making sense."

And I'd say I agree, it's not technically good to live each day as if it were one's last, but still I think it's good to be aware that we're guaranteed no tomorrows. Mostly in terms of making sure your relationships are on solid ground.

Anyway, then we made cookies. Aunt Meredith's chocolate chip peanut butter cookies. Delish.

Well, I'd better go find myself a potato sack race companion. It's so handy having Ben in on the action. Just a text to Ben and he makes it all happen. I think, actually, that the cast and crew have the day off (it being Sunday and all), so I may be able to find them all down at the bar at Mac's downstairs. I'll go check. Tomorrow I'm going to be an extra. Tuesday, I think they're filming an alien scene, out by Knot Mountain, over in that … I don't know, is it a plain? A valley? In that big flat area just on the northwest side of the mountain, toward Balky Point. The very uninhabited area, though I think it's actually somewhat near a cabin Ed owns, that he was talking about renting out to that family that was here over Christmas. My point being, I'm hoping work is really slow and my boss won't mind if I go off to be an alien extra. Or even just watch, though I don't know if they'd let me. They're pretty secretive about the scripts! Ben can't even be bribed, though I'm sure he knows more than he's letting on. If you were here you could be an alien too! Oh well.

So, here's the cookie recipe. Hello to Raine! Love you!

x

Chocolate Chip Peanut Butter Cookies
Ingredients
   1 cup butter, softened
   1 1/2 cups peanut butter
   1 1/4 cups dark brown sugar
   1 1/4 cups light brown sugar
   1 Tbsp vanilla
   1/3 cup milk
   2 eggs
   1 tsp salt
   1 1/2 tsp baking soda
   3 1/2 cups flour
   2 cups (12 oz) chocolate chips
Directions

- In large mixing bowl, cream butter, peanut butter, and sugars. Add vanilla, milk, and eggs. Mix in salt, baking soda, and flour. Gently stir in chocolate chips. Bake at 375° for 9 to 11 minutes.

March 7, 2011
Wishing Rock News
Millie Adler, editor
Letter from the Editor

Dear Rockers,

It's Walter's birthday today, for those of you who didn't know. Happy birthday, Walter!

What a week we're having! Have you all caught your breaths yet? After a long and exciting day filming the show in my store (what a day that was!), I'm just in from the bowling competition. Someone told me that apparently you want high scores in bowling, low scores in golf. I had that mixed up and was sure I had won. Didn't even get to keep the pretty shoes.

Congratulations to everyone who has won or participated so far. It's great that the cast and crew of "Inhabitants" have been getting involved in the games! Please remind anyone you see that Wednesday is our next potluck and our first National Wishing Rock Day. While everyone is encouraged to bring potluck items, we will for sure have more than enough to feed our guests, so make sure they know they are welcome. We'll be up in the fifth floor commons room, 6 p.m., be there or else! Walter is working on a Wishing Rock anthem – music only. I was working on words to put to the tune, but Walter tells me songwriting might not be my calling. I don't know why. It seems the world has been waiting for an anthem that includes the word "formaldehyde," don't you think? Rhymes with "by your side," so it made sense to me.

It looks like the weather might hold for a few outdoor events this weekend, so keep your fingers crossed. If tennis doesn't work out, we can always switch to ping pong. Lawn darts would have to be cancelled. I can't see that being a good indoor sport, no matter how you shape it. Regardless of weather, the much anticipated toilet plunger races will be held in the hallways of the fourth floor. I about peed my pants laughing while watching some people practice this one, so I recommend coming prepared in whatever way that means to you.

If it's not raining, closing ceremonies will be a bonfire at the beach. Otherwise we'll bring it in to the auditorium lobby. Potluck, of course. Bring your best.

It's late and this old lady must now get to sleep! Another busy day tomorrow. Since Alexandra and David are participants in the heated cup stacking competition, I will be officiating. No cheating! I am a ruthless officiator. Don't try to pull anything. Alexandra and David, I'm looking at you. Then Friday is the line dancing marathon. I hope every one of you will consider joining in that one. Get your scooting boots on and be there!

Millie

Text from Erin to Ruby
Sent: March 8, 2011

Hey, can you pick us up at the airport tomorrow night?

~

Text from Ruby to Erin
Sent: March 8, 2011

What the what? Who? Yes! Who? What? When? What??

~

Text from Erin to Ruby
Sent: March 8, 2011

Raine and me. I've been getting Millie's updates and I can't believe I'm missing these games. I want to be there! Raine said we should just come. Getting in around dinnertime. I'll forward my flight info.

~

Text from Ruby to Erin
Sent: March 8, 2011

Yes! Oh hooray! Raine, too?! Well, this is exciting indeed! Do you need me to air out your house or anything?

~

Text from Erin to Ruby
Sent: March 8, 2011

If you could set the thermostat so it's not freezing when we get there, that would be awesome. I'll figure out the rest.

~

Text from Ruby to Erin
Sent: March 8, 2011

Yay! Yes! Yay! For how long are you coming for, please?

~

Text from Erin to Ruby
Sent: March 8, 2011

Just about a week. I couldn't handle all the non-stop sunshine and warmth here, you know. Needed some cold and rain.

~

Text from Ruby to Erin
Sent: March 8, 2011

Ha! I'll bet. Well, yes! We'll take you as long as we can get you. I'll see you tomorrow!! Yay!!

~

From: Ruby
To: Gran
Sent: March 9, 2011
Subject: Home

Gran!
    It's the first Official National Wishing Rock Day! Or maybe it's unofficial. I can't remember. But it's today! Happy National Wishing Rock Day!
    I'm in my pajamas and ready for bed after a long day. So grateful to Ed, though, who made it less long than it might have been. I went to pick up Erin and HER BOYFRIEND Raine tonight at the airport, and Ed, bless him, scheduled for a friend with a little puddle hopper plane to pick me up here on Dogwinkle and fly me to Seattle. I picked up the Maui kids, got us back to the friend's plane, and he flew us back here. Saved us all that ferry-to-Seattle time, hours and hours, made it possible to get back here tonight even, which was fantastic. Not the cheapest route but this one time, for National Wishing Rock Day, Ed said it was his pleasure to take some pressure off me. Plus he was out of town for a couple days and we've already missed enough of the Games together.
    When we got back here, it was dark but not rainy. We turned on the lights out on the side lawn, and got out the lawn darts for practice. Note: lawn darts + nighttime = not the best combination. I don't think we killed any small animals or anything, but we quickly decided we couldn't see well enough to be throwing small javelins! Although I'm still unclear on whether it's illegal to own them, or just sell them or buy them? Or use them? Regardless, we decided to head inside. Ed fired up the fireplace at his home and the four of us converged for cocktails and catch-up. Ed and Raine hit it off right away. I'd say Raine is a little more serious, but once he felt comfortable he warmed up quickly. Erin clearly enjoys his company, all smiles whenever he was around and also when he was not. He was so attentive to her, getting up to get a napkin for her when she spilled salsa on the table, mixing her drink just the way he knows she likes it. Nice guy.

It was one of those bittersweet things. So glad she's back that it made me constantly aware of how much I miss her when she's gone. I just have to remember to stay in the moment and enjoy the time she's here, rather than wasting it on wishing she'd stay.

Life would be so much easier for me if everyone did what I wanted them to do!

We are getting so close to Pip's due date! I can't believe it. Is everyone ready over there? Pip says she's ready but who really knows, I'd think, right? That's a pretty big life change. At least Gavin has done it before and knows what to expect. I'm sure they'll all be all right. I hope I can get over to visit soon after the birth. We'll see.

Love to all,
Ruby

From: Roone
To: Erin
Sent: March 10, 2011
Subject: Yo

Hey –

Talked with Raine before you guys left. He says I owe you an apology. Do I? I apologize. We're all just getting by, friend. If I hurt you I didn't mean to. I'm darker than I like to let on. More edges, more cliffs, more dark caverns where no one should be allowed to go. My ways aren't the ways of the masses. Sorry if some of my issues seeped onto you. Plan BE is a work in progress.

I'm working on figuring out whether to figure things out with Ava. Maybe what we thought we wanted wasn't what we wanted after all. Maybe our future wasn't what our dreams were made of. There's a song in us, you and me, me and her, me. A song in every heartbeat. A song in every heartbreak. A song in every new day.

Hope we can be friends. Come visit me when you're back on Maui. Sunshine awaits. Glad to hear you and Raine are good. He's all right. A bit too responsible, if you ask me, but one of us has to be, right? The balancing of the universe, light and dark, hope and despair, yin and yang, responsible and carefree, Raine and Roone. And the love of one girl.

R.

From: Erin
To: Ruby, Claire, Carolyn, Alexandra, Millie
Sent: March 10, 2011
Subject: xoxo

Hey gals!

First of all, I just have to say it's been so good to see you all. You complete me. You fill up my heart. You raise me up! I'm going to break into song! I just wanted to tell you all how much you mean to me and how much I appreciate who you are and all you bring to my life. You don't realize these things until they're gone, as the saying goes. I miss you all so much, and being here reminds me how much I love you all. People like you are rare and hard to find. I don't tell you that enough. So now I'm telling you. You guys are the best.

So, Roone has written to apologize, though he wasn't really clear what he was apologizing for. I can't even tell what he's saying. Does he know what he's apologizing for? Do I know? I'm not sure what to say. What do I say?

Alexandra, I'm so glad I got here in time for some Olympics. Everyone is raving about it, how much fun they're having. I hope you're hearing it. I hope people are telling you. They are having a blast. Great job. You rock.

Erin

From: Alexandra
To: Erin, Ruby, Claire, Carolyn, Millie
Sent: March 10, 2011
Subject: RE: xoxo

Erin, such kind words. Thank you. Yes, people have been more than generous in expressing their appreciation. I could not have done it without so many people here, and especially without David.

What do you want to say to Roone? Is there anything he really needs to know? Do you have regrets? Do you want something different from what you have, from how things worked out?

~

From: Erin
To: Alexandra, Ruby, Claire, Carolyn, Millie
Sent: March 10, 2011
Subject: RE: RE: xoxo

Surprisingly, I'm totally fine with how it all worked out. I was pretty shocked when I found out about Ava, but then Raine came into the picture so quickly that everything sort of clicked. One of those lightbulb moments you hear about. Like, in my brain, I almost heard myself think, "Ohhhhh. I get it. This is why all this happened." Maybe I'm wrong about that, but it feels right.

I don't blame Roone for anything. He's just being himself. He can't be anything other than himself. I'm not sure I have anything to say to him right now. Not in a mean way. I'm just fine as we are.

I feel like I was always apologizing when we were "together" – if I can even say we were together. I was always trying to prove I wasn't who I am. But now, I feel really at peace with who I am. Like I can own it. Own all the pieces of me, the messiness and the insecurities and the things I've hidden from the world because I thought they weren't okay. It's just me. Love me or don't.

~

From: Alexandra
To: Erin, Ruby, Claire, Carolyn, Millie
Sent: March 10, 2011
Subject: RE: RE: RE: xoxo

If you don't have anything to say to him, then don't say anything. Let it sit for a while. The right time will come.

That time, however, is not now. For many reasons. One of these being that the First Annual Wishing Rock Cup Stacking Competition is about to begin, and David and I are about to, as they say, clean the floor with Ruby and Ed. I am assuming we haven't heard from the others because they're already at the event site. Make your way to the fifth floor commons room, Erin, and forget your woes whilst watching me win my due reward. See you in a few moments!

~

From: Ruby
To: Alexandra, Erin, Claire, Carolyn, Millie
Sent: March 11, 2011
Subject: RE: RE: RE: RE: xoxo

Whatever. So you won. Totally let you win, you know. Next year, Alexandra. Next. Year. Watch out.

~

From: Alexandra
To: Ruby, Erin, Claire, Carolyn, Millie
Sent: March 11, 2011
Subject: RE: RE: RE: RE: RE: xoxo

As you and Ed like to say: bring it.

~

From: Ed
To: Alexandra
Sent: March 12, 2011
Subject: Love, love will keep us together

Lex! My love!

First, I have to tell you, Ruby is serious about beating you at cup stacking next year. I think she's online now searching for cup stacking training regimens and protein diets and eye tracking exercises and who knows what. Had no idea my girl had such a competitive streak! Kind of sexy, you know!

Question, hypothetical. What is love? How do you know if the person you're with is the right person? Do you see a future with David? Do you ever doubt?

~

From: Alexandra
To: Ed
Sent: March 12, 2011
Subject: RE: Love, love will keep us together

Ed: Please tell Ruby to, I believe the phrase is, "dream on." It's very sweet that she thinks she has a chance at beating me and David in cup stacking next year.

I do see a future with David. I don't doubt. Mostly, because I don't worry about it. I don't stop and question and dwell or even really try to plan the future. I'm very focused these days, David and I are both very focused these days, on the present. The present is quite lovely indeed. If it doesn't work out, it doesn't work out. I've been through worse. So there's no need to doubt. Everything has always worked out for the best, in the end, so I trust it always will. Were I to spend all my time wondering about what will be, I'd rob myself of this time I have now. So no, I don't ever doubt.

How do you know if the person you're with is the right person? I'd say the answer to that is that there is never one right person. It's more a matter of deciding to be with the person you're with. If you're both committed to making it work, I really believe it will work.

Why, are you doubting?

~

From: Ed
To: Alexandra
Sent: March 12, 2011
Subject: RE: RE: Love, love will keep us together

Haven't doubted since the day I met her. I keep thinking I'm supposed to doubt, but I never have. Not since the day I met her, the day I helped move her in and went home and made her my famous macaroni and cheese.

~

From: Alexandra
To: Ed
Sent: March 12, 2011
Subject: RE: RE: RE: Love, love will keep us together

Ah, I'd forgotten about the infamous poison mac and cheese.

~

From: Ed
To: Alexandra
Sent: March 12, 2011
Subject: RE: RE: RE: RE: Love, love will keep us together

Your mistake, there, that would be the Famous Not Poison Mac and Cheese, thankyouverymuch.

It feels right. Ruby and me, I mean, not the casserole. It feels right in a way I never knew right could even feel. No fear. No doubts.

⁓

March 13, 2011
Wishing Rock News
Millie Adler, editor
Letter from the Editor

Dear Rockers,

Well. Well, well, well. The games are over, the medals have been doled out, the potlucks all cleaned up and dishes put away, the bonfire is out, and I'm here with my candlelight and my tea and my warm fuzzy feeling of joy. What a night. What a week. What an Olympics! Wherever you are, stand up and join me in a standing ovation for Alexandra, David, and everyone else who made this magical week happen! And for all our participants too, it would not have been the same without every one of you! I haven't laughed so hard in years – whoever thought up that toilet plunger race must have worked for an adult diaper company, how hard I laughed! – and I'm reminded once again, so completely and fully, why I live here and I why I love this place and you people so much. It's unfortunate that the tennis was rained out, but probably for the best that the lawn darts were, too. I saw Michael practicing one day and between you and me, that was an accident waiting to happen. Next year I think we may need to have a safety committee in charge of some of these games. Who would have ever guessed the most dangerous event would not be speed whittling but rather the office chair races? Followed closely by the potato sack race. (As a side note, thank goodness you were here for that race, Jake; Ruby was bound and determined to not just race but also win, and I don't think we would ever have heard the last of it someone hadn't been there to fill in as her partner at the last minute!) Congratulations to Ruby and Jake on a solid potato sack win. And once again, I'm so glad the cast and crew of "Inhabitants" joined in.

The final results:

Office chair races: 1. Carolyn; 2. Susan; 3. Ben

Speed whittling: 1. Walter; 2. Ben; 3. Lee-Ann

Potluck competition: 1. Carolyn; 2. Claire; 3. Millie

Idiotarod: 1. Dean, Paula, Donna, Cody, Dick, Beth; 2. Karen, Danae, John, Mike, Angie, Tony; 3. Ed, Michael, Ben, Jake, Tom, Claire

Walk/run: 1. Ben; 2. Damian; 3. Carolyn

Rock skipping: 1. Michael; 2. Meredith; 3. Millie

Potato sack races: 1. Ruby and Jake; 2. Claire and Tom; 3. Mike and Dori

Bowling: 1. Claire; 2. Tom; 3. Walter

Leg wrestling, men: 1. Tom; 2. Bill; 3. Ed

Leg wrestling, women: 1. Ruth; 2. Joyce; 3. Claire

Arm wrestling, men: 1. Hal; 2. Ed; 3. David

Arm wrestling, women: 1. Carolyn; 2. Dene; 3. Alexandra

Thumb wrestling, men: 1. Tom; 2. Michael; 3. Old Henry

Thumb wrestling, women: 1. Margo; 2. Lisa; 3. Ruby

Cup stacking: 1. Alexandra; 2. David; 3. Ruby

Line dance marathon: 1. Raine; 2. Erin; 3. Claire

Ping pong: 1. Ed; 2. Michael; 3. Traci

Toilet paper / plunger race: 1. Ed, Michael, Tom, Ben; 2. Sonja, Annie, Denise, Shannon; 3. Ruby, Claire, Carolyn, Erin

Start practicing now, everyone, because I have a good feeling we'll be doing this all again next year, same time, same place.

Tomorrow the crew of our new favorite TV show leaves. It has been great having you all here. I never thought I'd be a TV extra star! I can't wait to see how we all look (especially those of you who were aliens!) and the end result. Meredith, or anyone on the show, please be sure to let us know when the episode will air and I'll spread the word. It's been a pleasure. Come again soon, whether you're filming or not! There is always a room for you in Wishing Rock.

Then, Meredith herself, shining daughter of the town, will leave on Wednesday. Meredith, I have to admit I knew far too little about you before you came, and that's my fault for not asking your dad more questions about you. I can't say enough about how glad I am you came. The Brooks family has long been quite special to me – I'd say your dad even saved my poor beleaguered soul in some ways – and getting to know you has been like getting to know long-lost family. You, more than anyone, must come back soon. Our home is your home, in so many ways.

And with that, my darling Wishing Rock family, new and old, near and far, I bid you all a very fond goodnight. Sleep well, my friends.

Millie

From: Ruby
To: Gran
Sent: March 14, 2011
Subject: Friends and Family

Hi, Gran!

You have to come visit us soon. I insist. So many things happen where I wish you were here, living down the hall from me, so I could come over and cuddle up on your couch under one of the afghans you've knitted, with a cup of cocoa and a chocolate chip cookie, crisp from the stash in your freezer, and chat about the world and the people in it. I want to wake up tomorrow and make monkey bread and scrambled eggs with you and stay in our pajamas until noon, talking. I want to see you again. Promise me you will visit soon!

Ed's Aunt Meredith's TV show's cast and crew are on their way home now, after a fun-filled week. I had no idea how long those TV filming days could be! Especially if you have to go into makeup (as aliens do) at 5 a.m.! Remind me not to be an alien ever again. Although I suppose I could be a new generation of aliens, the kind that look exactly like humans. Maybe there are aliens that look like humans that just rolled out of bed? That's the kind I'd be. I'm ready!

Ed had a final dinner party for Meredith last night – Ed and me, Carolyn and Michael, Alexandra and David, Erin and Raine, Millie and Walter, and Meredith and her beau. Do you remember that a few weeks ago – right after your wedding – Alexandra was going up to Bellingham to meet her half-sister for the first time? And then we have Meredith here, after her having been completely uninvolved with the Brooks family for so long. It got us into a conversation about family, and what does "family" even mean? And friends?

"If you ask me," said Raine, "we don't have enough words for the different types of friends, the different types of relationships we encounter. I'm always needing to explain exactly how a person is related. Even the word 'relationship' is problematic. If I talk about my relationship with someone, people assume I mean an intimate relationship. When, in fact, a relationship is merely how two people are related to each other. That is, if two people are strangers, then that's their relationship: strangers. We just don't have enough words for how people know each other."

"I totally agree," said Millie. "Ruby, I got to know your grandma, Adele, purely by writing to her. I called her a friend, but people who didn't know either of us would ask how we met. Then I'd have to explain, 'well, we haven't met; we just write to each other.' Were we friends before we met? I think so. But people have an expectation of what that means."

"Is it all about how we meet then? How we have or have not met someone?" asked Alexandra. "My sister was my sister regardless of the fact that I'd never met her, didn't even know she existed for most of our lives. Why can't Adele be your friend, even before you'd met?"

Millie jumped to defend your relationship, Gran, don't worry! "Of course she was my friend. Back in my day we'd call her a pen pal. People used to do that; do they do that still? Friends who we just knew by writing to them, and no other way."

"That's the internet," said Raine. "People are friends on the internet without ever meeting. Maybe we need to call them internet pals."

"But why do we need to define it at all?" said Alexandra. "Why do we need the labels?"

"I think," said Erin, "the question doesn't come from needing to define friends. A friend is a friend is a friend, regardless of where or how you know them. The challenge," she said, "is in those people we know, but who aren't really friends. They're not co-workers, they're not family, you don't hang out with them, but you know them online and are friendly and enjoy chatting, but probably will never develop a 'real' friendship. Or what about friends of friends – people who are friends of your friends and therefore you've added as friends online, but you really don't know them and only added them because you felt you had to. What are they? I agree with Raine. If some cultures can have a hundred words for snow, then certainly we can have more options than just 'friend,' 'family,' 'co-worker.'"

We did not solve the issue, but it made for interesting discussion. I know I've struggled to explain my relationship (in Raine's not-intended-to-indicate-intimacy definition of "relationship") with people before. Who is this person to me, exactly? Well, I've gone on a couple dates with him but we didn't hit it off, so that makes him ...? I met her once and we started following each other online and occasionally we exchange jokes, so that makes her ...? It's complex, is what it is. Does it matter? I don't know. Does it not matter? I feel like it matters somehow, but I just don't know.

Meredith segued the conversation: there are also, she said, the people posing as friends because they want something from you. I don't think she was as much bitter as she was sad when talking about friends who changed their tunes once they found out she knew famous people, via her first husband.

"You find out who your friends are, and who just wants to be friends with you for the inside scoop," she said. "Suddenly the people you used to think cared about you are all talking about you behind your back, and the only thing you did was refuse to betray another friend's trust. The non-celebrity friends get mad at you for not spilling the beans on the private lives of the celebrity friends, and where they used to care about you (or so you thought), now you realize you are worth something to some of them anymore only in so far as you will fuel their gossip fodders. They no longer care about you.

"It hurts that you lose what you thought were friends, especially when you know what kinds of things they're saying about you. But because you're trying to stay professional and positive you swallow the hurt and the betrayal – because after all, you were betrayed too. You thought these people were friends but somehow they turned, somehow now you are the subject of gossip and not in a kind way. Somehow now your integrity, of which you are so proud, the trustworthiness that you afforded all your friends, celebrity and non-celebrity alike, means you think you're better than others; it means you're not a team player for not sharing what they want to know, even though you are certain they wouldn't want you to spread their own secrets. So you feel betrayed too, and hurt, but you can't say anything. And when you do say things, you talk about trying to remain compassionate because you know these people are all good people at heart, but even as you say those things you know they're returning no favors; they're not speaking of you with compassion but rather jealousy and bitterness. But you remind yourself that you've made choices about how to live your life, you've chosen not to let negativity and bitterness in, so all you have left is just this sad place, this sadness that people who you thought cared about you are now maligning your name when all you did was hold firm to your integrity, to your promises of trust, and now you're the enemy."

She sighed. "You'd think at my age, I wouldn't have to deal with that anymore, but the fact is, people are insecure at any age. If only they'd realize how much happier they'd be if they got their sense of importance out of things they're doing in their own lives, rather than from being 'in the know' about someone else's. It's all so toxic. It's toxic, and I had to learn to get away. It made me sad to have to leave some friendships, but if those people only wanted me for gossip and scandal, they weren't real friends anyway.

"You reap what you sow," she said. "People say it but don't look at their own lives. Sow misery, reap misery. Sow jealousy, reap jealousy. People will claim to be an innocent victim in a relationship but neglect to mention the hurtful things they themselves did. They are cruel and unkind and unfair and then they don't like it when the people they've hurt decide they've had enough, and leave. It's crazy."

Meredith smiled, one of those I-have-an-inside-joke-with-myself smiles, like she was remembering something, which it seems she was: "A friend of mine used to say 'It's too bad you can't make world peace and chocolate out of crazy, 'cause there ain't never no shortage of crazy.' So true."

And then she shook her head and laughed. "And that, my dear friends, is enough time – far too much time – spent worrying about that. Let's play charades!"

And so we did. Meredith and her man, with their practiced and refined acting skills, won easily, but we all had a great time. Let it be noted: the word "space" is all but impossible to act out. I'm just saying. Anyone who manages to get her partner to say "space" should automatically win. But, you know, it's not about winning, it's about having fun playing. Whatever.

The family thing, though, that made me think. About the choices we make. The people here at Wishing Rock have absolutely become my family, though I'm not related to any of them. What if I'd made a different choice? Would I have met these people eventually, these people I love so much? Was it destiny or chance? It makes me sad to think I could have stayed in Seattle or moved somewhere else and thereby missed out on these people – but what about the people who are there who I might have loved, but never met? You never know which choices will change your life. It's all sort of mind-boggling. I can't think about it too much. I'm glad for the family I have, though, no matter what the relationships.

Love you!

Ruby

~

From: Gran
To: Ruby
Sent: March 15, 2011
Subject: RE: Friends and Family

Hello, Ruby!

I agree, I must get to Wishing Rock soon, if only for these dinner parties you all throw with such joy and reckless abandon. I hereby make a Grandmotherly Ruling that anyone who manages to get her partner to say "space" (when "space" is the correct word, that is), should automatically win. Grandmotherly Rulings take precedence over all other rulings, of course, and so it is so!

Interesting discussion you all had over friends and family and definitions. I have to say, those things never occurred to me. I've referred to Millie, as well as Alexandra and all the others I've met through you, as "friends" without giving it a second thought. I like them, we communicate, we are friends. Does it need to be more complicated than that? Do we have to have definitions for everything, labels for everyone? As our dear philosopher Søren Kierkegaard said, "Once you label me you negate me." As a person who has never felt she particularly fit into any one niche or category, I've always deeply appreciated that quotation. I am who I am. You are who you are. Each of us in wonderfully quirky and unique and beautiful. Do we have to categorize everyone? I understand that it makes life easier, being able to quickly define someone, but none of us is truly so easily defined. Don't you agree? Labeling people, pigeon-holing everyone, yes it's a shortcut and helps us more quickly understand the world around us, I suppose, but I'd rather we slow down and take the time to understand individuals. The joys of the world are not in the ways everything is similar. The joys of the world are in all the ways we are different.

Which is not to say that we don't need to recognize our similarities, too. Liam and I were discussing the other night how polarized our world is becoming. It's human nature, I suppose, to pick a side and then fight for it. That's why sports teams are so popular. We want to have a side, and then we will support and defend that side against all enemies. It's one thing with sports, but it has become so prevalent in politics these days, defining how we approach each other. Again, it's about labels. We label each other, we label ourselves, and from there we decide how we are going to treat each other. But this polarization does us all such a disservice, when we argue from the standpoint of how we're different, rather than how we are similar. Take the environment. Everyone knows the environment is the domain of liberals. But is it? You can't tell me that conservatives want their children to drink polluted water. I wish we could all start to have conversations from our points of common ground rather than labels. That we could approach a conversation and say "I am left and you are right (or whatever polarities the two conversants might have), but let's have this conversation starting from where we agree. Let's say that whatever is said here doesn't threaten my being left nor your being right. If you agree with me or I agree with you, that doesn't mean we have to turn in our left and right cards. Let's put away labels and find the common ground, and start from there." I fear for our future if we can't do that. We have to put away labels, categories, assumptions, and start finding common ground.

Well, enough of that. Alexandra mentioned she is working on living in the moment rather than the past or future, and I think that's the best advice of all. The point of life is not to figure it all out once and for all, or to get bogged down in definitions. The point of life is to keep living, keep moving, keep making mistakes and keep picking yourself up. What is the meaning of life, after all, if it isn't even lived? Trust me, you don't want to get to the end of your days and wish you had sixty more years to make up for the time you didn't take advantage of, all because you were afraid of taking a wrong turn. And you don't want to take up too much of your life hanging on to things when you should have let go. Just live, focus on kindness and compassion and love and joy, and the rest will fall into place. Now I'm off to a dance with Liam. I love how much people dance in this country. I never understood the concept of "bad dancing." People talk about bad dancing like it's something to be embarrassed about. I've never regretted dancing badly. I've only regretted not dancing.

Love to you from me and Liam,
Gran

~

From: Ruby
To: Jake
Sent: March 16, 2011
Subject: Holding on, letting go

Hey, Jake –

So, where to begin. Gran wrote me yesterday, and one of the things she talked about was how to live. And about not hanging on to things when you should have let go.

I think I've been unfair to you. I've been hanging on to you in a way that wasn't fair. I mean, I don't know, but I think you sort of hoped things might change between us, change back to how they were, and because I got confused about Ed, because I get confused about things so easily, I think maybe I've led you on. You're like a safety net. And that's totally not fair to you. So I feel like I need to let you know, I'm letting go.

I don't even know what that means, or why I'm telling you. What I want, Jake, is for us to be best friends forever. I love you, I totally do, I care about you from the bottom of my heart, but we're just meant to be friends.

It's such a funny thing, relationships, the ending of relationships. There's this person you once cared about so intensely, and suddenly even friendship is difficult. Why? I mean, I know why. The sum of why relationships fail: one person cares too much; the other cares not enough. That messes with our hearts and our fears. We want to hurt the person who hurt us so we strike out. Then everyone's hurt and everything falls apart when in fact, at first there was so much love. Why can't we put aside the things that don't work, and focus on what does? It's all self-protection. It's all about making sure we don't get hurt again.

I know I hurt you, and I'm so sorry, Jake. You're a wonderful person. You're so kind and giving and thoughtful and generous and funny. You're smart and full of love. I don't want to say some woman will be lucky to have you one day, because that sounds so trite that it's almost mean. But it's true. Only an amazing woman will be deserving of you, so hold out for that. Hold out for a woman who is as powerful of a force for good in the world as you are, someone who fills you up with joy. Don't settle for less than you deserve.

You've been so good about being a friend since the day I broke up with you, but part of me thinks it's because you hoped we'd get back together. I hope you'll want to be as good of a friend now that I'm telling you that's not going to happen. I know, you might need space and time. Millie once told me that our old Meriwether had a saying, time and tides carry away all our woes, was that it? So take the time and let the tides heal. I'm not going to be contacting you but it's not out of not wanting to. I'll be staying away so I don't steal that time from you, whatever time you need. If and when you one day feel ready to be friends, you are so welcome in my life.

I wish you all the best, always.

Ruby

From: Jake
To: Ruby
Sent: March 16, 2011
Subject: RE: Holding on, letting go

Hey,
    Thanks. Can't say I wasn't hoping still. I respect that, though. Yeah, it'll take some time.
    Take care.

~

From: Erin
To: Alexandra
Sent: March 17, 2011
Subject: Home .... I mean, Hawaii

    Well, tomorrow's the day. I'm just about packed, as is Raine. Thanks for offering to take us to the airport. One thing I like on Maui is I don't have to travel a whole day just to get to the airport! Can't expect Ed to save us every time, I suppose. That was so nice of him when we arrived. I need to thank him again. Tell him thanks for me if I don't see him before we go, will you? He took Ruby out earlier; I don't know where they went. Do you? I haven't seen them for hours.
    I'm so torn here. It's been amazing seeing you all. I love Hawaii, I love that I met Raine and I wouldn't have met him if I weren't there, but you guys are home. Being here reminded me of that. The people you love, that's home.
    But I'm not done with Maui yet and Maui probably isn't done with me, either. I need to see Roone again and talk things out with him. Closure. Why do we always need closure? Can't we move on without it? What is closure, even? I guess it's just feeling like you said everything you needed to say, and got the answers you needed to get.

Which means it's all about needing, and I don't think that's very Zen of me. I need to move past needing and just start accepting, I think. Still, I need to talk to Roone again.

Don't get rid of my stuff here just yet, though. Turns out a good part of my heart is here. Raine is somewhat nomadic, so he could move with me, but it's far too soon to ask him to move for me. Even if he did move here, there's no saying whether he'd stay.

I'm going to miss you guys. I miss you already.

~

From: Alexandra
To: Erin
Sent: March 17, 2011
Subject: RE: Home …. I mean, Hawaii

Closure is a strange thing indeed. Ruby sent a message to Jake; that was about closure. I think maybe closure is another word for forgiveness. Forgiving ourselves and forgiving the other person. I don't know if you can get through a true relationship – friendship or intimate relationship – without ever hurting each other, or at least saying the wrong thing on occasion. Mostly unintentionally, but we're all so easily bruised. Closure is just a way of saying those hurts aren't going to have a hold over you any more, and you're moving on, I guess.

Give me a call when you're ready to head out.

~

From: Ruby
To: Gran
Sent: March 18, 2011
Subject: Rock

So this is what happened.

Yesterday, Thursday, I was getting ready for work, but about eight Ed texted me and said I had the day off. I asked why and he wouldn't explain, said to just relax, have a leisurely breakfast, and he would to come get me at ten, and to dress warmly.

So, I dressed warmly. It's been cool but not rainy lately and that was the forecast for yesterday, too, so I had breakfast, and layered up my clothes, and waited. Just before ten, there's a knock at my door. Ed, standing there with a goofy grin.

"Ready?"

"Ready for what?" I asked.

No answer. More goofy grin. He took my hand, locked the door behind us, and led me away. Down the elevator, out the lobby, to the dock, to his boat.

"Where are we going?"

Goofy grin.

We got in; he started up the boat; we headed out. I wrapped my scarf tight around my face. Though it wasn't raining, with the wind it started to get mighty cold.

Soon I started to recognize where we were headed.

"Are we going to your island?"

Goofy grin. Extra goofy grin, I'd say.

Sure enough, we soon pulled up at the dock. Michael and Carolyn's boat was there.

Ed broke his goofy silence. "Michael wanted to come here for a hike," he said, somewhat awkwardly. "He's been working in his shop a lot and wanted a break," he said. Goofy grin. "Anyway, welcome to Eternal Cove. It's like Eternal Love, except it's a cove." He smiled at his joke, as did I. He'd asked me a while back to help him name this cove, and I'd totally forgot about it.

"Aw. Eternal Cove. I like it. That's perfect," I said. I looked around. I've only been to the island once before but it felt like something had changed. I finally settled on the dock. "The dock looks different from last time I was here," I said. "Did you fix it up?"

"Yup," he said, mighty pleased with himself. "Well, I had people fix it up. Yes, it's fixed up." Grinning.

"It's lovely," I said, somewhat amused with his exuberance over such a small thing. "So, what are we doing today? A hike? Something that will warm us up?" I was happy, but chilled to the bone. I hadn't thought to bring gloves, and my fingers were ice.

"Let's go inside," he said, taking my freezing left hand in his hand and into his pocket.

"Inside?" I asked. Puzzled. There weren't any buildings on the island. Not the last time I'd been there.

I was answered with a goofy grin.

And so we walked along the dock and up a new boarded pathway I hadn't noticed before. As we walked, we could start to see over the little crest of the dunes, and through the little opening in the dune where the path led, and I saw …

… I saw a castle.

I stopped in my tracks. Jaw gaping.

Ed, so pleased with himself, I'm surprised he didn't start to dance.

"A CASTLE??" I said. "You built … a castle??!"

He shrugged a mighty pleased shrug. "I didn't build it. I had it built," he said. Whatever smile goes beyond ear to ear, that was his. He smiled with his mouth, his eyes, his chin, his shoulders. His body, one giant smile. "But yes. I built you a castle."

"You built ME a castle?" I said, stunned. "This is for me?"

"Not haunted, either. I promise," he said.

And he went all silent again, except for his extremely loud smiling, and led me along the path. Once we were on the other side of the dunes, the path was lined on either side with dozens of little votive candles in clear glasses – not dozens, hundreds, flickering in the light breeze, leading the way to the enormous castle door.

This castle, Gran. Do you remember once that I said if I owned an island I'd put a castle on it? He remembered, and he made it happen. When his ex-girlfriend Julianna came to visit and he found out she was an artist, that's when he started talking with her to put his ideas onto paper. That's why he was talking with her! Totally innocent. And, as it turns out, all for my benefit. Anyway, this castle. It's not tiny, but it's also not huge. (Who needs a huge castle?!) It's only two stories high, plus turrets and towers and whatnot, but the way it's designed it looks like it's four stories. Each story has two sets of windows stacked on top of each other, so from the outside it looks like four stories. It's made of stone, as all good castles are; solid dark gray stone over most of it, and then in between the two floors, it's faced with a stripe of white granite in a ring all around the castle. Like a giant wishing rock castle. A perfect giant wishing rock.

I almost wept at how perfect it was.

We walked through the enormous, elaborately carved wooden front door (so tall it took up nearly one-and-a-half floors, which from the outside looked like three), and Ed gave me a tour of the interior. "It is not easy," he said, "to get a castle built in this short of a time frame, especially on a remote island. Just letting you know in case you want another one. It'll take longer next time. I had to pull quite a few strings." He smiled. "But I think you are worth one castle, anyway."

I replied with a goofy grin.

Our tour ended at the grand dining room, which was laid out with dozens more candles around the room and on the huge natural live-edge dining room table, handmade by Michael (who apparently made or designed or helped make a lot of the furniture in the house). Later Ed told me one of Carolyn and Michael's duties was to light and then keep an eye on the candles until we arrived, to make sure nothing burned down the castle! (Ed wasn't lying about Michael being there for a hike; he just had Carolyn along too. They did go on a hike afterward once we arrived, to give us privacy.)

The table was set for two, with champagne glasses and silver-dome covered dishes (labeled, in Carolyn's handwriting: "appetizer," "salad," "main dish," "dessert"). Ed pulled out a chair for me at one of the settings and I noticed he'd brought over those Wisdom Rocks Alexandra gave me for Christmas, and taken a few dozen of them and shaped them together to form a Wisdom Rock heart. I can't remember all the words, but I know "happiness" was there, along with "bliss," "balance," "laugh," "respect," "appreciate," "trust," "heal." The word "love" holding it all up from the bottom tip.

I sat down, ran my fingers over some of the words on the smooth gray-green rocks, then stared, admiring, taking in the coziness of the room, and the roaring fire I had missed when I first looked around. Ed, with Carolyn and Michael's help, had thought of every detail.

"This is so gorgeous, Ed," I said, my eyes a little teary. "This is amazing. You have built the world's most perfect castle, I think."

His eyes beamed. He pulled the silver dome off the "appetizer" dish, to reveal … a jar of olives.

Not that I was disappointed by olives, of course; I love olives. Somehow, though, having already sensed Carolyn's touch on the day, I expected something else. Crab cakes, or wild salmon canapé, or who knows what.

"For you," he said, handing me the jar.

"You're giving me jar of olives?" I said with an uncertain smile.

He looked at me, shook his head. "I'm giving you a jar of olive juice. The olives just happen to be in the jar."

Olive juice. How it all began.

"Olive juice," I said.

"Olive juice, too," he said. Mutual goofy grins.

Turns out there was another tray of appetizers that I hadn't seen – none other than wild salmon canapé, of course. Carolyn never disappoints! Followed by a delicious pecan-goat cheese-cranberry-spinach salad, and then … macaroni and cheese.

"My very own recipe," said Ed. "Not poison."

"It's my favorite," I said.

When we finished, Ed suggested we wait a bit before dessert. We moved over to the fire. I sat on a lush, thickly padded chair, and Ed sat down on its matching ottoman, in front of me.

"Ruby," he said, and suddenly his smile grew nervous. He wiped invisible sweat from his brow.

He started over.

"At the time when Gramps named Wishing Rock 'Wishing Rock,' I was pretty young and pretty stupid," he stopped and laughed. "Maybe the latter is still true. But at the time he named the town, names didn't mean much to me. Years later, though, I was maybe sixteen or seventeen, I got to thinking about it, and I had a conversation with Gramps about the town name. At that age of course I thought I knew everything, and so I told him naming anything after wishes was stupid. Wishing was stupid. Why wish, when you could just go out and make things happen? Wishing is so passive, I explained calmly, slowly so he might understand. Wishing is for people with no aspirations, I told him.

"Gramps smiled at me, that benign warm Meriwether smile. 'Ed,' he said, 'Ed, I see what you're saying. Maybe I have a different perspective on it, though. Wishes aren't passive. Wishes are the beginning of action. If someone says to you, 'You have three wishes,' what does that do? It forces you to focus: What matters to you? What are the three things you long for so much in life that you would wish for them at the cost of all other wishes? We cannot get anywhere in life without first knowing: What do we want? This is what wishes do. Wishes bring our longings and desires into focus; they help us realize our true dreams and goals. Wishes are how our hearts speak to the universe. Of course you have to then go out and do the hard work to make the wish come true. Almost everything worth having takes work. But you have to start by knowing what you want.

"'Wishing, Ed, is the beginning of all wonderful things,' he said.

"'You see, Ed,' he continued, 'when I named Wishing Rock, I was telling the universe my dream. I wanted a place to heal my broken heart. I wanted to build a place where people would come together and love each other and watch out for each other and be kind. A place where community and compassion were more important than pettiness and anger. The kind of place, really, that we all dream of. It's not utopia. It's a choice. People come here and make a choice to be kind to each other, and what do you know, people are kind back. People make a choice to engage with their neighbors, and community is born. People make a choice to have fun, rich lives, and what do you know, we're happy. My wish was for a place that would break through all the fears we all have – fear of being rejected, fear of not being loved – and be a safe place to rest our hearts.'"

Ed went on. "And so, after that talk with Gramps, I started wishing. When I didn't know what to do next, I'd wish. When I knew what I wanted, I'd make a wish. When I didn't know what I wanted, I made a wish. It always helped me to focus, to figure out what I wanted." He paused, got down off the ottoman and onto one knee. From his left pocket, he pulled out a little black jewelry box, and opened it.

"Ruby, do you remember when we were on that martini float, in the Dogwinkle Days parade?" I nodded, tears forming in my eyes. "When we were on that martini float, I made a wish. Before I knew you, I had so many wishes. After I met you, there was only one wish. You, Ruby, are all those wishes come true. Will you marry me?"

And I said yes. Actually, I think I said "Yes! Yes! Yes!! Yes yes yes!!" and started crying and hugging Ed and kissing him, and the rest is either a blur, or is more than anyone needs to know.

The ring, it's incredible. Brushed silvery-gold with a band of moonstone, like a wishing rock on a ring, with a fiery "cushion cut" diamond embedded into the center. Photo of ring and of the castle attached.

Gran, I so well remember when I came here. Do you remember it? My heart was so heavy when I first stepped onto this island. I thought it would never heal again. But the people of Wishing Rock made it whole again. Rather, they made it something greater than whole. They made it complete. And now, this. Everything I didn't even know I was wishing for.

We're not planning a long engagement. I'll keep you updated.

You see, when I tell you to come visit me, I mean it. One way or another, I'll get you here.

Love,
Ruby

Epilogue

April

From: Ruby
To: Ed
Sent: April 13, 2011
Subject: Unto us a baby is born

She's here! She's here! Baby MacAlpine is here! I just got off the phone with Gavin. Pip's resting. Everyone is fine. They named the baby after Gavin's mom: Mairi Rose MacAlpine. Rose is kind of like Ruby, so I'm going to say she's named after me, and no one can tell me otherwise.

I hope your conference is going well. Say hello for me to anyone I know. Look over those color samples I sent you if you have time. Do you have a preference? I kind of like the white / brushed-silvery-gold / deep midnight blue combo. Or maybe the plum and "candle-light" (previously known as "ivory" then "eggshell"; keep up, please). What do you think?

Do you think we're old enough that we can get away with having just one person each in our wedding party? I don't need a whole flock. What's a group of bridesmaids called anyway? Gaggle? Probably not, that would be wrong. Swarm? No, no, wrong again. I looked it up; looks like it's just "wedding party." That's boring. Let's think of something else. Muster. Mob. Murder. You know, like a murder of crows. Ooh, bats are a "cloud." A cloud of bats. A cloud of bridesmaids? Maybe, with some of those awful frou-frou pouffy dresses. Anyway, whatever it is, I don't need one. Do I even need one? I sort of don't think so, but then I wouldn't get to force anyone into some awful frou-frou pouffy dress, and this is my one chance where someone has to wear exactly what I tell them, specifically with the purpose of making me look prettier by comparison. I don't know if Pip will want to fly with a three-month-old; I sort of doubt it. Which begs the question: If I have just one, who will it be? Who will be the one true bridesmaid?

Pulling out my hair already. Elope?

Love you,

Ruby

May

From: Erin
To: Alexandra
Sent: May 20, 2011
Subject: Home to home

Hey, lady –

Well, it's decided. Raine and I are moving back to Wishing Rock. Or, more accurately, Raine is moving to Wishing Rock, and I'm moving back.

We'll keep separate homes for now (which reminds me, I need to give Raine Ed or Michael's contact info so he can arrange to rent one of those rental units, until he decides if he wants to buy, marry me, or move on). We're not ready for co-habitation, and besides, all those studies say couples do better if they don't live together first. Raine wrote one of those articles once, so he's pretty convinced. Just my luck. Wait, does living in Wishing Rock together count as co-habitation? Something tells me it actually might. We'll have to see if he can at least get a room on a different floor. Maybe fourth floor, up with you, so you can keep an eye on him for me? Just kidding!

I finally had a chance to have a good talk with Roone. I don't know if we were avoiding each other or the topic or what, but somehow even when we made plans to talk, we ended up having to cancel, reschedule, you name it. But finally, we sat down and talked. And we're friends.

Ironically, or not, if I'm using that wrong, but ironically, he finally broke up with Ava, "for good." You never know with them if it's final, so I suppose only time will tell.

Do you think that's just what love is, Alexandra, hurting each other and forgiving each other, over and over, a never-ending loop of hurting and forgiving? It feels like it sometimes. You only hurt the one you love and all that.

So, we'll be back by June, I think, in time for me to do some of my Maid-of-Honorly duties, once we tie up loose ends and enjoy a few last Maui treasures here. There are things we haven't done yet – whale watching from a boat rather than a balcony, an official luau, going on a run along the Red Sand Beach, finding the infamous Little Beach, hiking around the Iao Needle area – and while I know we can always come back, we also want to enjoy these places, and each other, while we're here. I gave my two week notice at my various jobs today, which means my last day will be June 3. That reminds me that I need to contact Ed to see if he has any job openings … Hmm. Raine can still work as a freelance writer from anywhere. Quite handy. He's intrigued about us, meaning Wishing Rock, and said he just might write a novel about a group of people who all live in the same building. I can't imagine it would be all that interesting, but if he does, I'd read it. So long as he changes the names to protect the guilty!

Dang it, in the course of writing to you I thought of and then proceeded to forget about a dozen things I need to do. Must stop and make a list. Chat soon.

x

E.

From: Alexandra
To: Erin
Sent: May 21, 2011
Subject: RE: Home to home

I'm glad you finally had a talk with Roone. To answer your question: No, that cycle of hurting and being hurt and forgiving and rinse and repeat, I think that's less about being hurt and more about being scared. Scared the person won't or doesn't love you back like you love them. Eventually, you know the person well enough and you're not scared anymore. That's the test; to see if you love enough to trust through the fear. Eventually, you start understanding. You stop being hurt because you understand the person's intentions. We all mess up but that doesn't mean our intentions were hurtful. It takes a lot of trust to get there. Faith. Courage. You have to believe in the person you're with more than you fear being hurt.

Potential big news here soon regarding me and David and the future. No, not marriage. I think we have had enough of those lately! I'll let you know when plans are less muddy, more firm.

Anything you need to help you get back, let me know. I am here for you, as are we all. I'm so glad you're coming home.

Love you,
Alexandra

June

From: Millie
To: Adele
Sent: June 24, 2011
Subject: Wishing Rock latest

Dear Adele,

Well, here we are, almost July! The wedding month is nearly upon us. I'm just tickled pink and peach and all assorted colors that you are finally coming to Wishing Rock! Claire has her best room all ready for you and Liam up at the Inn. I know she's insisting on not charging you for it. Don't fight her. It's making us all happy beyond words to have you here. You may not know it, but you're something of a legend in Wishing Rock! It's like having Queen Elizabeth come visit us. Everyone is excited.

So much has happened since I last wrote; my apologies. Where to begin! Speaking of Claire, Alexandra and David have joined forces with Claire and Tom and the Inn. David's love of adventure has infected Alexandra completely, so now the two are starting a sort of adventure business that they'll market to Inn visitors and anyone else on or coming to Dogwinkle. David will offer spelunking excursions and is trying to figure out the logistics of operating a ziplining business, or convincing someone else to do it so he could partner with them. I tell you, Adele, do you remember that I went ziplining last year when I was on my cruise, and swore that while it was fun, I'd never do it again? Either my memory has faded or I'm going crazy in my old age, because if he gets that zipline up and running, I may just do it again. To see my dear Dogwinkle from the sky as I fly through the air, I'll say that would be quite a treat.

Regardless of the zipline possibilities, though, David plans to offer hikes, bike riding, and more; pretty much any adventure a visitor wants to go on, he'll lead it. Pre-designed or custom made, David is your man! And Alexandra will offer the relaxation on coming home: yoga classes, meditation, and she might hire someone to help with spa treatments, if there's demand for it and things go well. They've hired Ben to help them manage the day-to-day operations since Alexandra is still doing her psychic stuff as well. They are a busy bunch! Alexandra thought they might even incorporate some of the games and races we did during the Wishing Rock Olympics, into something guests could do as groups somehow. Ideas flinging around left and right, it's more than I can do to keep up with all the goings on!

Jake is officially home for the summer again. A far cry from the mood and happenings last summer; much more low-key and low-drama this summer, I'd say, and thank our lucky stars for that. It's great to see him and Ben together, good friends, after the way they used to pick on and fight with each other. And Jake and Ruby, well, they're not close, I'd say, but there's peace there, or at least the undercurrents of peace.

Even Roone, Erin's ex-friend or I don't even know what he was, has joined the peace: He wrote a song for Ruby and Ed for their wedding. I don't think they're having it sung during the ceremony, but it's such a nice gesture.

As Meriwether used to say, in his infinite wisdom, time and tides carry away all our woes.

I am just too excited for you to arrive. I may have to go on heart medication. When will you get here? That's too bad Pip can't come but I certainly can understand not flying with such a tiny baby. Isn't it something that Ruby and Pip will have wedding anniversaries one day apart? Maybe having his anniversary on the same day of the month as his birthday will help Ed remember it. I think Ruby is the type to remind him, though, never fear.

Oh, the excitement. We are at excitement level ten in Wishing Rock. Come join us!

Millie

July

From: Ruby
To: Pip
Sent: July 10, 2011
Subject: Honeymoon bound

Happy anniversary, Pip! Wow, just one year? You have had a busy year! We all have!

We are at the airport, on the long trudge from Seattle to Italy. Who decided to go to the Cinque Terre and Tuscany for our honeymoon? Oh wait, that was my suggestion. I'm sure I'll be glad when we get there but for now I'm feeling that overtired shaky muscle slightly nauseated thing you get when you're overtired. Or that I get when I'm overtired.

But it's a good overtired.

The wedding was wonderful. I'm so glad Ed talked me out of having it at our castle – what an endeavor that would have been! Getting all the guests to Eternal Cove would have taken forever, boats running back and forth all morning, from Seattle, from Wishing Rock, ladies with scarves over their perfectly coiffed hair, then packing the bathrooms at the castle to try to fix the wind-swirled messes. And then the reception, where did I think we'd have the reception? We could have had it outside, but not if it had rained.

Anyway, all castle/island disasters were averted by simply having the wedding on the Wishing Rock grounds. All the poker ladies did an amazing job of transforming our little humble town into a gauzy tulle-y deep plum and natural candlelight (that's a color) spectacular. (The "natural candlelight" actually turned out to be a little darker than I expected, sort of an earthy shade of off-white, hard to describe but beautiful – see pictures, attached.)

I had totally forgotten that I'd have to hand my bouquet over to someone at some point (duh), so I'm glad we decided to go with having one attendant each. Erin was beautiful, of course; she looked stunning in the deep plum dress, with her hair up and stray curls cascading down. I, too, was told I looked quite fine, and I'd like to agree, if I do say so myself. Ed was the most handsome man in all the land, and Best Man Michael cleaned up well, too.

Vows were quick and heartfelt. We decided not to write our own, after all, but just chose some really nice ones from a book I found. I mean, after all, people have been declaring their undying love for thousands of years; why reinvent the vow wheel? One less thing for us to worry about.

Rather than unity candles, we did something Erin had heard of at another wedding: we had a wooden box made with love by Michael, and before the wedding we each wrote a love letter to the other, but didn't show them to each other. At the ceremony, we put the letters in the box along with a bottle of Wishing Rock Brose, and then we nailed the whole thing shut. The idea is that when we have our first big fight, we'll open up the box, pour the liquor, go to separate rooms, read our letters, and be reminded of how much we love each other, why we're in this. A really sweet idea, I thought. I'm curious to read what Ed wrote, but at the same time I hope it's a really long time before I find out.

Afterward, with our lovely weather we were able to have the reception outside, which had also been transformed into a plum and candlelight wonderland. Carolyn and Claire had offered to do the catering but we wanted them to enjoy the day rather than work through the whole thing, so we hired a company out of Moon Bay, and they did a great job. The cake was divine, four simple layers expertly iced with real frosting (who likes to eat fondant?), with the top and third layers "draped" with "pearls" (icing), a perfect fondant (well, sometimes you have to) bow, in the deep plum color, wrapped around the bottom of the second layer, and the top layer laden with frilly deep-plum frosting flowers, and repeated at the base of the fourth layer. Ed had a special groom's cake commissioned, too, which I didn't know about until I saw it – an exact tiny replica of our castle! (More fondant on this one, but what can you do.) I don't know much about the groom's cake tradition; Carolyn was telling me it's traditionally cut up and given to guests? If that's the case, we didn't follow tradition. It's in the freezer at home now, waiting for our first anniversary, I guess, or some other occasion. Maybe I'll bring it out for a castle housewarming, if we ever get around to that. It's so perfect, I can't imagine slicing into it, but that is, after all, the cake's destiny. That's what cakes are for. We all have our roles in life, and a cake's role is to get into people's tummies.

The music was also spectacular. Do you remember my first date with Ed, after the Dogwinkle Days parade, we went to The Fiddler over in Moon Bay and there was this violin/vocal duo called "Sephira" playing? Ed, dear darling attentive Ed, remembered how much I loved them, and hired them to perform a couple songs at the wedding ceremony itself and a couple more at the reception. They played on a little platform that was set up under a canopy, a very light cloth that was held aloft with a couple dozen plum and candlelight helium balloons, held down to the earth with invisible strings. Like it was floating in the air above their heads! So creative and beautiful. We also had a D.J. for the dance-along songs. People got up and got down and swirled and sweated. The party eventually moved inside to the auditorium lobby so we could all dance late into the night and into the wee hours this morning. Then, Ed and I sat up on his – our – newly constructed rooftop deck, bodies and hearts entwined, and watched the stars in blissful silence.

I've had about four hours of sleep. Very much looking forward to sleeping on the plane.

Oh, also, I got the mini-Brooks family reunion I'd been working so hard for, for so long. Everyone came. Ed's parents were both there – Mitchell and the mythical Kathy from Iceland – and of course Aunt Meredith came back, which was fabulous. It was just a small group, but they hadn't seen each other for ages. It's a start. They sat together at a table and talked for hours. I kept watching them and I am so happy to report I saw lots of smiles. They've been away from each other long enough that the old wounds have healed over and they were all able to greet each other with that fondness you have for someone you've known a really long time, no matter what the details. I'm hoping we can have a bigger reunion for them sometime, maybe not this year, the year is flying already, but next year maybe. Maybe they can all come back for the Second Annual Wishing Rock Olympics and serve as Grand Marshals or something. At any rate, a fresh beginning, a new start.

So, that's about it. We're weary but joyful, sitting in the airport lobby and getting ready to start our first days together as a married couple. Is it supposed to feel scary? Because it doesn't. It feels right.

We'll come visit as soon as we can. Who knows, maybe we'll stop over on the way home. If we do, act surprised.

All my love to you and the whole family, and a special hug and kiss to my wee niece.

Ruby

August

From: Millie
To: Adele
Sent: August 12, 2011
Subject: Joy

My dear Mrs. MacAlpine,
    How have you been? I thought I'd better check in as it's been a while. Ruby and Ed came by this morning to show me pictures of their beautiful niece, your gorgeous granddaughter. They tell me you and Liam are starting to plan your next adventure. That travel bug hits again! Let me know where you decide to go!
    They've been married just over a month now, as you well know, and we started talking about that and then about how Ed proposed, how Ed told Ruby about Meriwether's story about wishes and Wishing Rock. Took me right back to those days when Meriwether and I would sit on the beach in those old Adirondack chairs, whiling away our summer evenings with conversation, solving the problems of the world and becoming entwined into each others' lives.
    Meriwether. That's the thing about life, isn't it, Adele? It ends. There's no getting around it. It ends. It ends, and there's nothing to be done about it but love each other while we're here.
    I remember so vividly that day, so long ago now, when I was a store clerk and I served a snooty woman who was talking about a

strange town on some island, a town where everyone lived in one building, and how my interest was piqued, and how it led me here, and how here I have stayed.

It's not perfect here, certainly. We have grumpy Old Henry, we have people who don't really want to get out and participate in all the activities we work so hard to create. We have people who come to every potluck and never contribute a thing. We have people who never sign up to help with clean up or set up. No place is perfect, and everyone has different expectations of where they live, and that's okay.

But it's a good place; a rare place these days, I'd say. It's a place where you can trust that no one is going to poison your macaroni and cheese. A place where you know when you leave town, five people will step in to water your plants and take care of your house, and everyone will gather together when you're back to watch a slideshow and share in the joy of your return. A place for love, and a place for forgiveness. A place where who you are overall is more important than who you are on any given day.

Living in this small town means if you get mad at the world you're soon literally mad at everyone. We have to learn to forgive and let live, or otherwise be miserable. In the process, I think we all learn more about forgiving ourselves.

It's a place for second chances. For healing.

Another thing I learned living here, Adele: People have so much more joy in them than they'll let you know at first. People have tremendous inner abandon, but they keep it hidden because they think they'll be judged. Most of us weren't cool in school so we know better than to do anything uncool, lest someone come along and look down their nose at us and we're forever relegated to eating lunch alone on the outskirts of campus. But most people, most people, given permission, will laugh with abandon, will dance a hoedown, will participate in an Idiotarod, will take part in a tacky talent show, will race through the hallways on office chairs and look ridiculous in a toilet paper / plunger relay. Once you let people know we don't care whether they're any good at it; we just care that you show up, they show up. And that's when the magic happens.

On that day, years ago, when a broken Meriwether Beauchamp Brooks sat at the edge of his future town and stared and thought and pondered until slowly his vision grew in him, his dream of this place he would create, I believe that what he dreamed of, what he wished for, was that very thing we all dream of and wish for: a place where we're accepted for who we are, where life is rich and full, where the people around us provide a soft landing when we fall. At its simplest, it is a place where our hearts and our ideas and our hopes are welcome and safe. A community of friends, where you never have to be alone if you don't want to be. There's always someone around to double your joys or share the burden of your sorrows. It's a place where fun and happiness and laughter are cultivated and therefore grow in abundance. It's not just a place, but a way of thinking, an approach to life. A way of treating people with compassion and respect. Choosing to find the humor and fun in each day. Not taking anything or anyone, including yourself, too seriously. Learning from your mistakes, knowing your people have your back.

It's a place of love.

In the Wishing Rock of today, I see Meriwether's wishes have come true.

I am so glad you joined us for the wedding, Adele, and got to visit our little town. Even if a person has never stepped foot in Wishing Rock, I believe at this town's best, at the core of what we're about, anyone who carries the dream of Wishing Rock in his or her heart can claim it as Home.

Love,
Millie

Ed's Famous Not Poison Macaroni and Cheese

Ingredients

- 1/4 cup butter
- 1/4 cup flour
- 1 tsp salt
- 2 cups milk
- 1 to 2 cups medium cheddar cheese
- 2 cups macaroni

Directions

- Pre-heat oven to 350°.
- Prepare macaroni according to directions.
- Stir butter, flour, and salt in the top of a double boiler until it's all gooshy.
- Stir milk into gooshy butter/flour mixture. Mix until smooth, and then mix some more until it has thickened.
- Add cheese to mix, and melt it as much as you like.
- Pour prepared macaroni and cheese mixture together into a large casserole dish. Bake for 20 to 30 minutes.

November

Text from Ruby to Ed
Sent: November 11, 2011

One minute! It's almost 11:11 on 11/11/11! This won't happen again for 100 years! Get ready to wish!

~

Text from Ed to Ruby
Sent: November 11, 2011

No need, my love. Nothing left to wish for. You are my happily ever after.